9/05

MW00978579

MZUNGU MJINGA*

**A memoir of a hunter's first safari to
Tanzania's Masai-Mara
seeking *Mbogo*, or Cape Buffalo,
often referred to as
The *Black Death***

***in Swahili, mzungu mjinga means
"crazy white man"**

Rick Boyer

High Sierra Books
Silver City, NM

MZUNGU MJINGA

Rick Boyer

To my over-the-mountain friends Jim and Linda Carmichel, who asked me all the crucial questions concerning my forthcoming safari, then gave me all the perfect answers--

Swahili Glossary

arakasana—hurry up!

banduki—gun, rifle

chui—rhymes with chewy, which is apt: Swahili name for the leopard

faro—the Rhino. Second largest land mammal, this relic of the Pleistocene has the IQ of an oyster, but can wreck a lorry in a head-to-head collision.

jambo!—hello! Welcome! Whazzup?

kunata—*stick*. Kunata upepo is a wind stick, or wind chaser used in hunting to determine wind direction.

kuki—spear, especially the Masai spear with a four-foot iron blade used for killing *simba*.

kufa—*dead.*

kupiga—*to shoot, to shoot at.*

kupgia banduki—*to shoot a rifle at.*

kwa heri—Goodbye!

kwenda—"we go," or, let's get going

Masai—famous herding/warrior/hunter tribe in northern Tanzania, southern Kenya, who live solely on their cattle's milk, meat, and warm blood. Tall, handsome, and arrogant, they are polite but not to be messed with.

i

mbogo—African Cape Buffalo (not to be confused with the water buffalo)—meanest of the "Big Five"

mjinga—confused, misdirected, ignorant, *crazy*

Mzungu—European, white man (woman, etc.) *Mzungu Mjinga* means **"crazy white man"**

ndio—yes

nyani, or nugu—the baboon. Traveling in large troops, these dog-apes are ugly, ill-tempered, destructive, and sometimes deadly.

piga—to hit (same as kupiga). To connect—usually with a bullet.

Sante, ahsante, ahsante-sana—thank you. All the native Africans we met had perfect manners and gentle dispositions.

simba—the lion—needs no introduction. They rule the plains, and take a back seat to nothing except *tembo*.

tafadhali—please

tembo—elephant, biggest of the "Big Five." Also, in the author's opinion, the noblest animal that has ever walked the earth.

upepo—wind

Kamba, or *Wa'Kamba*—hunting, semi-nomadic tribe in East Africa. Famous for using poisoned arrows. Good trackers and gun bearers.

Kikuyu, Wa'kikuyu—farming tribe of Kenya. Jomo Kenyatta's tribe. These people, assumed so often by the British to be the least warlike of all tribes, became the backbone of the feared Mau Mau rebellion in the mid-Fifties.

PREFACE

The following account is a factual memoir of my first African safari, undertaken in the late summer-early fall of 1995 in Tanzania, East Africa.

The names of the participants—excluding me—have been changed to protect their privacy.

The man presented herein as Glen Schacht (pronounced *shot*), while a man of strong convictions and iron discipline, is nevertheless a nice guy underneath and one of the very finest PH's in the business. The same can be said of his assistant, Aaron Broome. Anyone fortunate to book a hunt with this team will be amply rewarded.

MZUNGU MJINGA

PROLOGUE
British East Africa, 1899

I am walking behind and slightly to the left of Alan. Flies are buzzing around my head and in my ears. The air comes off the red earth in hot waves. Breathing hurts. My eyes sting. Alan's shirt is sweat-stained; his felt hat is soaked at the brim. On his left shoulder rides the Westley-Richards 470 Nitro Express double. The breech is broken, the rifle resting on his shoulder. The barrels are forward; I can see into the chambers. The wide brass cartridge bases sit in them, each as wide as a penny—the cartridges big as panatelas.

Mkouli is on Alan's right. In his hand he holds a *kunata upepo*, a wind stick. It is a two-foot long mopane branch that holds a small linen sack filled with wood ashes tied at its end—a miniature hobo's bundle. When he waves or taps the stick a trail of gray powder emerges and points the wind's direction. When you hunt *tembo* you need the witching stick. To walk the wrong way in the wind can get you killed. Once tembo catches your scent you have no option but to keep shooting between those billboard-sized ears until he goes down. You hope to God, because you can't outrun him. And if you climb a tree he will pull you down with his trunk and flatten you.

Behind me the two German clients, reeking of stale beer from the previous night, pant their way up the slope. Their rifles have grown heavy over the two hours since we left the ox wagon. They are Germans all right—fat and red and sweaty and noisy. And bossy.

I glance to the top of rise where the topi are standing, watching us. Their curved horns resemble those of Mbogo, the Cape Buffalo, but are much smaller. Topi are medium-sized antelope. Now I see them close-up. They are covered with flies, and constantly shake their heads and stamp their feet. On the far slope I see a lioness at half-crouch. She leans toward the topi, waiting. As they stamp and shake their heads in discomfort she walks five quick steps, holding her belly inches from the earth, then freezes again. Two hyena are watching, waiting for her to do the work. In the white-hot sky above a twenty-pound lappet-faced vulture is nailed in the rising air, wheeling in slow arcs, descending now to above the acacia and baobab trees. Closer now, his outstretched wings never moving, the papery rustle of fingerlike primary feathers coming to me in the hot wind.

Kumi the scout appears at the rim of the hill we are climbing, making his way down to us fast, his broad bare feet kicking up clouds of red dust. He approaches Quartermain, holding his kuki upright in his left hand. "Tembo, Bwana!" he pants, flashing the fingers of his right hand open four times.

"And their teeth? What about the teeth, you mangy ragamuffin? Their ruddy *teeth,* you heathen!"

Kumi grins for an answer. Again he points. We reach the summit of the rise and the great dry red-brown valley yawns below us. Acacia trees grow thick on the banks of the brown river winding through it. Through the scrub I see brown shapes moving. Round reddish-brown figures shambling through the scrub forest. From where we stand they look like dogs. Huge, slow-shambling dogs. Bigger than ninety-five percent of the all the dinosaurs who ever stalked the planet. We are going down the slope now. Mkouli is swaying his stick in the breeze. The dust trail is pluming back in our faces: all is well.

What's that? A sound, ever so faint, comes up the slope to my ears. A ticking like a giant far-off clock. Or a tapping. Perhaps a black New Orleans minstrel-man doing a softshoe breakdown on a wooden stage. It is a dry thumping, a soft scraping, a syncopated *tickity tick. thud, thud, tickity tick—*

A sound like the slapping of wet leather—

Quartermain turns his angular face in my direction. "Drums, laddie. Hear them? It's the Wa' Kamba. You know what they're saying?"

I shake my head. Feeling my pulse race.

"They say Ricky Boyer is brave boy—that's what. Now mind, you stay next to Mkouli, who will stand behind me. I'll be with Hans and Fritz up front. If things get dicey do exactly as Mkouli instructs. Clear?"

"Yes Alan."

He leans over and whispers to me: "lucky bastards, these krauts; several of the bulls in there will carry teeth that will top one-fifty apiece. Let's hope they don't muck it up. There's a good lad. Now off we go."

Now we are walking into the trees, in the speckly shade cast by trees whose leaves are thorns. Like all things African, it has become a nastier version of its cousins to survive. The herd stops and mills around, nervous. A huge bull in the rear turns and faces in our direction. I want to run but force myself to remain still. The bull is seventy yards away—a distance he can cover in seconds. A cow behind him trumpets and flaps her ears. Great clouds of red dust swirl around the animals.

Quartermain brings up the first German. Right away I notice he is not nearly as brave and full of bluster as he was last night at the campfire with eight beers in his belly. Now he is shaky, and sweating more than ever. His breathing is fast and heavy. He cannot take his eyes off the elephants. He raises his Mauser but his arms are shaking. Then it is too late for words or warnings or anything because it all happens so fast. The alpha cow comes charging through the herd dead at us. Now we see—way too late—the calf she has been protecting. Since the lead cow runs the herd the bulls follow her, and then it is just a wall of great beasts twelve feet high and heavy as three locomotive engines steaming down on us. The German gets off a shot; it thumps in a puff of dust off the dome of the cow's skull. She keeps coming. Alan raises the Westley-Richards and fires, striking the cow between the eyes. First the puff of dust and then her great knees buckle. She skids to her belly and her hind legs leave the earth from her sudden stop. The two bulls stop short and wheel, turning to the fallen mother, whose calf is bawling.

I realize I am crying—

The German client, puzzled, works his bolt and asks Alan what's happening. He is grinning his stupid, red-faced, beery grin. Alan breaks the breech, extracts the spent shell, and inserts another cigar-sized cartridge.

"I hope you enjoy her," he says briskly. "You got your bloody trophy."

"But what are they doing? The others? What do they do now?" He is pointing at the bulls that are on their knees, inserting their tusks under the body of the fallen female.

"They're trying to save her, carry her off to safety. The fools."

As we make our way through the clearing to the edge of the trees where the dead mother lies Kumi comes up to Alan and whispers in his ear. Alan turns to him; his face tells me he doesn't like what he's heard.

"About face chaps. We've got to go back. Unfinished business." And then to the second German: "Klaus—did you shoot as well?"

The man nods, grinning, but the grin infuriates Alan. "Well, it's gotten away from us—that's why I want *one client at a time to shoot*, understand? You shot when he did, and we thought that ended it. Now Kumi says there's another bull out in the bush, wounded. We can't leave him there; we must go back, and now it's your turn to find out what it's like to be hunted."

Immediately the grin leaves Klaus's face. Suddenly he is not at all thrilled with prospect of going into thick brush after a wounded bull elephant.

With a grimace Alan disengages the safety on the Westley-Richards. "Oh you needn't worry. Mkouli and I will clean up your little mess. After all, it's what we're paid for isn't it?"

Kumi and I sit on the hot dirt under the baobab tree. The Germans are behind us and I have already forgotten them as I watch Alan and Mkouli walk up to the dead cow.

Then I am turning to say something to Kumi, but before I can get the first word out I hear a scream and see both clients jump up and run away. They have left their rifles behind. I turn again and see a bull bearing down on Alan and Mkouli. I know it is the wounded bull, but he is going so fast in his rage I know he will not stop. Mkouli, crouching over the cow, is the first to leap to his feet. Standing now, he raises his *m'kuki* and draws his arm back. But I know he is too late and there is no kuki on earth, even in the hands of the strongest, bravest Masai Moran, that can stop a charging elephant with a spear. Maybe a lion, but never an elephant. Just before I shut my eyes the elephant is coming so big and so fast and so loud he is taking up my whole vision—taking up everything. Then he is lifting Mkouli up with his trunk. Mkouli is screaming, his arms trying to pry off the massive trunk. I am screaming too.

"Take me home!" I scream. *"Take me home!"*

I have turned away from the screen, my face buried in my hands. All the people in the theater are looking at us, and my mother clutches at me, saying it will be all right. But I have to get out of the theater now, this very instant, or I will die of fright. Then she is carrying me through the crowded aisle—people standing up to let us by, my older brother also crying now because he can't see the rest of the film. Now outside and she is walking us home. I am still gripping tightly to her hand trying to recover from the shock of that elephant charging right into the movie house.

What I failed to realize was that it was also charging into my life. Forever. *King Solomon's Mines* was the motion picture adaptation of H. Rider Haggard's classic African adventure tale, starring Stewart Granger as Allan Quartermain and Deborah Kerr as the widow of the ill-fated Henry Curtis, who disappeared into the unexplored region to the west of Kenya looking for a lost diamond mine—the supposed treasure trove of King Solomon...

The year was 1951. I was seven, and already hooked on Africa. But I didn't know it yet. I do remember this: the horror and beauty of the opening scenes had enough impact on me so that my brother, my mother and I went back to Evanston's Coronet theater for another go at it. This time I stayed. Stayed right through the elephant scene, holding onto the seat arms in a white-knuckled sweat. But I made it. Made it through all the other adventures as well: the raging brushfire and subsequent stampede of plains animals that wiped out half the safari staff (there were more panicked critters jumping over the huddled heroes than Noah had in his Ark), the abandonment of the bearers, the murder of the lead askari by the murderer Kurtz (played by Theodore Bickel), Poor Ms. Kerr's close calls with the giant spider, the python, the crocodile, and the leopard (how any one woman could be such a magnet for menacing creatures seems ludicrous now, but then nobody in the audience showed the least surprise), the meeting with the strange outcast king from the West Kingdom with the cobras branded on his belly, the perilous trek through the desert, and finally arriving into the prince's native land—Rowanda/Burundi, home of the magnificent Wa'Tutsi— and the diamonds.

And through it all was the music: the wonderful singing of the Africans: the work chants, the fireside sagas set to rhythms, the plaintive wailing of toil and pain—all of these had a haunting beauty. And of course too there was that thumpity-thump, tickity-tick, clack clack clacking of the wooden drums...the sound like the slapping of wet leather.

It was scary, it was vast, it was strange, it was beautiful. It was magnificent. And I was at far too tender and impressionable an age to resist even a bit of it. I saw the entire movie, and strode home elated.

Not only that, I went back twice more before the Coronet changed features. And after that I saw every African movie that came to the Midwest. *African Queen, Ivory Hunters, Mogambo, Something of Value, White Witch Doctor, Zulu…*

Later on I read Hemingway's *Green Hills of Africa*, and everything Robert Ruark wrote about the Dark Continent (which I think was better than even Hemingway's stuff). Then there were other authors from centuries past. Men like, Gordon Cumming ("the mad Scot"), a fellow countryman (also either crazy or totally fearless) named William Bell (named *Karajomo* by his native bearers), John Hunter, Arthur Neuman, and Peter Hathaway Capstick. Capstick was probably not as fearless and skilled as his books would have us believe. But nobody could write better prose or create a mood better than this former stockbroker. His books *(Death in the Silent Places, Death in the Long Grass, Death in the Lonely Lands, Maneaters, Death in the Dark Continent)* are riveting and extremely informative, whether or not all the action in them actually involved him.

I suppose I should have realized my fascination with African safaris was for real when, sometime in the late 1980's, I began buying big bore hunting rifles and toting them to the local gun club to accustom myself to the heavy recoil and awesome power of these "big brute" firearms.

Then, in 1993, as if ordained by fate, the last pieces clicked into place. First was a hefty royalty check from one of my publishers—more than enough to cover the cost of a first-class tent safari in a premier game-rich destination in the Dark Continent. With it I bought a new camera system, a new medium rifle (most North American hunters would consider a 300 magnum a heavy rather than a medium—but this was for Africa), some luggage, top-grade binoculars, and enough clothes to fill a steamer trunk (I was later forced to sift it down to a duffle).

But the biggest break came when a former college friend came by chance to visit his mother in Brevard, a nearby town, and suggested we call our old mutual friend Larry Dietrich, now a famous (and deservedly successful) general surgeon. He was also a lifelong, born-in-the-blood hunter, now living in the heart of the Mississippi flyway. We called him. I sent him some of my books, and along with these, some heart-stopping videotapes of hunting Cape Buffalo in Tanzania.

Within two weeks Larry called back Steve saying he'd sent the tapes to his hunting buddy Dick Manning out in Idaho. Dick called me two days later. I asked him if he liked what he saw on tape. He answered in the affirmative.

"So do you want to go?"

"Do I want to go? Of course I want to go; I've wanted to go to Africa since I was twelve."

"Same here, only eight, not twelve. I think it's time. What does Larry say?"

"He's up for it."

"Well then?"

"I know a great guide who lives here. He hunts Africa in the summer months. Best there is."

"Best there is. In *Africa?* Only the Brits and Dutch are best."

"Bullshit. Glen's better by half than all of 'em. You'll see. Gotta go now; have a patient. We'll be in touch—"

In the second week of August, 1995, after weeks of rifle practice at the range, running and lifting to be in top shape, 18 major vaccine injections and countless oral medications, I drove from Asheville NC to Chicago, took a cab to O'Hare field toting 2 rifles in a monster aluminum gun case, a four-foot stuffed canvas duffle, a safari hat and hunter's jacket, and boarded a KLM flight to Arusha, Tanzania via Amsterdam with Larry and Dick.

As the big 747 lifted off, tilted northeast, and began its climb I cracked two miniatures of JWR and took mighty sips, hoping the scotch would quell my thumping pulse and adrenaline rush.

Didn't work.

Tanzania, *here we come—*

CHAPTER ONE
ARRIVAL

After 17 hours of air travel from Chicago (via Amsterdam), we touched down in Arusha just before midnight. It was my first time in a bona fide third world country. We slugged our weary way down the boarding gate and into the terminal, which was seething with people, mostly black, but interspersed with whites who accosted the new arrivals. Once such man made his way toward us. A tall, blond man with a deep tan and Cockney/Brit accent presented himself before us with two attendants.

"Party of Dick Manning?" He glanced at the three of us in rapid succession.

"Guilty," said Dick, and they shook hands. He introduced himself as Aaron Broome—Assistant P.H. with Swanapoel & Scandrol Safaris, Ltd. We all shook hands and staggered after him in the din of the reception area, which stank of stale beer and sweat and echoed with the deep basso voices of African men talking and shouting in Swahili. You're not in Kansas anymore, Toto.

I asked Aaron where the customs line was. I dreaded waiting in line bearing a 50-pound duffle on my shoulder. But Aaron assured us it had been "taken care of," and whisked us along until we saw our aluminum gun cases spin onto the loading dock. Aaron's attendants picked these up. One was average height and wiry, the other darker, short, and wiry, and came up scarcely to my shoulder. I was later to discover that these were Julius and Boogie, Aaron's gun bearers and trackers. Little Boogie could scarcely heft Larry's gun case, but he managed without complaint. This was our introduction to these indomitable fellows. I discovered over the course of the two and a half weeks we were "on the ground" on the Dark Continent that each one of them was a prince. We were continually amazed at the Africans' stoicism and ability to weather the worst hardships without complaint.

Outside the terminal it was warm and humid, but not as hot as I feared. We all got into Aaron's long-wheelbase Toyota Land Cruiser and sped off to town, driving on the left lane and narrowly missing three collisions on the way. As in the case of so many other things, we would all grow accustomed to this NASCAR mode of driving. I could feel myself falling asleep as we entered the outskirts of the city. By the time we reached the Impala Hotel I was out on my feet. Not a good flyer even in the best circumstances, the two-night trip on the Flying Dutchman had done me in.

My recollections of the Impala Hotel that first night are faint, surrealistic. I remember a boy hauling my eighty- pound aluminum rifle case up to the security locker after I signed the registration sheet, then grabbed a Tusker beer to take my nightly dose of larium. In my small room I crawled between the sheets. How great it felt to actually stretch out full length! The air- conditioner hummed and I was on the brink of sleep when I realized something else was humming as well. I reached over and turned on the bedside light. Looked around. Sure enough, I was being stalked in my room by the deadliest animal on the African continent. Just then a knock at my door and Dick peeped in.

"Sorry to wake you, but Aaron gave me this to pass around. They already got me twice."

I took the can of spray and dosed the room with it. "You take you pills yet? Don't forget. Just one lapse and you could be a victim."

He thanked me for warning him and left. I made sure to lock the door behind him (sure—the Mau Mau insurrection was forty years ago.....*but you never can tell...*), returned to bed, and passed out.

Muuuhhhhhhhaaa! Muuuuhhhhhaaa! Ahhhhlahhh Akbahhhh! Ahhhhhhhhlahh Akbahhhh!

"What? What the hell? Somebody's screaming in the street below me! Sacrificing a baby? Deflowering a virgin? Impaling a kid for *thinking* about stealing a crust of bread?

No doubt about it, these Muslims were keen on discipline. I slid out from the sack and made my way cautiously to the window.

I crept up to the window. The victim was definitely a guy; I could tell by his voice, or what was left of it. Jeez, it was loud. Of course, he obviously couldn't keep it up for long—not with what they were doing to him. I just had to see what it was. I was drawn by the horror of it. I mean, one doesn't get to see a disembowelment every day, does one? Especially before breakfast. But peering out the window I could see nothing but cars and taxis below, and an occasional lorry. Porters and pedestrians walked to and fro. Where was the action? Then the screaming commenced again. Right over my head!

I looked up. A white tower with loudspeakers attached seemed to be the source of the racket. Of course—the call to prayer! I had forgotten that Africa was overwhelmingly Muslim. But couldn't they call the faithful in a more melodic style? Loud knocks on my door led me over to it.

Let's get moving; they've started breakfast," said Larry. I grabbed my camera gear and followed him.

"Did you hear that racket?" I asked. He nodded. "Yeah. I'm glad we're getting out of here today. Change of plans. Aaron says Glen is tied up in the bush with his client. I guess they're going after lion."

"Well, when will he return? I mean, we've waited almost two years for this trip."

"We'll have to wait three or four more days, looks like. But don't complain, Boyer—we get those days extra, at deep discount. This means we get another half-week at virtually no cost. So we can't complain now, can we?"

Downstairs we found Dick sitting at a table laid out for us talking to the owner, a pleasant native man with a wide smile who greeted us and talked about the menu. I had fresh OJ and bacon and eggs—everything but the grits and redeye gravy. So what was really so exotic about Africa? This owner was quite the entrepreneur, that was obvious.

After breakfast we packed all our gear except our guns (which were still locked in their gun gases and secured in a locker room) and met the man named Muad (pronounced like *good*) who was standing proudly beside his white Toyota SUV with a customized, slide-back top. Muad was to be our driver on our four-day photo safari in the national parks prior to the real one, which would commence as soon as Glen returned to town from his base camp in the bush. Muad was pleasant from the start, and remained so the whole trip.

As we left the neighborhood of the Impala and headed for the outskirts of Arusha, we got our fist shock. The scenes we saw on our way out of town were a baptism to this way of life. The road soon turned to dirt and dust broken only by rivulets of brown water made filthy by cow dung. Women were washing clothes (rags, really) in this water, which was also probably used for drinking. Houses were shacks of timber scraps, cardboard, and tin. Scuffles and fistfights could be seen in the no-man's- land behind the huts and up the banks of the littered ravines. Semi-wild dogs, gaunt and slaver-jawed, with hollow, yellow eyes prowled the undergrowth and garbage heaps. A truck carrying cases of empty soda bottles stopped in front of us. Instantly a young man rushed up, grabbed a case, and ran away with it. He would get a few cents from these. It was all dirty, desperate, and degenerate.

After a few miles, however, the scene changed once again. Here cabbage palm trees lines the wide road, which had become paved once again. Iron fences guarded stately, wide lawns. Big whitewashed houses set back on these well-tended lawns had tall fan windows, pillared porches, terraced patios. No doubt this was where the European colonials resided-formerly German, now British and Dutch. As in all such countries, it was obvious Tanzania had no middle class.

It was a relief to be sure when we quit the city and hit the open country, passing the complex of shops on our left. One was a native gift shop that Muad said was first-rate, selling genuine, quality stuff at much better prices than the shops in town. There was another place right next to this. The sign said: SEE THE SNAKE FARM.

...more on this later—.

Three hours out of town we saw a sign for Lake Manyara National Game Park. Meanwhile, even before entering the park we had seen ostrich, impala, zebra, giraffe, gazelle, warthogs, cranes, and the Secretary Bird, a giant-sized relative of our roadrunner. He is so named because of the numerous tall plumes sprouting from his crown. These look either like a lopsided Indian headdress or a collection of writing plumes on a desk— hence its name. We saw a dust devil or two

26

storming up the dry plains in our wake. We stopped to take a leak, and a mangy heard of humpbacked cattle approached in the distance. We watched as the tink-tonk of their bells grew closer. Then we saw him: the herdsman, a boy of ten or eleven years old. This boy, armed only with a wooden staff, was the sole guardian of these cattle, alone in the outback. How he coped each night with the prowling lions and hyenas I'll never know. He gratefully accepted magi (water) from our plastic jug, and sat on his haunches talking with Muad in Swahili while we watched and took photographs. Life in African bush (as Thomas Hobbes so aptly stated) is nasty, brutish, and short. We left the kid and his cows with a bottle of cool Fanta orange and best wishes. He was barefoot, and clad only in canvas rags. Good luck kid.

There were many spectacles on the safari, but I'll never forget our first. We drove for perhaps half an hour up a mountain slope. As we proceeded we could feel the air become cool and moist. Vegetation thickened. The thorn scrub and savannah grass gave way to bamboo and creeper vines-dense forest growth that shut out light. Eagles and kites perched in the trees along with the ever-present hornbills. There was also a bird's cry that repeated itself endlessly. I realized I had been hearing it ever since we left Arusha. It went breeep-breeep! Breeep-breep! I asked Muad to identify it.

"It is the go-away bird," he said. "When he calls, he is saying go away. Or some say he is saying that he is going away." When pressed to tell us about other important avian life whose calls we should know, he mentioned two in particular.

"First, There is the hornbill, it makes that honking sound we hear constantly. It is everywhere, but not very important. The most important bird by far is the bee-eater because, since it eats bees, it will guide you to honey. It will seek out people and sit on a branch near them and call, then fly away because it knows the people will follow it and dig out the honey, and he can eat as well, you see?"

What about the others?" asked Larry. "You know I want to shoot birds as well as game. I know there are doves here, and grouse, and partridge."

"There are all of these, and you will see them down on the plains. You don't need to know their calls. But the bee-eater will also lead you to water, because bees need water to make their honey. That can be extremely important out here. A matter of life and death."

When we topped the hill Muad told us to get out of the Toyota and take our cameras with us. We weren't prepared for what we saw.

In grandeur and scope the only thing I can compare the view to is that of the Grand Canyon. We were looking down into a vast caldera of an extinct volcano. Big trees appeared as mere specks. Rivers as small brownish lines that curved and rolled across the valley like dropped string. I returned for my binoculars. Through their power I could then see the animals. There were down there, free and wild, contained within this natural circular wall. Miniature giraffes, standing silent sentinels in small groups. Herds of elephant, zebra, wildebeest all moving in slow cadence across the veldt like miniature toys. Fleas in a flea circus. Eagles soared in the air above us on the hot thermals rising from the flat valley floor. Thousands of feet above them vultures and carrion- eating Marabou storks were nailed in the white sky on motionless, outstretched wings.

We wanted to get down there. Larry had loaded his camcorder the previous night and Dick and I had our still cameras. Muad slid back the top of the Toyota. It was a giant sunroof. Standing in the back of the swaying vehicle, the three of us could look and shoot in complete safety as we cruised close to wildlife. Well, not complete safety. A lion could jump up there. Or a leopard. Not to mention a black mamba. But these were unlikely culprits; Muad explained that the animals in the park were used to cars and humans and could not be hunted. Therefore, their tolerance of us was great and we could venture quite close without either spooking or arousing them. I was glad to hear this, but disappointed to discover that exiting the vehicle was strictly forbidden. I had lugged a new heavy tripod and 500 mm lens all the way from North Carolina in hopes of getting some National Geo-quality close-ups of the animal life, and now it was not to be.

The car ground its way down the switchback roads for over an hour before we entered the park and soon found ourselves in a forest that looked as if a bomb had hit it.

"What the? Hay Muad, what happened here?" asked Dick. "They making a subdivision here or what?"

He shook his head. "Elephant."

"Elephant what?" asked Larry.

"Elephant do these things. Elephant eat trees. Destroy the forest."

"That's awful."

He shook his head and explained that without elephant herds the trees would soon take over, obliterating the grasslands. When that happened, the game disappeared. "Look at Uganda. After the wars there the poachers went crazy and killed all the elephants. Now there is no plains left…. and no antelope, zebra, lion, buffalo. Nothing. We need the elephants eating trees. It is their job."

It was then that he led us out of the car. And there we were, unarmed, walking in the place itself, the great African bush. What the Brits call MMBA. Miles and Miles of Bloody Africa. And beyond the first line of trees and mopane grass I could hear the *craaaa-ck* of big limbs being wrenched from trunks. Sometimes a monstrous deep crackling and groaning as an entire tree was pushed over, and then the hissing and high crackle as it fell onto the forest floor. Those big eight-ton animals were moving around in there. We could hear them. Hear the muted grinding of their gigantic molars, and their deep basso rumbling as they communicated with each other in their weird infrasound, just as whales do in the ocean. With dread I realized we had not stopped walking. We were going into the bush where the huge bulls and cows were. I ran up and grabbed Muad by the elbow of his khaki shirt.

"Where are we going?" I hissed at him. "Are you out of your fucking mind?"

"Don't worry," he smiled back. "I don't think that they will charge us."

I stared at him. Didn't think they would. *Didn't think they would.* Great.

I thought of all the African books stories I had read by people like the great ivory hunters of the 19th century, like John "Pondoro" Taylor, Denis Fitch-Hatton, John Hunter, William "Karomojo" Bell, Arthur Neuman, and the rest, who so vividly recounted what an enraged pachyderm can do to a person unlucky enough to be in its path. Being stomped into jelly or impaled on a giant tusk were the obvious ones. But how about trunk decapitation? An elephant's trunk-all muscle-weighs between 7-900 pounds and is quick as a fly swatter. Pondoro Taylor knew several instances when friends of his were approached from behind (you absolutely *cannot* hear en elephant sneak up on you if it wishes to remain silent) and had their heads flicked from their shoulders by a trunk being whipped back and forth as a teenaged boy "flicks" a towel at another's buttocks in a school shower. Ka-whappp!

Then there's Tembo's version of She loves me, She loves me Not, in which the human interloper is grabbed by the trunk and flung to the ground upon his back. Then a great tree-trunk foot is placed upon his chest, and-again using the prehensile trunk— his arms, legs, and head are yanked in sequence from the torso and flung to the four winds. Since there have been no survivors to date, it is unknown if, during this ritual, the elephant hums the tune or not. ..

Doesn't think they will charge...

But after all, wasn't this what I had come for? The electric fear and thrill of being on the animals' turf with no bars or moats between us… Stiff upper lip, Boyer. Once more into yon breech and all of that-tally ho! Cheerio!

I had to take a leak. I went over to one of the fallen trees and unzipped only to see a troop of baboons emerge from the forest and head our way, their dog-snouts and yellow eyes aimed right at us. The baboon's name is *nugu*, or *nyanyi*, and he, unlike other monkeys, is not cute or pleasant. These half-dog monstrosities, sporting 3-inch canines and a foul temper (not to mention the foul odor) can weigh 200 pounds, move like lightning, and disembowel you with fang and claw in a wink. Fortunately, the troop traveled on, picking grubs and other detritus from the ground as they went. The babies (who were cute) rode sitting up on mamma's back just in front of her tail or clinging below on her chest. I was glad when they split. Going back to Muad I noticed Larry and Dick had returned to the Toyota. Apparently their camcorders had run out of tape or something. Anyway, I was anxious for a few slides. I advanced with him. A cow elephant appeared on our left, throwing a trunkful of dust across her back. She swung her massive head and looked in our direction. "*Whheeeeeach!*" she said, and stamped her foot. Then, blowing through her nose with a sound like a car-wash vacuum hose, she swung around and reentered the forest.

And then HE came out. And there we were, just me and the five-foot five, unarmed guide, staring face to face with Tembo, the biggest (by far) of Africa's Big Five. Ten and a half feet at the shoulder. Probably ten tons. Two big teeth projected down on either side of the massive trunk. One was broken off about halfway down, but they were still huge.

A poacher would indeed risk life and limb to shoot this animal with the primitive muzzle-loaders they employed to get this much ivory .The bull fanned his billboard-sized ears at us, then let go an aromatic shower of bowling-ball-sized turds. I realized then I was finally here, face to face with Tembo with no moat, no bars, no circus ring, no nothing between us.

And that he could cover the sixty yards or so between us with shocking speed if he chose. And if he did, there was nothing in this world we could do to escape death. Not climb a tree, not get in the truck (that was one-fifth his weight!)—and certainly not outrun him.

Because even strolling along the escarpments of the Great Rift Valley at what appears to the green observer as a casual walk, the elephant herd is covering a steady eight miles per hour. And they do it 12 to 15 hours each day. Try jogging that speed for even two or three miles and see why humans are no match for the animal on the ground.

So just how fast can the elephant—a big bulky bull like the one standing in front of us—run the hundred yard dash from a standing start? How many seconds? Care to guess? After all the excitement I could stand we returned to the vehicle. We drove around the park for awhile, then headed up a mountain road toward the high ground again. Muad told us he had an interesting surprise for us. We drove to the lip of the crater again only this time viewing it from another direction. Below us lay a large lake, obviously Lake Manyara. But unless we had been fed hallucinogens for lunch or had lost our minds, what we were looking at was an utter mystery, for this lake, less than a hundred miles south of the equator, was rimmed with ice.

"I don't think it's ice," said Larry. "I mean, it can't be ice."

"Snow," suggested Dick. "Freak snowstorm. They get them all the time around Salt Lake City."

"No, then it would be salt," I said.

"Wait, that's it. It's salt. Right Muad?"

But the small man simply grinned, gunned the engine, and began driving down the twisty switchback road to the bottom of the crater. Before we were halfway down, the three of us had agreed it had to be salt, which usually deposits itself in just such places. I'd never flown into Salt Lake City, but approaching San Francisco from the air one can see vast fields of salt lying to the city's south and southeast.

In less than an hour we were there. Muad pulled the Toyota to a halt and told us to view the lakeshore through our binoculars. We did, and became still more confused. The salt appeared to be lumpy…and the large lumps appeared to be *moving!*

"Okay Muad, what the hell's going on?"

"You will see, sah!" He took off at a good clip; we fairly raced at the lake now. The deposits of salt boiled up, and became airborne.

"Birds!" we all shouted. And birds they were. Giant white flamingos. Clouds of them. Flying oceans of them. I never expected to see these birds, associated with the Florida coast, in the interior of the Dark Continent. But there they were. We asked Muad how many he thought were in this flock and he simply shook his head.

"I'd guess a couple million," said Larry. I said I would guess at least ten million. Hell, maybe there were 20 million. All we knew is that the flying birds, that were so thick together in the air you could not see through the flock, took well over half an hour to leave the lake.

We watched until the lakebed took on a normal, dun-colored hue, then set off for our home for the night. It was a working coffee plantation about an hour's drive from the park.

Though I had done precious little walking that day, I was exhausted. No doubt the jet lag had not left me, but more than that was the enervation of continual new stimuli. That…and the excitement—okay you could call it fear—of the encounters with the animals.

As we left the park gates behind I eased back in my seat, closed my eyes for a short rest, and contemplated the answer Maud had given me to the question I posed earlier about the elephant.

Eight.

Eight seconds—

CHAPTER TWO

MBOGO

That evening we rolled out of Lake Manyara Park and headed towards our digs for the night. Muad insisted we would love this place, and we were looking forward to it. We soon left the green confines and hilly terrain of the park and returned to the dry, dusty Savannah country that makes up most of this country, roughly the size of Texas and New Mexico. The land is flat to gently rolling and dotted with Acacia thorn trees, Kasaka brush, and grass of varying lengths and hues. Soon the ground rose again and big greenish trees towered into the air against the dark blue sky, They looked oddly familiar; I'd seen them before and was trying to place them.

"This place is a working coffee plantation," said Muad, his hands flying on the wheel as he fought the truck around the hairpin turns. We climbed up the mountainside which grew greener and more fragrant with each minute. It was the aroma which triggered my memory of the trees.

"Eucalyptus! Muad, I thought they grew only in Australia and the U.S."

"And here. They imported them here as well. They grow very fast—"

"Uh huh," said Dick, "and burn even faster with all that oil in them. They practically explode."

The truck halted at a pair of wrought iron gates while Muad reached out through the window and punched a number into a keypad. The gates slid open and we drove through, continuing uphill on the narrow road that was now lined with gorgeous flowers on either side. The grass, where visible, was flawlessly trimmed—likewise the shrubs. We pulled up in front of a colonial-style building with arched windows and a terrazzo patio in front. The coffee business was good. Muad told us to wait in the car while he checked to see if our quarters were ready. Soon we were unloading our gear onto big comfortable beds in a spacious ground-floor room with a tile floor, swing-out French doors and windows, and ceiling fans. It was cool. Quiet, and clean.

Muad reentered to shake hands goodbye. I didn't want him gone.

"Where the hell do you think you're going?" I said. "You can't leave us here in this strange place. God knows what'll happen—"

"Stop being such a chickenshit," said Larry.

"Yeah Rick, we're sick and tired of your whining."

"Me too," I agreed. "I'd call for help but there's no phone—"

"C'mon everybody," said Dick, "Aaron's supposed to meet us out in front for beer before dinner. Let's get going."

So Larry and I followed him out and around the pleasant shaded walkway that skirted the plantation house. The yellow-white narcissus popped at our eyes from the gloaming—their aroma was heavy, and thick. We met Aaron and his fiancée Christina sitting at a rustic wooden table on the front lawn. Above us, behind the tall shrubs and Italian cypresses rose the stucco and timbered house, in whose basement apartment we were to spend the night. We sat and dug into the *Tusker* lager that lay in a huge ice-chest at our feet.

"Are we supposed to down all this tonight?" I inquired hopefully.

"Absolutely not, Boyer. Part of the camp stash. I've bought four more; they're in Christina's lorry yonder."

The beer was excellent. But what would one expect from a former German colony? We had cheese and bread with the beer while Aaron explained the drill for the next day.

"We'll go to Norngoro Crater tomorrow. I'll be with Christina and her little brother in their truck. Tell Muad you want to rendezvous with us at the big fig tree near the lagoon at noon. He'll know the spot. Got it?"

We nodded our heads. I lighted a cigar and gave Dick one. We opened more beers. Christina was a lithe, sexy thing who looked to be just under thirty, with light skin and the hint of freckles and very long, light-brown hair worn in a ponytail draped forward over one shoulder. Her father was a German-born mining engineer, and Christina had lived in East Africa all her life. What struck me most about her was her calm self-assurance. No doubt she had faced more interesting—not to

Mzungu Mjinga

say dangerous—situations in her life than I had.

It grew dark and the mosquitoes made their appearance. Aaron and Christina got into their Jeep, leaving the beer with us, which we stowed in the room. We went upstairs to the main floor of the house, which had a European elegance, and sat down to a dinner of fried plantains in caramel butter, broiled Irish potatoes, leek soup, and Gazelle chops with Béarnaise sauce. Two South African reds came with the meal. After finishing up with a Bavarian-style torte cake and ice cream we made our way, pleasantly oiled, back down to our quarters where we reflected on the day's events.

Larry told me to sit down; he had something to say to me. "Listen Boyer, if you keep saying stuff like *'hey, look at the fucking horns on that antelope!'* or *'holy shit!—look at those teeth!—'* we're going to seal your mouth up with duct tape, understand? We're sick of our videotapes being ruined by your mouth."

"I believe my comments add a certain *panache* to our enterprise," I opined. "They enhance the whole *Gestalt.*"

"Yeah? I might get the urge to add a little Gestalt to your skull," said Dick, "and enhance your puss with a baseball bat. How'd you like that?" He left us to go to the john. I turned to Larry.

"Now I ask you, is that any way for a physician to talk?"

Next morning I was up ahead of the others, coffee in hand (this was the famous "Estate-Grown Tanzanian" coffee we see in all the upscale cafes and gourmet food shops) ambling along the garden path. I spotted Muad and another chap (you notice my picking up on the Brit expressions? Cheeky, eh what?) leaning against a lorry.

Muad introduced him as Ohljme, and we shook hands. Again, there was that soft African handshake, almost a caress with its gentleness. Whereas we REAL MEN here in the states, whose only danger is dodging traffic and worrying if our credit cards are maxed out, we give REAL handshakes. Yeah!

"Where are the others?" asked Muad.

"You mean my friends?"

"Ummmm—" he murmured dubiously, stroking his chin. "Last evening, as I departed, they told me they were no longer your friends, Bwana Rick."

35

"You don't say. How odd. But don't worry," I said with a nervous laugh, "they're only fibbing. After all, I was the one who organized this expedition."

"Really? I would not have thought it, Sah."

"Hmmmph. Just shows you're not observant, my good man. Try to stay on full alert from here on. What say?"

"Very good Sah."

"The other two louts are still sacked out. I'd like to chat with Ohljme here out in the sunshine if you wouldn't mind rousting them."

"As you say, Sah."

Muad sped off in the direction of the apartment door as the big man and I fell into conversation. We talked about hunting mostly, and he was interested in what we were seeking. He was not surprised we were after buff since that's the biggest draw in Tanzania, and the reason safaris are so expensive in this country.

"A lot of buff around this season?" I asked.

He nodded. "Always plenty. Are you going after lion as well?"

"No. A cat license requires a two-week minimum stay."

Another nod. "Well, since this is your first trip, perhaps it's best you're not going after lion too. That might be too much for the first time out. Buff are dangerous, but lion I believe even more so. A lion killed my uncle last year."

He added this last anecdote casually, as if giving me background information on a local tourist attraction.

"What? Killed your uncle? How did it happen? Did he stumble on a nursing lioness or what?"

"Oh no. Nothing of the sort. He was simply walking to the next village to see his girlfriend and a lion—we think it was a male by his pugmarks—jumped him from behind. From the tracks left by my uncle we know he never heard him coming. Just leapt upon him and bit through his spine. He didn't suffer."

"That's terrible. An unprovoked attack. I didn't think lions attacked unprovoked."

"You have no doubt been watching those American and British wildlife films on television, have you not?"

"Oh definitely. Want to be prepared you know."

"I've heard there are a lot of those kinds of wildlife films in the states. They give you the impression that wild animals aren't really wild—that they're rather like house pets on the loose. Don't you believe it—this is a thoroughly rough place."

"Was the animal starving? I've read that's when they become man-eaters."

"A true man-eater, yes. But to kill a man, all they need is to be in foul temper. The lion did not eat uncle Jhanja. Scarcely touched him in fact."

"Then why kill him for no reason?"

"The usual reason: territory."

He pronounced the word British fashion: TERRA-tree.

"Lions are the most territorial animal on earth. You've got to be extremely careful where you go—especially alone and unarmed."

This short exchange rather threw a damper on the morning's reverie. I thought again about Tembo and how fast he could move once he got his great bulk moving.

"Tell me Ohljme, can you give me a rough estimate on how fast an adult lion can run a hundred meters?"

His face broke into a wide grin. "I can give you better than a rough estimate Bwana. Our game departments collect close data on such things. They prove to be more than useful. They can be lifesaving."

"Okay. How many seconds?"

"Three and four tenths, Sah—

—I turned on my heel and headed back to the inn.

"I say, did I offend you Sah? Where are you going so fast?"

"No you did not..... And, inside to get a Bloody Mary. The day's not starting out right."

Within an hour we were cresting the high ridge of the caldera that surrounded Nrongoro Park. A caldera is the crater left by an extinct volcano. Most are a few hundred feet across. Big ones are maybe a mile or so across. Nrongoro is 86 kilometers across, or roughly 50 miles in diameter. There is a lot of space in this crater, and the high walls of the caldera form a natural wall that keeps the plains-dwelling animals inside the confines of the crater. The bottom of the crater is flat to gently rolling, the surface hard-packed gravel and sand, perfect for vehicles. After descending the interior wall of the of the crater we found ourselves in blazing sun, driving along at 20 mph, a cloud of dust behind us and always, in the distance, three or four dust devils dancing about the plain, these miniature tornadoes swirling in high, thin inverted cones of sand and dust. Herds of Wildebeest, Grants and Thompson's Gazelles, and zebra were the most abundant mammals, but we also spotted two prides of lions, several warthog families, and the occasional Hyena *(Fisi..* . and yes, the name fits) running in its spastic, hobbyhorse shuffle on stunted rear legs through the low brush. We saw giant crested cranes walking in pairs, solitary ostrich running ahead of the truck, pumping their two feet. An ostrich more closely resembles a man when it runs than any animal alive.

In the far distance big hulking shapes stood out against the bright gray dust, resembling battle tanks. There were never more than one or two of these in any given location. Through our binoculars we could see they were rhinos. The rhino (called *Faro* in Swahili) is, as most people know, a remnant of the Pleistocene Era, as is the elephant. But unlike Tembo, whose brain kept growing as the animal evolved, Faro's seems to have succumbed to this challenge and remains the size of a walnut. Since it probably takes this much brain-matter merely to run the bodily functions of a 4-ton animal like Faro, there isn't much room left over for the higher thought processes. So the rhino, alas, is a dumb brute—capable merely of short, nasty displays of temper or the warm feelings of a devoted parent, which it truly is. And also, I must say it is beyond me to understand why anyone would want to shoot one of these increasingly rare giants. The meat is tough, the gestation period and growth rate slow, the trophy huge but ugly, and the much-prized horn (despite superstitious claims to the contrary) as valuable as fingernail clippings or barbershop floor waste. Poor Faro! Bluff-charging, blundering and snorting his way into extinction.

Another animal whose death I cannot condone is the elephant's. True, the meat is good (and God knows there's plenty of it; an elephant carcass can feed a village for several weeks, and for months afterward on the biltong), and the ivory precious. But Tembo (unless your trophy room is as big as a gymnasium) makes a silly trophy, and none of the things we humans can take from an elephant we have killed can remotely justify taking the life of a creature so vastly intelligent, so infinitely tender and caring of its own, so courageously protective of its young, or so willingly helpful to people when trained or kept.

The elephant, in every sense, is noble. It is the true King of

Beasts, and the Beast of Kings. It is **Royalty.**

But on the other hand, having said this, I also think we should take every hyena and baboon we can get our hands on, throw gasoline on them, and set them afire just to watch the ruckus. I was brought out of my reveries by Muad, who turned his head around and asked:

"Don't you want to see the animal you are here to get? Want to see Mbogo?" We answered yes of course. A hearty yes. An enthusiastic yes.

An hysterically-anxious yes.

I had my doubts then. We all seemed just a little too eager...

Before long we began to see more zebra and giraffe. The horselike zebra is Africa's quintessential grazer, the giraffe its ultimate browser (along with the elephant). Their presence meant that high grass and trees probably lay ahead, and Mbogo, liking the grass to feed upon and the trees for shade and concealment, would probably be waiting for us.

We were not mistaken.

Less than an hour later we saw them, at first faintly as low dark blotches against the light brown grass. We approached slowly in the truck, all three of us watching through our glasses. The buff were lying down in the high grass chewing their cud, jaws working in that queer, circular motion as their molars re-chewed the six to eight bushels of fiber they had bitten off earlier in the day before the heat set in. When they saw us, which was from far, far off, all heads turned in our direction. The jaws stopped moving. We saw the bosses on top of their heads where the great sweeping scimitars of polished black thick horns met. Both males and females of *Cincerus Cafer Giganticus* wear huge horns. On the female they are set high on the head and curve outward then in, sitting on top of the head much like cow's horns, except they are black rather than gray. But on the bulls the horns are set low, emerging from the boss at the sides rather than the top, and drop outward and down as the animal ages. The oldest of the bulls—those sought after trophies with the thickest bosses and longest horns—are outcasts who live alone or in small groups of fellow outcasts. These are called *dagga boys.* Like all buff, they generally aren't much to worry about if they are healthy and undisturbed. Live and let live is their motto.

But when you hunt them the ambience shifts. And if and when

39

you put a bullet in them, a sudden and amazing personality change occurs. No author described hunting Mbogo better, or more accurately, than Robert Ruark. He gives the following account in his most famous African hunting piece, *Suicide Made Easy:*

Some people are afraid of the dark. Other people fear airplanes, ghosts, their wives, death, illness, their bosses, snakes or bugs.... Each man has a private demon of fear that dwells within him—the kind that makes the hands sweat and the stomach writhe in real sickness. This fear numbs the brain and has a definite odor, easily detectable by dog and man alike...

I have a fear that crowds into my dreams, a fear that makes me sweat and smell bad in my sleep. I am afraid of Mbogo, the big, black Cape buffalo. Mbogo, or Nyati as he is called in the South, is the oversized ancestor of the Spanish fighting bull. He is so damned big, and ugly, and ornery, and vicious, and surly, and cruel, and crafty. Especially when he's mad. And when he's hurt he's always mad. And when he's mad he wants to kill you—he won 't be satisfied with less.

From a standpoint of senses, the African buffalo has no weak spot. He sees as well as he smells, and he hears as well as he sees. And he charges with his head up and eyes unblinking. He can run as fast as an express train, haul up short, and turn on a shilling. He has a tongue like a wood rasp and feet as big as knife-edged flatirons. His skull is armor-plated and his horns are either razor sharp or splintered into horrid javelins. The boss of the horn that covers his brain can induce hemorrhage by a butt. The horns are ideally adapted for hooking, and one hook can unzip a man from crotch to throat. He delights to dance upon the prone carcass of a victim, and the man who provides the platform is generally collected with a trowel and placed in a coffee can, for Mbogo's death-dance leaves little but shreds and tatters.

But mostly, Mbogo refuses to die. He will soak up enough lead to sink a carrier and keep on coming. Leave him alone and he is mostly cattle and will gallop off at a loud noise.

"Shooo!" Kill him dead with a first shot through the nose and up into the brain, or get his heart and break his shoulder, and he dies. But wound him, even mortally, and he engenders a certain glandular

juice that makes him all but impossible to kill. I don't know the record for lead-absorption by a Cape buff, but I do know of one that took sixteen 470 Nitro-Express solid rounds through the chest and still kept coming. I know another that was shot twice through the heart and went more than two miles. Don't ask me how; he just did.

(On one hunt...) I lurched up and looked at Mbogo. . . and Mbogo looked at me. He was fifty to sixty yards off, his lead low, his eyes staring straight down my soul.

He looked at me as if he hated my guts.

He looked at me as if I had despoiled his fiancé, murdered his mother, and burned down his house.

*He looked at me as if **I owed him money—***

With these jolly thoughts in my head we crept closer to the herd.

"They don't look all that bad," mused Dick.

"That's what I'm thinking," Larry said. "They look like cows to me. I mean, a cow is a cow, right?"

"Uh huh. A cow is a cow is a cow." Wasn't it Gertrude Stein who said that?

Dick again: "I don't see what the big deal is, assuming we can get a good shot. Look: they aren't even getting to their feet. There's no threat response."

"Maybe they're used to trucks," I suggested.

"Well, then so much the better. We get in close, get out of the truck and place the shot, then maybe we can hop back inside if things get dicey," suggested Dick.

"The only problem with that is," said Larry, "they seem as big as the truck."

I studied the big black shapes again, each the size of a bass boat. Noticed their wide, wet muzzles, the shiny sweep of their black horns. The huge hump of bunched muscle on top of their necks.

"He looked at me as if I owed him money..."

There was a few seconds of silence before Muad turned his head around again and looked at us.

"Is this your first time hunting these animals?" he asked. We answered that it was.

"Um. Then I am not surprised."

"Surprised at what?" asked Dick.

"That you all think it will be so easy. I fear you may find it otherwise."

Uh oh...

"Well then how will we find it?" Larry was leaning over the seat now, in Muad's face, so to speak. "How will it be otherwise?"

Muad swept his hand across the windshield, indicating the herd of bovines lying placidly chewing their cud in the afternoon's heat. "Here we are in the midst of several big game preserves. In places like these, animals are not hunted, and they act accordingly. They do not fear man. Nor trucks, as you see. They do not hide, but stay out on the open—even in the daylight—to feed. Without man to worry about, they have no enemies."

"Not the lion'?" I asked.

Muad scrunched his lower lip and shook his head slightly.

"Not really. It takes two or three females to bring down a bull buff, and when one is attacked the others go to his aid. The same is true of a female. And if a calf is set upon the entire herd turns on the intruder. Buffalo kill lion on a regular basis. The big cats rarely bother them— they're better off, and safer, going for zebra."

Now for the big question, and I had to ask it. "So, how are they different where they're hunted?"

"First of all, you will never see *Mbogo* bed down on the open grass in daylight when you hunt him. That's one. He'll be in the thickest brush he can find. What we call *Kasaka*. It's low-growing thorn shrubs that you can scarcely crawl through. And it crackles around you like firecrackers when you push against it, so *Mbogo* can always hear you coming. But strangely enough, you can never hear him. Except when it's too late."

We were all leaning intently over the seat now, our faces rapt, inches from Muad's. I realized I had to take another leak.

"*Mbogo* will be holed up in the brush or deep in the swamp reeds all the day long. He will come out only after twilight to feed. When it is cool and dark and safe. That's when you can find him."

"In the *dark?*" I asked.

"Yes Sah."

"Fuck that," I said.

"Exactly, Sah. Fuck *all* of that—"

"And the only place we can get to him during the day is to crawl

42

through this *Kasaka* shit?" asked Dick.

"Yes Sah. The hunters and gun bearers generally duck-walk through the brush. It is very tiring—you have to stoop over low, ducking and twisting—"

"How the hell do you get a clear shot then?" Larry asked. I could hear a slight quaver in his voice. To this Muad shrugged his shoulders and held up his palms. "Do not ask me Sah. Per-son-a lly, I do my best to stay *out* of the brush and *inside* my vehicle."

Since I had been curious all day about the land speed capabilities of various fauna,my next question was obvious.

"Muad. How fast can a person go through this brush?"

"I can't really say," he shrugged. "I suppose a half mile an hour at the most, if you don't get stuck."

"I...see. And how about the buff?"

"Oh they slow down considerably Sah. I doubt very much if they could exceed ten or fifteen miles an hour in there."

There was silence in the Toyota as Muad turned us around and headed back. I believe it was what is referred to as a *pregnant* silence.

The silence and gloom lasted until, after a forty-minute drive through wind and dust of the plains of Nrongoro, we spotted the big fig tree in the distance.

Arriving on the scene, we saw that the tree owed its longevity and girth to a huge pool that lapped along its extended roots. The pool was deep and long, and perhaps in the rainy season became part of a river. In the brownish water huge gray shapes bobbed and collided. Now and then a pair of comical bulbous eyes would break the surface, accompanied by a pair of wriggling ears and puffing nostrils. Hippo. Those clownish-looking fatties that kill more people on the Dark Continent each year than any other mammal save the lion. A hoot to watch—from a distance Muad told us—just don't ever get between them and their water. Especially if they have a calf with them.

Beyond the hippos a large flock of Egyptian geese had landed. They resembled our Canadian geese except they had brighter plumage, which shown with flecks and stripes of iridescence.

We opened our lunch boxes that Christina had made up for us. In each box was an orange, a banana, a mango, a beef sandwich in a semi-stale French baguette, a hunk of some kind of German cheese (we were, after all, in the former German East Africa), and big candy bar of Lindt chocolate. To round it off was a small cooler if iced Tuskers lager.

It certainly looked tasty. But when I grabbed the sandwich and began to raise it to my mouth a pair of sharp pincers grabbed at it. At the same time something soft and slick butted and slid against my neck and head. I recovered my shock in time to see a pair of large flapping wings heading for the fig tree.

"What the—?"

"Mmmm. Red Kite," laughed Aaron with a stuffed mouth. "They're always good for a laugh when newcomers try to eat their lunch here."

I looked around at the crowd of people who had disembarked from a big touring coach, and another just come over from a big lorry with canvas sides. Everywhere I could see the big reddish-black hawks swooping down on the sightseers, making off with bits of their lunch. I was amazed at their boldness.

"Do they ever hurt anyone?" I asked.

"No. An occasional scratch on the hand is all. But Christina swears they're what gave rise to the legends of the Harpies. I don't know who they were, but you might."

I nodded. "But it's strange. I mean, the boldest birds I've been in contact with have been seagulls. They'll take fish out of your hand, but it takes a bit of coaxing to draw them near."

He looked off dreamily past the fig tree, the hippo pond, the flapping geese and the acacia trees to the far purplish horizon. "Yes Rick, it must seem strange to you. And your friends. But it doesn't to me simply because I was raised here. You must realize that this is Africa, and things are strange here. Basically the struggle for survival—survival mind you, not dominance or happiness or fulfillment or any of that rot—but basic survival—takes up almost every moment of every day for most creatures here. People included. There's not much time for delicacy, refinement, or manners here. It's steal or starve. Kill or be killed."

Christina came up and put her arm around Aaron. I had a burning question I was anxious to know the answer to. Now seemed as good a time as any.

"Muad was explaining about the thick brush here he calls kasaka.

Is it truly as unnavigable as he claims?"

"Pretty much so, for a person anyway. It's a great haven for small animals…even big ones."

"Yes, like Mbogo."

"—hey, you're catching on to Swahili."

"So what do we do if he goes in there and hides when we're hunting him?"

"Why then we go right in there after him. Great sport."

"I was afraid you'd say that. Listen: what encouraged me to come over here were those videos on buff hunting. They sure made it look exciting and all. But nowhere in them did it show the hunter wading into this kasaka brush to get his buff."

"No?"

"Absolutely not. It showed the guide and the client on the fringes of vast plains, scoping out herds of buff through their field glasses, then deciding which one to aim at. No kasaka on these videos, Aaron. No duck-walking through scrub at half a mile per."

"Shame, that. I reckon they left you a bit in the dark."

"Well? Are we going to have to crawl thorough that stuff or not?"

"Absolutely not."

"Well thank God."

"Not unless you'd like to get a buff that is—"

"Aaron!" cried Christina.

"Just kidding…"

"But really," she continued. I think you should be honest with Rick. And the others too, you know. It won't do any good to have them surprised and.. .thrown off balance by the unexpected. Along those lines dear, I do think you ought to tell him about the snakes."

"Snakes'?" I queried, brightening. "Did I hear the, uh, enthralling word *snakes?*"

"What she's eh, trying to say is that the *kasaka* is a favorite hang-out for our legless reptiles."

"Are they poisonous?"

"That, uh, depends on what you mean by poisonous." he said, sounding remarkably like a former President.

"*Aaron!*" shot Christina. "Why that's—"

"—now listen everyone," said Aaron—giving his fiancé's arm a quick little pinch—"there's really no point...no point at *all* in anyone here giving our snakes a *second thought*. Is there dear?"

He said this in his most soothing tone. I must say he had a soothing tone for a thirty-year-old kid who had been (we later found out) wanted in every country from Kenya to Mozambique for poaching. Perhaps in the states he could wrangle a job delivering singing telegrams to parents whose kids had just been in fatal car wrecks.

"I suppose not...not when I really pause to consider it," Christina sighed, rubbing her arm.

"Well, that makes me feel better at least," I said.

"Besides, I've never been that afraid of them anyway." I stood up from the table and dusted off my shorts. "Well Aaron, Christina; Muad's waving me on; I guess I'd better return to the truck. So long."

"Cheerio!" said Christina.

I walked to the truck with a lighter heart knowing I wouldn't have to give the African snakes a second thought. Good thing. I mean, there was enough scary shit to worry about on this adventure already.

We left the fig tree and headed off to see more game and scenery. Muad told us he had a nice place booked for us to stay that evening. It was more rustic than the plantation house, but he assured us we would have all the conveniences. He didn't lie. In late afternoon we arrived at a locally-run lodge overlooking a waterhole. The lodge was built on stilts to offer a good view of the local waterhole and at the same time prevent flooding and "intrusion of native fauna" (read: leopard in the nighttime). Muad made it clear at the outset that this was not where we were to stay the night, but eat our dinner. The bar/restaurant was an open porch extension of the lodge, with exposed hand-hewn rafters and beams and rustic railings all around. It was deserted when we arrived. We ordered beer and bread and looked down at the waterhole. A group of Massai "Morran," or warriors was washing themselves in the pond. It was to be the first of many times I was to see this ritual. The Massai were clean as well as brave, and (most notably the men) tremendously vain as well as handsome. After a great meal of antelope chops, curried loin of warthog, fresh pineapple-mango chutney, fried yams, and ice cream, the three of us sat back under the humming ceiling fans. I lighted an Upmann Petit Corona. Dick set fire to a Macanudo Royal Ascot. The rich, tangy smoke drifted around us. I felt the taste of the Upmann right in the top of my nose, just below my eyes.

"Life is good," I sighed.

"It's not bad," Larry agreed.

Dick glanced in my direction. "Why are you saying life is so good, Boyer? You're the guy who's been whining this entire trip. And we haven't even come to the fun part yet."

"If the 'fun' part includes duck-walking into the kasaka to root out Mbogo and his wee kiddies, count me out. I ain't the brightest guy who ever came down the pike, but I'm no idiot."

They looked at each other, then at me.

Larry said, "I wouldn't place a bet on that."

We left the lodge behind us when the sun was low in the sky. The Acacia and Baobab trees were casting long shadows across the brown grass and red earth. The sun was bright orange in a purple sky. God, Africa was gorgeous! Too bad it hid so many. . . surprises.

It was around eight when we approached a compound of rustic structures on wooden platforms surrounded by a rail fence. There were ten of them, two rows of five. The structures were thatched roofs under which canvas tents were set up. This was, I assumed, the combination of the rustic and convenient that Muad was referring to.

A black woman of thirty named Beatrice was the owner of this campground. She showed me to my tent (the three of us each had our own private tents) and explained how the shower, flush toilet, and sink worked, showed the refrigerator, and departed. Beatrice spoke perfect English and was very polite. I was constantly struck, throughout the trip, by the patience, manners, and gentility of the natives in this land of harsh brutality and continual threat. I don't remember much about that evening—not because we were drunk but because we were tired, not to say exhausted. It was not from physical exertion; all we'd done essentially was ride around in a truck. It was the stimuli. Too much input too fast. And a lot of the input was the heavy-duty variety, the kind that keeps your imagination buzzing with unpleasant scenarios. Dick was in the next tent over; Larry was sequestered in the one behind me. I lay on the stiff bunk and smoked another Upmann while I finished my evening Scotch and water. I lighted the candle on the table and turned the lights off, listening to the night sounds. Funny. For all its wildness, Africa was strangely silent at night. Not at all as noisy as North Carolina, for example. I heard some bugs singing in trees, and

47

the occasional call of a night bird, but no yipping Hyenas. No lions roaring to bring the sun up, as in the *Short Happy Life of Francis Macomber*.

I thought again of the snakes that weren't worth a second thought. Then promptly let them drop. That at least was good news. I closed my eyes and went to sleep.

CHAPTER THREE

ARUSHA

The next day we rolled into Arusha just before lunch. When we arrived back at the Impala Hotel we were told that Glen had finally returned from the Selous Reserve with his clients and was now at his camp—the same camp we were bound for—in the Masai Mara. He would make his way back to Arusha tomorrow, finish up his paperwork, and we would leave for the local airport the next day for camp. To get maximum hunting time we would fly in because the camp was seven hours from Arusha by road—if it could be called a road. By aircraft it was less than 40 minutes.

Meantime we had a day and half to kill in this second-largest city in Tanzania. Muad pulled the Toyota into the courtyard of the Impala and we disembarked. I was struck by how beautiful the courtyard was. Perhaps I had been too rushed and wound-up to notice it on our outward journey. But I noticed it now. The courtyard was paved in bricks that resembled the pavers on the streets of Paris. A pergola of heavy wooden poles stretched over the patio walls, creating a beam-like effect beneath, and were covered with waxy green vines, choked with dark shiny leaves and bright blooms. The air seemed cool and fragrant after the dusty heat of the savannah. I was glad to be home, no matter how briefly.

We unloaded our gear from the Toyota and first time I noticed a decal on the rear window. It said:

JESU JAI!

I supposed this to signify some sort of Christian spiritual experience or conversion, but I didn't pursue it. I turned to shake Muad's hand. Or perhaps to give him a hug. He seemed more like our little brother by this time rather than our guide. But he told me we weren't done with him yet; tomorrow was to be a full day of seeing local sights.

"In fact Sah, I was planning on taking your party out to see the craft shop and the snake farm in about an hour—right after you finish your nap."

"Why that's a good—I say Muad...have my ears deceived me or did I hear you utter the words *snake farm*?

"Yes Sah!"

I turned and made for the lobby door. "Okay sport. See you in a few—"

"Sah!"

I went up to my room which I hadn't seen in three days, took a long hot shower, changed clothes, and lay down. I was awakened by Larry knocking on the door, saying it was time to head out. Dick and Muad were waiting in the Toyota, and once again we drove that dusty red road out of the city, through the outskirts, past the colonial mansions, and into the country. We passed an ostrich farm on our left. The sight of hundreds of the huge, upright gawky birds behind barbed wire fences seemed surrealistic to me—like a Bergman film. By and by we saw a large building just off the road and a big sign in front proclaiming native crafts and gems for sale at discount rates.

"I know the owners person-al-ly," he said as we got out and walked in the scorching sun across the parking lot. "They will give you a far better deal than anyone in the city, and they also take credit cards."

Since nobody I had seen in country—with the exception of the Impala, which did 90% of its business with foreigners—had even seen a credit card, this was a definite plus. I had a travel wallet and a money belt bulging with high-denomination American bills and traveller's checks (local printed currency was practically worthless). I hated this, for obvious reasons. If these got filched I would be stranded in Tanzania and probably forced to join the nearest Masai village. This would be bad enough, but after they discovered I couldn't chuck a spear worth a hoot, I'd be led out of the boma at the first full moon and left to the Hyena Welcoming Committee.

So I was glad I could splurge a bit with my plastic and not deplete my wad of Dead Presidents. We entered the shop to the warm greetings of the salesmen who hugged Muad and gave up the same African handshake: the soft caress of their cool hands, with no grip pressure. This was not a show of strength on their behalf, but a true gesture of welcome.

One entire wall of this big shop was devoted to gold, silver, and gems. Especially gems. I was told before I left that the hottest new precious stone was the Tanzanite, a variety of sapphire that was first cousin to a diamond and that had a faint purplish hue. I wanted a Tanzanite for Jenny. Muad had assured me en route that I could buy her a giant specimen for a reasonable price, ie: in the neighborhood of one grand. After twenty minutes or so I decided on (or he talked me into) one slightly larger than I intended for $1200. Muad (who I *assumed* was not getting any kind of kickback on the sale…just as I *assume* that French elections are fair and the government of Mexico is a model of stability) assured me that it was the buy of a lifetime. So, with my credit card noticeably lighter I made my way around the store. Frankly, nothing much in the way of native crafts interested me. With the exception of course of the two huge elephant tusks on special consignment. These, mounted on special teak bases and trimmed in brass on the their bottoms, framed each side of a doorway, and reached up beyond the molding.

"Record tusks, Bwana Rick. They were taken fifteen years ago by a Hungarian Count."

"You know, Muad, I don't believe in killing elephant. They're too noble. But since the owner of these magnificent tusks has already handed in his dinner pail, so to speak, would you mind telling me the asking price? They'd look good in my study."

"Thirty thousand U.S. Cash."

"Hmmmm. So much for that. Let's see how our comrades are faring. Then we'll take in the much-heralded serpent display."

We found Dick and Larry lounging near the doorway, so we were ready to go. It didn't even necessitate the Toyota. We simply ambled next door and there it was, with a big sign: SNAKE FARM in English outside. Reminded me of those roadside quasi-zoos one sees on the way to Florida.

Outside the walled farm two camels reclined on the dust, I assumed awaiting their masters. If you've never had the opportunity to get up close and personal with a camel, you have no idea how huge they are. These beasts, lying on their stomachs and tucking their knobby forelegs under their chests, were twelve feet from head to tail (the neck was a good four feet of that). On their single humps rode saddle frames made of cross-timbers that straddled their bony backs in an inverted V. Over this framework were fitted high-backed cushions. I approached them closely, ready to dodge back if they showed any signs of aggression, for I heard camels are notoriously ill-tempered. They will spit at you, bite you, or kick your brains in. But I knew they couldn't do the latter because they were sitting on their forelegs. They eyed me passively as I came up to them and blinked their eyelids—the four-inch lashes sending waves of air currents over me. God, they were huge! It's no wonder they're called the Ship of the Desert.

We entered the enclosure (it had no roof) under crossed timbers of native design and met the curator, a fellow in the olive drab whose name was Michael. He introduced himself and collected our money. I was to see similar olive drab uniforms everywhere in this country, most notably on the Tanzanian soldiers, who were a very visible presence, riding through thrown and about the countryside in their open lorries, assault rifles slung across their chests.

We began by watching Michael collect various small green snakes off the trees in the compound and hold them in his hands, caressing them. Some of the larger ones, which I could tell were boas, he draped around his neck. They snuggled up there beneath his neck in a cozy hold. Since my son had owned two ball pythons while in high school, I was used to these antics and was unfazed. Larry even volunteered to hold one of the smaller green snakes. It was pleasant in this garden. Silent for one thing. Behind low stone barriers lizards the size of Gila Monsters moved slowly as minute hands on a clock.

Leaving the garden, we entered a cool, dark stone building whose only source of light came from rows of small eye-level cages. In these thirty or so types of snakes were confined behind thick glass. We ambled past these in cavalier fashion until Dick let out a groan. I saw him pointing to the cage he had just come adjacent to.

"Oh God—look in there guys…"

Larry looked in and shrugged. "So?"

I looked in and shrugged. "So?"

"Keep watching; you'll see."

We were looking at two medium-sized serpents, each about two and a half feet long with speckled grayish-black heads and backs. They seemed to be a mated pair, entwined around each other and moving in that creepy way snakes have, where one part of their length is busy coiling and undulating while the rest of it appears dead. Still, I saw nothing to get excited about, and kept to Aaron's dictum of 'not giving our snakes a second thought.' That is, until this pair of lovebirds spotted us, moved up to the front of the cage, and raised their heads. Then they flared their hoods.

"Cobras!" whispered Larry. "Holy shit!—I knew they lived in India, not here."

"Oh, the cobra lives many places," said Michael, who had oiled up behind us to give these good tidings. "The King Cobra lives in India, but many others are scattered throughout Asia and Africa. These, you see, are *spitting* cobras."

"Oh, they spit but don't bite?" I said. "Well that's good because for a second I was—"

"They spit *first*, Sah." interjected Muad. "They spit their venom through their fangs, and can hit you from twelve or fifteen feet. If the venom gets in your eyes, you will be blinded."

"Temporarily, of course," corrected Dick, who was, after all, the best known ophthalmologist in Pocatello, Idaho.

"Permanently, I fear."

"Oh…I…see…"

"And then of course, after he blinds you he usually bites you."

"Ah, but then there's antivenom," countered Larry.

"Yes Sah," said Muad.

"Good to know."

"It never works; the venom is too quick and powerful."

"…I…wasn't aware of that…"

We moved along. The inhabitant of the next cage was bad; I could tell by looking at it. The scales stood out like tiny loosened shingles on an old roof, giving the snake the appearance of a flexible wood rasp. The color was brownish red, with some faint lighter markings that were hard to distinguish. The head was, well, singular. It was wide, with swellings at the mandibles much like a pit-bull's biting

53

muscles. It was powerfully muscled, and had scaly protrusions over the eyes.

"What's this little gem?" I inquired.

"The puff-adder, Sah. Also called the hundred foot snake."

"*Hundred foot snake?*" Larry wasn't going for it. "C'mon Michael! I know a little about snakes. The biggest snake on earth, the Anaconda, is only about thirty feet long. That's plenty big. A hundred footer? No way! How could this snake ever hope to get—"

"—you are quite correct Sah— this snake seldom exceeds five feet in length."

"Well then why do you call it the—"

"It gets its name because no living thing, once bitten by it, can go a hundred feet before falling over dead."

"...I...see....."

A deep depression was spreading over me. I noticed too the friendly banter and idle conversation of our little group was fading. In its place was a silent void, a series of anxious glances and downcast stares. Fondling the small, hard bundle in my pocket that held the gorgeous Tanzanite, I wondered if I would ever see my Jenny again. Or my children. Alas, it seemed increasingly not to be. No doubt I would perish in this remote and inhospitable land...writhing in agony from a serpent's strike, my last conscious moment watching the huge, stinky Griffon vultures winding their way down the air currents to devour my entrails, leaving the remainder to my favorite animal, *fisi*.

It sucked.

"I'm going out for a breath of air," I told Larry.

"The hell you are. C'mon, we might as well see the rest. I mean, they can't be as bad as these fellas. Besides, these things can't hurt us, they're in cages—"

"It's not these I'm concerned about; it's their relatives out there—slithering around in the sand."

"He's right Rick. Let's move on to the next cage," said Dick. So we did. I peered inside, and instantly knew what monstrosity lay there. I felt the dry heaves coming on; the curators should have had sense enough to tape a vomit bag to the cage.

Now, allow me to insert something at this point in my narrative: many people feel a universal revulsion to all snakes. I am not one of these. I think most snakes are fine. Some are even pretty. I don't regard them as inherently ugly or monstrous, or evil. Spiders, yes. Snakes, no.

But there is one snake so malformed and malevolent-looking that it can turn the stomach of a goat. Make the Marquis de Sade do volunteer work in a nursing home. Cause a hardened atheist to drop to his knees in supplication. You get the picture.

I advanced and peered into the glass again. Yep. No mistake. There it was: the **Gaboon Viper.** A serpent less than a yard long, but weighing over thirty pounds. Less than two inches high along the back but at least five inches wide. A serpent that to all appearances has been run over by a steamroller. The head is huge, wide, with prickly horns on the snout and swollen poison sacs at the back of the jaws. The fangs are the longest of all the serpents and monstrously thick, with enough potent venom in those balloon sacs to float a war canoe. It is a bundle of flattened muscle covered with a perfect camo pattern of scales that makes it invisible. The venom is beyond deadly and has no antidote.

"This is the Gaboon Viper gentlemen," intoned Michael. "and it is—"

"—don't say it; let me guess," said Larry. "Poisonous in the extreme, with no hope of recovery."

"Absolutely, Sah! Thank you for your interest."

"My pleasure."

With dry mouth and pounding heart I peered down the row of cages. Mercifully, along this wall there was only one left. "And now gentlemen, we have the most interesting for last. In this last cage you will see the most dangerous snake not only in Tanzania, but the whole African continent. Not just the African continent, but in the entire *world*—"

I paused with baited breath, expecting perhaps a fanfare and a drum roll. I could blow lunch.

We peered around the corner of the cement wall and into the cage. It was a large cage, as big as a bathtub, with several dead logs inside and a water dish. Entwined around the wood was an exceptionally long, thin snake that was metallic pale green in color. The head was small and well shaped, unlike the swollen-jawed, pit-bulldog head of the pit vipers. Nor the horrendous flared-hood variety of the kraits and cobras. Actually, this snake looked fairly benign. Rather like a long green garter snake.

"I must say Michael, that looks rather like a long green garter snake."

He turned to face me. I saw his lower jaw tremble.

Oh *no*, Sah. I wish it were so. But this snake is a nightmare come true. For this… this is…the *Black Mamba*."

"Wait a sec," interjected Dick. "Isn't the Mamba a dance?"

"No stupid; that's the *Sam*ba," corrected Larry.

"On the contrary," I stated. "I believe you're referring to the Mam***bo***."

Poor Michael was looking back and forth between us shaking his head. He was muttering something.

"Well speak up man, what is it?" I asked.

"Mzungu Mjinga."

"Come again?"

"Mzungu Mjinga."

"What's that mean anyhow?"

Michael remained silent. But Muad was laughing.

"Muad, what's he talking about?"

"I don't know, Sah."

"Hell you don't. He's talking about us, isn't he?"

"I would not think so, Sah."

"Now Michael, is it Mamba, Mambo, or Samba?"

"Or perhaps even ***Sambo?***"

"*Shhhhhhhhhhhh!*" Shut up Rick. Black people don't like it when you call them Sambo.

"And also, why's it called the *Black* Mamba if it's green?" Dick asked. I thought this a fair question. The only good one, in fact, since we'd entered this venom-venue.

"It's called Black Mamba because the inside of its mouth is black. Black as coal. Pray to your Christian God you never see the inside of a Black Mamba's mouth, Sah!"

"I also hope so. But listen: we've just seen a fine smattering, if you will, of your more disagreeable snakes. Have you any good ones?"

He shook his head.

"Ohhhh-kay. Well, we've become acquainted with the Spitting Cobra, the Puff-Adder, the Gaboon Viper, and the Black Mamba. Anything else?

"Oh, there are perhaps a score or so more, like the Green Mamba, for example."

"And also the Boomslang, the Hairy Bush Viper—"

"Not to mention the Night Adder…but these are the headliners."

"Now tell me, if bitten by one of these little cuties, I take it there is absolutely no hope of recovery. Is that correct? "

"I am afraid so, Sah. But the Black Mamba is particularly ferocious. It has a terrible temper, and although the head appears small, the snake carries a very large amount of toxin. The mambas are tree-dwellers, and have very keen eyesight. It is not uncommon for these snakes to lie among the branches in a tree, high up, where they can watch everything that passes. If they see something, or someone, that infuriates them they spring from the tree and make through the tall grass at lightning speed, far faster than a person can run."

Just what I needed to hear: another land speed record by a killer beast.

But something in his description had me doubting.

"Muad, tell me this—even if they have great eyes, how the hell can they see what they're going after when they're in grass that's *three feet tall?*"

"Simple you see: they do not crawl or slide like most snakes, Sah. No—the mamba carries himself in a series of leaping bounds, arching high up over the grass so it can keep its victim in full view. Once it strikes, death comes quickly. It is said the best thing to do when bitten by a mamba is to sit down and light a cigarette. Needless to say also, the victims final minutes are not pleasant ones—"

I turned to Muad, clenching and unclenching my hands. I wanted to wrap them around his scrawny neck and squeeze. "Listen: do you mean to say you've dragged us all over creation here without telling us that *death lurks beneath our feet* even as we walk? That one misstep will prove fatal?"

"Of course, Sah. But this is Africa. The reason so many of your countrymen go on safari here. The thrill of danger."

I stalked out of the building and out into the courtyard. I went out to the road and scanned the highway hoping to thumb a ride back to town. Then to the hotel to pack my bags, and to the airport where I would board an early flight home. To hell with it! I waited for several minutes with no vehicle in sight. I went back into the courtyard where the two camels were still reclining on the hot sand chewing their cud. Or whatever they do. I approached the nearest one and prepared to throw my leg over the saddle frame. The beast turned his big head and blinked at me, working his huge lips. I've heard camels spit at you when they're pissed off. I assumed Joe here was working up a big goober to send my way.

"Hey Rick, what the hell you doing?"

I turned to see Larry standing in the doorway.

"Heading back to Arusha. I'd thumb a ride but I don't trust these military dudes in their half-tracks." I took a chance and swung my leg over the high saddle; the huge animal began to surge beneath me. As it rose high I felt like a rodeo rider, wondering if I could stay on for eight seconds—the time it took an elephant to do the hundred yard dash. No dice—I jumped off, almost spraining my ankle in the process.

"Why are you going back there?"

"Catch a cab to the airport, then the first plane back to the Lower Forty-Eight. I'll see you guys. *Happy fangs.*"

"You can't just ditch out like this."

"Hell I can't. And I'm going to sue the clowns who made those adventure videos. You betcha. Or maybe put a mamba in their mailbox. Talk about hate mail—"

"Rick, Goddammit! We're heading back into town. Now hurry up or you'll *walk* back, and think about what could be waiting for you along the sandy road. Eh?"

Dejected, I followed Larry and Muad back to the truck where Dick was waiting.

"I need a drink," I said.

"Don't we all," said Dick. "Hey what happened to you back there anyway?"

I told him I had a sudden urge to impersonate Lawrence of Arabia. We headed back into the bowels of Arusha (I use that metaphor deliberately) again and stopped at an intersection in the heart of the city that was definitely *native* (read: no white people for miles). As soon as we exited the car we were surrounded by street people and beggars so assertive it has hard to tell them from shakedown artists. One tough in particular stalked us, trying to sell some sort of gewgaw that definitely was worthless. He tried me twice, and each time I fixed his stare directly with mine and made eye contact for a full two seconds before I shook my head and said NO. He left me alone after that, but Larry caved in and bought it, whatever it was. I must admit that he fell a bit in my eyes after that.

Behind these street-corner types was a shop with an open-air front (much like the ones in Latin America) that are closed and locked only with a slide-down shutter grate. Inside a man in the far back was sewing a Masai-style tartan robe with an old Singer treadle sewing machine. His big two-tone foot pumped rhythmically as he expertly stitched the garment for a customer who waited by his side. But it wasn't the tailor who caught my eye. It was the old man seated in a chair at the head of the shop facing the street. He faced the street, listening to the foot and motor traffic. But he obviously could not see it. His eyes were filmy white, the irises covered with an egg-white sheen that made them opaque and ghostly. His legs and feet were swollen beyond belief, and the skin there was riddled with scabs and running sores. Since my comrades in arms were both physicians (and one an ophthalmologist, no less), I asked them what they thought ailed the old man. They answered they had no idea. That it could be anything from advanced scurvy to parasites to elephantiasis. We left the place and headed back to the Impala Hotel again, but I knew I would never forget that street corner scene, and the obvious suffering that the old man bore so silently. Truly Africa is a rough place.

In the Impala's bar we had more than our share of Tuskers and headed up to our rooms for a lie-down before going out to dinner that evening. I awoke in a groggy state and met Larry and Dick in the lobby, from whence I was summoned. We saw Aaron waving us outside to the courtyard where we climbed into his truck and rode in the deepening twilight to the place Christina and company had chosen for us to dine. The restaurant was the best (and also, apparently the *only*) place to get a really good meal in town. *L'Entrecote,* we were assured, was worth the wait and the expense. We entered and found it jam-packed with European tourists. Not a black face to be seen. This, I was told, was the primary attraction. We were given places to sit at the bar—the last thing we needed—and ordered drinks. I decided to stick with beer since I guessed the wait for food might be somewhat protracted. In this, I was not mistaken. Most of the patrons were drinking booze: gin and tonics, pink gins, gin and bitters, Scotch and sodas, martinis, the usual liver-lancers.

"Well then, are you one of the new clients?" said a very British voice to my immediate left. I turned to see a gentleman in late middle age hunched over a gin and bitters, slice of lime, smoking a cheroot. He wore a wide brim hat, glasses, and a trim salt-and-pepper moustache. I gave my name and said we'd signed on with Glen Schacht.

"Great. He's a first-rate PH. I'd say he's the best in Africa right now. None better. And a Yank as well."

"I know; Aaron told us."

"Lives in Jackkson Hole, Wyoming. Guides for Elk and Mule deer when not over here. Awesome shot. Doesn't stand for any foolishness though. Mind you do what he says or he'll let you know."

As I was to discover only too personally and powerfully later on.

"So what's your name?"

"Peter Swannapoel."

Well well. The Legend Himself. Swannapoel, of Dutch extraction and born and raised in Zambia (as was Aaron) was the cofounder of *Swannapoel & Scandrol, Ltd.* This small firm is probably the most respected outfit on the continent. I told him so and he nodded humbly but proudly into his glass. "Well, we've worked damn hard getting it that way. Though God knows how long the hunting will last over here. Be a damn shame when it all goes."

"You think it will go?"

"Almost positive. The locals—even the more competent ones—haven't the patience or sense of planning to keep the game. There's immense pressure from all native populations to turn the parks and preserves over to farms and grazing land. When that happens, it'll only be a matter of a few decades at the most. And the irony is this: sport hunting is Africa's trump card, its goose with the golden eggs, don't you see. Nothing brings in more hard cash to these poor strapped nations than hunting fees…except maybe the diamond and gold mines."

"Well then it's a good thing we came when we did and didn't postpone it."

"Oh absolutely. The only thing you have to watch out for this year is an outbreak of Rift Valley Fever. Other than that it's—"

"What's Rift Valley Fever? I assume it takes it's name from the place Leaky discovered the fossils—"

"Exactly. But take it from me, you don't want to get this malady."

"Like malaria, eh? Well, I assume they have medications and all that?"

"Yes and no."

"What are the symptoms?"

"I don't think I'll tell you; you don't really want to know."

"And why is that?"

"Because it's a hundred-percent fatal."

At that moment a waitress stuck her head over our shoulders and directly between our heads. "Your table is cleared and ready gentlemen. You can go and place your order now."

And so, with that cheery news, we rose and left the bar.

The order was forever in coming, and we passed the time by downing more Tuskers and booze. This stopped only when they brought the wine. By the time dinner arrived I was at that point at which the world had gone into slo-mo and shapes and voices were blurry and far-off. I was vaguely conscious of my plate beneath me, which I pawed at with my utensils now and then. The strip steak was a perfect *au pointe* and covered with Béarnaise Sauce. Delicious. But I was looking at the girls. When I get buzzed they seem magically to come to the forefront, and now in the dim light I was trying to check them out. Christina looked radiant. She was pretty anyway, but in the dim light and with the booze working in me, she was terrific. The waitresses looked pretty too, which meant they were at least passable in normal conditions. We stuffed ourselves, laughed and joked a lot, and finally closed the place up. We all pitched in to pay the bill; the damage to my wallet was fairly astounding.

We staggered out into the night air to board our respective vehicles. On my way out into the full darkness of a tropical night I bumped into a lean, dark man with a moustache that arched around his mouth and down each side of his chin. He wore a billed hat with a logo I could not see in the dark. He glared at me with intense, burning, black eyes.

"Whoa, Bwana—watch where you're going."

"Sorry. Didn't see you."

"Didn't see me? Your vision that bad? What's going to happen when we get out to camp and the shooting starts?"

"Rick, this is Glen Schacht, our P.H," said Aaron.

I offered my hand and he took it. Somewhat reluctantly, I thought. The man was a shade under my height and noticeably lighter built. Lean rather than thin. Didn't smile once. Gave the impression he took his job seriously and didn't suffer fools. Turned out I was correct in this assessment and, being basically a fool (at least much of the time) I would therefore suffer for it. But he did have an aura of self-assuredness. He reeked of confidence and courage, and that was comforting. Lord knows after what I'd discovered about the Dark Continent the past few days I needed some of that. Before I realized it we were piled into another Toyota, this one Glen's. I was seated beside him, of all people, with Peter Swannapoel behind me. Dick and Larry were riding with Aaron and Christina.

We bounced and jounced along Arusha's ruined streets at way above speed limit, passing a serious car wreck on our right. Injured people screamed in the night. A rescue vehicle of some sort was attempting to come to the scene but was blacked by clots of onlookers and looters.

"Major *kufa*," murmured Glen.

"What's a *kufa?*"

"It means dead. I tell you, this place is fucked. Totally *fucked.*"

"You mean the whole country?"

He shook his head. "Naw. The bush is all right. But it's doomed. But the cities are all totally fucked. I assume you've seen a bit of it."

"Oh yeah. Wouldn't want to live here."

"Hell no. And the more whites they kick out the worse it gets. Then they ask the U.N. for more aid and we foot the bill, all the time being blamed for this kind of shit—" He waved his arm in the direction of the street ahead, shaking his head. There was a pause then as we rode. Then he asked me a question. "So tell me. What game have you hunted? Especially dangerous game."

"A few years ago I shot a wild hog. From a stand."

He stared at me. "That's **it?**"

I nodded. He sighed. "Major *kufa.*"

We arrived back at the Impala after midnight. I staggered up the lobby stairway to the second floor, found my room, and crashed. I didn't even think to spray my room first. I considered my situation briefly. Here I was in Deepest Africa, supposedly the land of my dreams as an adventurer. But adventure was one thing—suicide another. I wondered if there were still a chance I could backtrack to the airport and make a connection with the next jumbo jet winging back to Chicago via Amsterdam.

Sure, I'd be ridiculed.

Rejected.

Sneered at.

Spat on.

But hey, I was used to that. I could handle it.

And I'd be *safe*. Safe from the likes of *Mbogo. Tembo. Simba, Chui,* and *Fisi,* and all those other cuties, like the Four Friendly Fanged Fiends at the serpent emporium. Spare me! In the slightly twisted words of Tiny Tim:

"God Help Us, Every One!"

CHAPTER FOUR

FLIGHT

The next day was all business. Glen was up early and had eaten before we got down to the lobby. When working clients, the typical PH gets about 4 hours sleep. He must be up before dawn to supervise the help in getting the vehicles fueled and the breakfast started. Throughout the day there are innumerable details that demand his full attention. By dusk he is exhausted, yet must stay up long enough to plan the next day's hunts, making sure that the trucks don't interfere with each other and that each shooter has maximum opportunity for shots—and can therefore fill his tags.

On this morning Glen had several clients who were due to take the evening plane and he had to finish their paperwork. Like most Third World countries, Tanzania made up in paperwork and bureaucratic tedium what it lacked in substance and competence. And this in a former German colony. I hate to think what it would be like had it been a French colony. At any rate, throughout the A.M. we could see Glen at the terrace tables in the back patio head-to-head with various clients, fillings out reams of forms detailing each animal taken, vouchers for trophy fees received, transfer forms for the salted hides and skulls, and so on. At strategic intervals one client, a beefy, blond man wearing a conspicuous gold Rolex with diamond encrusted dial, would lean forward and affix his signature when required.

When Glen went in for a coffee refill we started talking. Turns out he was a banker from Seattle, and this was his fifth safari. I asked him what game he had taken and he told me crocodile, python, marabou stork, griffin vulture, hyena, and several others. I winced inwardly. I was curious as to why he'd sought these animals out (and gone all the way down to the Selous Reserve to get them) since they are neither edible nor particularly attractive. He replied that they were the only animals from this part of the continent he did not have in his trophy collection. I then envisioned Mr. Rolex striding around in his gigantic trophy room (or rooms), inspecting his miniature African landscape. I decided I didn't like this guy a whole lot. Dick, Larry and I spent the rest of the morning milling around, glancing at our (Japanese) watches. Glen had mentioned we were going to take a flight to the camp since the way by road was six hours plus. The flight was going to cost each of us an extra $250. That was not a huge sum, but I kept thinking that in chunks about this size my stash of cash was being inexorably eaten away.

"Goddamit, what the hell have you been doing?"
Glen was standing in the Impala's lobby, hands on hips, chewing us out. We stood in front of this dark, skinny guy like errant schoolboys.

"Well? I told you the plane leaves at *one*. It's now quarter after twelve. What if we miss it? Nigel may have another fare by then, and then we're stranded here. Now go up to the lockers and get your gun cases. I want you all down in Aaron's land cruiser in ten minutes with all your luggage and your guns and ammunition. *I'm sick of all this fucking around here—"*

He turned on his heel and left. I ran through my mind all the Professional Hunters I'd seen in the movies and read about in the books. These depictions always presented the P.H., first of all, as a Brit. A man with the courage of a lion, the manners of a count, and the heart of a nanny. A gentleman through and through who could be counted on to do the right thing. And do it with style and grace. A chap who, over pink gins at night round the fire, congratulated you on your skilled marksmanship, despite the fact that you'd turned to jelly and soiled your breeks while following a wounded Dik-Dik into heavy cover. That sort of thing…

Then here comes this blue-jean-clad, baseball-capped, hard-on from Jackson Hole, Wyoming who is definitely NOT one of the above.

"So why are we going with this guy anyway Dick?" I had asked him eighteen months previous. Dick had booked Glen on his own, bypassing a booking agent and saving us the ten percent booking fee. He had made it clear at the outset, though, that thrift was *not* his motivation.

"Hell, I live only about ninety miles from him," he told me. "And hunted with him maybe six times. Glen always gets the game. *Always*. If he doesn't it means there's just none out there. Simple as that. Besides, he's not a bad guy really—just gung-ho."

It was with a heavy heart that I ascended the stairway with Aaron and made my way into the triple-locked security room that had held our firearms while were on the photo safari with Muad. Hunched over in the small locker, we hauled out the big aluminum cases and opened them in the hallway. We were to leave the metal airlines cases behind—they were much too bulky and heavy for anything but shipping. I drew out my two magnums: a 300 Winchester and 458 Winchester. The latter is the most powerful commercially loaded cartridge available. It is used for the big heavy stuff, like *Tembo, Faro,* and *Mbogo.* The lighter 300 magnum is smaller-bore powerhouse capable of putting down zebra-sized game or bigger, but it's especially effective as a high-speed, straight-line shooter that can reach far out to nail antelope, warthogs, and the like.

Within half-an hour's time we were lined up outside the lobby in the courtyard, each surrounded by duffels, camera bags, and our rifles slung over shoulders on slings. The rifles weighed a ton, and I was glad when Aaron pulled up in his Land Cruiser to take them off our hands.

These Toyota long-wheelbase Land Cruisers were to be our second homes in the days to come. Open jeeps, they had drop-down windshields in front, a driver's wheel on the right side, and a row of elevated seats behind the front pair. The elevated seats were a full foot and a half higher than the first and held three men. Separating then from the front seats was a tubular gun rack that held long guns horizontally above the driver's seat back. The top of this rack was also useful for those riding in the second seat to hold onto for stability on rough roads or fast driving, both of which happened a lot in the bush. Behind the raised second seat was an open bed perhaps six feet long. This space had no seats; it was reserved for the gun bearers and trackers to stand in, hands gripping the seatback of the elevated second seat so they could see over everybody and watch for game. When game was killed the tailgate was dropped and the carcass hauled into the truck bed for transport. On each side of the bed two spare tires were fastened vertically to the sides. As many as four-to six men could ride in the bed, either standing, leaning on rails, or riding on the lowered gate.

We hauled ass out of Arusha for the third time. But now there was different feel to it all. We had been tourists before. Now we were *hunters*; the artillery swarming all over the gun racks proclaimed it. I noticed the natives looked at us as we passed, many of them giving us a lot of space. I supposed the early European colonists with their black-powder rifles felt the same superiority, and it just never died.

At the airport we watched while Glen fumed and fussed again, this time at Nigel.

"Where the fuck is he? The Limey bastard—"

But in short order the pilot appeared, clad in khaki jacket and wash pants, carrying his flight bag. His plane was a beaut, a turboprop model that could haul eight people and their gear. I remember it wasn't an American-made job, I think it was a Fokker or DeHaviland or one of those. Anyhow, we all struggled aboard and hauled our stuff behind us, stowing it, as Nigel instructed, in the various racks and between bulkheads where it wouldn't go flying around if things went amiss.

Flying is one of the things I'm really afraid of. But of course, it should now be obvious to even the most chowder-headed reader that I'm afraid of practically everything. But flying in particular gets me, mainly because it's so totally beyond my control. Once you settle into your seat and strap yourself in and the craft becomes airborne, that's it pal. It's *out of your hands.* And you're totally at the mercy of things like turbojet engines—which may or may not be in good repair; unknown pilots—who may or may not be secretly schizophrenic or on drugs or just recently completed a suicide pact; control-tower personnel who may be bombed, pissed off at their wives, eager to finish that all-important crossword puzzle—you get the picture.

Once you're on, you're fucking **on,** and there's no stopping and getting out.

But now, I was strangely nonchalant about getting aboard that turboprop to fly a couple hundred miles out into MMBA. And later I discovered the reason: there were so many other nasty things sprinkled in our paths in this place that a mere airplane ride was child's play. And also watching Nigel as he revved each engine in turn, checking the gauges, talking to the tower, and taxiing to the runway, made me feel all was well. Once at the end of our runway he locked the brakes and redlined both engines. I could feel the aircraft vibrate as it strained to go forward, but he held back until the last possible moment, then released the wheels. We sped down the tarmac and I felt the tail come up to horizontal, then we reached rotation—the wings pitched up, the tail dropped, and we climbed into the Wild Blue.

Well, flying over the Dark Continent was simply the Cat's Ass. I'd seen films taken from the air: herds of elephant running beneath the monstrous moving shadow of the aircraft, no doubt terrified by the horrendous noise form this giant bird overhead. Impala, Wildebeest and Impala racing in giant bounds. Giraffes, necks outstretched and humping along at 50 mph at a stride per second. Throughout the flight we all sat tight at the windows, foreheads pressed to the Plexiglas so as not miss a second of it. The Acacia trees went on forever. I don't believe we were flying above 3000 feet at any time. This was really MMBA, rolling away beneath our wings. We saw snaky brown riverbeds almost dry, with herds of elephant and hippo in them. Giant hunting birds soaring on still wings, and great flocks thundering in rapid flight toward those two things all animals on this planet seek above all else: food and sex. On the parched plains meandered zebra, wildebeest, impala, topi, and hartebeest. Far over our left wing was a snowcapped volcano resembling Mt. Fuji. It was Mt. Meru, and marked the fast-receding location of Arusha.

We began to drop, and before long level plowed fields appeared below us. The soil was flowerpot red, and I assumed—incorrectly it turned out—that the soil was a typical red-laterite clay soil like that in the Southeast. I was mistaken; the red color was the result of a high mineral content common in volcanic soils, which are among the very best crop-producers in the world. Glen leaned over and shouted to Dick and me. In that small turboprop shouting was the only was to hold a conversation.

"The farm we use as a landing strip here belongs to Thomas Montgomery and his cousin Colin Jones. It's an impressive spread; the soil's so good they grow seed plants there. There it is, right underneath us now. See?"

I looked down to see a flat plowed field with a thin pole standing upright in its center. Suspended from its top was an air sock. Nigel moved his arms and threw the plane into a steep turn. We were circling the field now, and still dropping. Before long I saw a straight dirt road bisecting the crop field. Our runway. We dropped and circled again, straightened our course, and came in for a smooth landing. We popped open the passenger door which was above the wing, stepped down on it, and walked back to it's tailing edge where we scooted off onto the ground. The rear fuselage door was also open now, and Glen and Nigel handed bundles down to two natives who stacked them in piles. The rest of our personal luggage was slid down the wing for us. All this time the engines were still running at idle with the wheels locked. A jeep appeared on the horizon approaching us from a distant farmhouse. Two white men got out. Jones and Montgomery we presumed, and we were right. They took our stuff and drove us to their farmhouse, a white-stuccoed building with a covered front porch with a shiny tile floor. What drew our attention, however, was the nice collection of skulls and horns on the walls flanking the front door. In America the preferred—and more expensive—form of taxidermy is the skinning and mounting of the animal's head, complete with skull, skin, and artificial eyes. These look absolutely lifelike. In Europe, however, a more common form of trophy preservation is simply the mounting of the animal's bleached skull and polished horns on a plaque. When the horns are slightly darkened with dye and polished with wax the effect is simple but stunning, and one need not worry about insect or mite infestation or cleaning the trophy. The animals represented on Monty's and Jones' front wall were greater Kudu, Impala, Topi, Grant and Thompson's gazelles, Wildebeest, and two big Mbogo. I studied the buff horns carefully, and noticed my companions were doing the same. Looking closely at the expressions on their faces and studying their body language, I had the distinct feeling that I was not alone in my trepidation regarding these monsters. Perhaps I was the most vocal about my self-doubts, but that didn't necessarily mean I was the only one who felt them.

The two farmers invited us in for beers. The interior had the same cool, shiny tile floor and thick white stucco walls as the porch. I assumed this was to fight the tropical heat. I was somewhat surprised to see a huge television against the far wall. I thought Tanzania would be one of the last places on earth to have television networks.

"Oh, they don't, except for a government propaganda station in Dar es Salaam. But we run this off our satellite dish. Hell, we get tellie from the States, Europe, Australia, South America…you name it. I sipped the cold Tusker. There was no other brand in East Africa except Safari, which wasn't as good but it didn't matter. Tusker apparently originated with the German colonists, using the same formula and methods they used in other countries like Mexico (Dos Equis), Brazil (Brahma), the Philippines (Carta Blanca), and even China (Tsing Tao). All these beers are excellent, and Tusker no exception.

The interior was neat, and clean as a surgery station. The partners were obviously particular about their home and, by extension, their business. A PC was on one desk, and was apparently used to track the day-to-day operation of 1200 acres of prime volcanically rich soil and the seed plants which it produced. These, they told us, were shipped to all parts of the globe where the demand for newly developed hybrid seed was insatiable—and lucrative. We were to bump into Jones and Monty many times during our fortnight in the bush, and always met with good humor and cooperation. But always I felt there was something hanging over them, and later discovered it was the possibility, if not the actual threat, that should another strong-man leader (it is a sad fact that in most African nations the so-called 'elected leader' is simply a thug with charisma and cunning) emerge in Dar es Salaam, the country's policy toward European landowners might change at a moment's notice and they would find themselves kicked off the farm they had spent decades building. Even worse, they might be imprisoned as spies or traitors to await an even more drastic fate. But for the present they both seemed to shrug this off and took life on the farm one day at a time, hoping for the best.

After a half-hour's visit we left the house, gathered our gear from the front porch, and headed for Glen's Land Cruiser, which he had parked at the airstrip prior to flying back to Arusha. Aaron was on his way from Arusha via his truck even as we started the road journey to camp.

So, rifles racked and duffels stacked, we bounced and jounced along the rutted road toward Mushandi, or Whitefaced mountain, under which, we were told, sprawled our camp, our home for the next ten-plus days and night.

71

This is it then, I thought as the dry, hot air blew through my hair. *All the watching of hunting videos, the buying of new gear, the painful practice bench-shooting a 458 Magnum elephant gun, the eighteen shots and vaccinations, the daily dose of larium starting a month before departure, the increasing phone calls between the three of us, the fourteen hour drive from Asheville to Chicago, the funeral arrangements for my recently-deceased father and comforting of my mother, the meeting of the triumvirate at O'Hare, the seventeen hour flight, the three-day photo safari, the horrendous snake farm, the increasingly fearsome tales of Mbogo...all of these were over now and it was the beginning of mano a mano—hand-to hand combat against this beautiful and frightful place.*

Was I up to it?

Time would tell.

Less than thirty minutes later, under a darkening cloudy sky, a steep smallish mountain appeared on the horizon. "Mushandi," said Glen, pointing over the dropped windshield. Soon the truck wound up a gently curving slope in the road that brought us to the foot of the mountain. There, at the base of Mushandi, just below the large boulders and scrub growth of the scree slope, nestled amongst a grove of old Acacias that spread a gentle, flat-planed peacefulness over the scene, lay base camp.

Glen drove to the far end of the camp, which was a much greater distance than I had imagined, to a series of large wall tents. We disembarked and dropped our duffels on the dusty ground.

"Your tents gentlemen," he said. "One single and one double. We'll eat in two hours. Until then you can unpack and stow your gear. Leave your guns on the stick tables outside the tent. You can see the shaving mirrors and basins on the outside of the tents. That—" he pointed to a curious structure of cinderblock and sticks topped with a 55-gallon metal drum affixed over the top, "is your toilet and shower. I request you take showers only when you need to. Every other day is plenty for most of us. The generator is on until ten thirty, then it's blackout, so if you want to read or write a journal or anything, do it before then. Wakeup is at four thirty. Breakfast is at five to five to five thirty. We're out of here before sunup. And we don't get back until dark. People ask me why my clients always get more game than anybody else. The answer is simple: I work my ass off and expect you to do the

milk, etc.), the luxury items (read: Tusker beer and Black & White Scotch), a kerosene-powered refrigerator, and a large rectangular dining table. The tent flaps were kept open—pulled back and tied to the sides of the tent so the interior was plainly visible. I believe this was Glen and Aaron's way of discouraging pilferers from sneaking in there. Despite this precaution, however, the level in the Scotch bottle dropped at a steady rate despite all Glen's dire threats and policing efforts. He ranted and fumed, of course, but I think underneath he viewed the whiskey sneaking as a universal weakness of mankind and viewed it with an almost humorous tolerance. The dining tent was the meeting place and nerve center of the camp. The only native allowed in or near it was John the waiter.

The fire enclosure was a forty-foot wide circle with the fire pit in its center, surrounded on three sides by a wooden slat fence to keep the wind from blowing smoke all over the clients and to prevent grassfires. Since all the books I'd read about African safaris depicted the campfire chats and bull sessions as the best part of the experience, the three of us were dismayed at the discovery that we would be spending almost no time boozing and bullshitting around the flames, listening to the roar of lions and leopards and the sickening giggle of hyenas.

Our fearless leader would not be there even of we elected to stay up; he retired after dinner and was up at four every morning whipping ass and checking the vehicles. When we returned each day (*night*, rather—excuse please) it was full dark, we were dog-tired and starving, and dinner was waiting. After a cold Tusker or two at the most we ate, then usually passed on the fire tradition and staggered into bed.

I know I resented this at the time, especially during the first few days since I had been so primed for it. But looking back, and especially considering the bill for this little excursion, I realize I'm grateful. A first-class tent safari in Tanzania—by far the best country for trophy buff—runs about two large per day. If all we did was sit around and drink and brag, it would have been an expensive party, nothing more. If we wanted to fill our tags in ten days, we had to bust hump. And bust hump we did; Glen and Aaron made sure of that. So we went to bed at nine and rose at half-past four.

Now, a word here about calls of nature in the night. Ordinarily this is something no camper worries about. And it is to be admitted that the shower and shitter provided for Larry and me was efficient and comfortable. It was built with cinderblock walls, and the toilet was placed over a concrete cistern. Glen and staff had worked all through most of the summer (it was now late August) to complete this camp. There was no stink and no mess. Ever.

But the problem was in the unique design: the bathroom had no door. And no roof. *El Problemo* here. The Dark Continent has three nighttime visitors you definitely don't want to show up to sing you a lullaby. Because they can, and will. And it's for keeps.

Number one is the lion. If *Simba* gets a hold of you in the night you're toast. It's that simple. The only saving grace to this finale is that it's fast. So fast it's probably pain free. Just as happened with Ohljme's uncle, the big cat gets you from behind and sinks his fangs through your neck or skull so fast it's like getting hit with four 30-06 slugs all at once—one for each fang. Bingo. *Lights out.*

Visitor number two is *Fisi,* (to rhyme with fece, and deservedly so). The Hyena is everybody's favorite vision from hell. He is a coward, so he goes in packs, making up in numbers what he lacks in character and courage. The only strength this brute has is its bite—the most powerful of all land animals. Why? So it can crush the bones of dead animals and eat them. Fisi is a carrion-eater, and probably proud of it. This spotted, red-eyed, hobble-gaited misfit will attack anything defenseless. A favorite "hunting" tactic is to wait at the hindquarters of calving Wildebeests, then grab the birth sac of the emerging calf and pull it from the birth canal before the mother can defend it, eating it alive. Sometimes, after they've had Junior for the hors d'eourve, they add Mommy to the menu for the main course.

Speaking of mommies, women are a favorite quarry…but not as preferred as children. The number of children killed in populous India each year by Hyenas is unbelievable. Fisi will attack a sleeping man, ripping off a foot or most of his face before fleeing. If you see a native with one stumped foot he's either a victim of a crocodile or a hyena, even odds. But if he has half his face torn off, and presents a nightmare visage in which you can see his exposed cheekbones, his gumless mouth, torn eyelids, or see through his missing jaw to his soft palate, there is no doubt as to the identity of his attacker. And if a sleeping man is too threatening to this coward, then it will rob graves to feed its young.

Oh, Fisi is a *splendid* piece of work! There's not a native tribe that doesn't agree that God was having an extremely bad day when he created this monstrosity.

And above all, for Fisi, NIGHT-time is the RIGHT-time.

Visitor number three is the most dangerous of all. No, it is not a snake. Some African snakes do come out at night, particularly the adders and cobras. But mostly, being cold-blooded (in the biological sense as well as the behavioral sense), they stay underground at night where it's warm. Thank God for small favors, Africa. Nighttime visitor number three is *Chui*, (to rhyme with *chewy*, and deservedly so) the leopard. The leopard, the deadliest of all cats. The one cat that is not only the best at killing, but the one that kills for the *love* of killing. Chui's family motto ought to be:

KILLINGS R US

Here's an animal that can kill prey that outweigh it by 40 percent, grab it in its jaws and leap a ten-foot fence. An animal so sneaky, so slippery, so slick and quick it can hide in brush lower than your knees. That stretches out on a limb over a path he knows you'll walk down (he knows because he's been *watching* you without you knowing it—watching you for days and days, and knows what you'll do next before *you* do), then drop right on you and bite through your brain... An animal weighing not much more than a big Lab that can kill a 2700-pound Eland antelope. That can hide in an alley in Nairobi, under your Land Cruiser, in your tent...in your damn *sleeping bag!*

The early British settlers learned about Chui's sneakiness and lethality the painful, personal way. Quintessential dog lovers, they arrived with their spaniels, pointers, and retrievers. Their hounds, their bullterriers...even their mastiffs and bullmastiffs. Certainly besides providing companionship, dogs made good sense in this wild place; they could be counted on to sound the alarm against intruders, be they human or otherwise. The big ones could attack not only wild game but also anyone or anything that would attempt to come into compounds or houses uninvited. Yes, dogs made a lot of sense...

Until they began to turn up dead and dismembered.

Or simply never turned up.

It didn't take long to discover the culprit was Chui. Furthermore, it was discovered that not only were the very biggest dogs no match for leopards, they actually attracted them. Every predator in Africa seeks out the easiest, tastiest prey it can find, and Chui had found his in *canis familiaris*.

So from then on: **NO DOGS ALLOWED**. And also all children, and even adults, were to stay indoors after dark.

Which brings us back to the calls of nature in the dead of night. First of all, a piss is one thing, a dump is another. When I had to piss badly—usually after four or five Tuskers—I soon learned that it made no sense to walk all the way to the privy—a good thirty yards or so, to pee down into the commode. So I simply learned to walk twenty feet or so and take a leak on the ground. The ground was dry, it soaked right in, and since it smelled as much like alcohol as urine there was no problem. Then it was back to the tent and the cot, and back to sleep. But if I had to shit, there was no way in hell I was going to squat down on my haunches and let loose anywhere near the camp. I could not hide it; it would stink; either the staff might think it was hyena shit and panic or Glen would hold an inquest after the discovery and find out I was the guilty party. He seemed none to fond of me anyway. I had two strikes against me; an episode like this would only give him more ammunition.

So there was no way around a visit to the bathhouse when I had this to contend with. I remember putting on my field jacket, unzipping the mosquito screen, stepping gingerly out into the nighttime chill (and it was downright *cold* at night—at 8000 feet and in dry air, the heat left the place as soon as old Sol took a dive), and walking quickly to the john. The cold night air was good though, it made for deep sleep and fewer belly-crawlers.

Of course I was nervous. Who wouldn't be? Who could tell how many pairs of eyes were studying me as I walked to what could possibly be my death? I was doing a tiptoe-through-the-tulips step I was so nervous. Anyhow, I made it to the toilet/shower at last. I entered the structure on its far side—the side away from the tents and camp. No doubt this was done to afford even greater privacy, but it also would allow one of our three nighttime visitors to enter undiscovered much more easily. Once inside the cinderblock walls right lead to the shower stall, left to the shitter. It was simply a standard commode with no flush lever set on the concrete slab that was obviously a cover to the septic tank. So the vict—uh, excuse me—the *bathroom patron* (slip of the tongue don't you know…) would sit there in utter silence listening for (and often hearing, in his head anyway) the sounds of approaching paws. All the while knowing of course, that these would-be singers of the lullaby-of-lullabies could simply amble in through the nonexistent door, or else, if it were our slick and agile pal *chui,* simply leap over the wall and into your lap…

Believe me, this was not pleasant. However, I'm certain Glen was convinced in his heart of cold hearts that it was yet more "thrilling experience" we were getting as the result of his careful planning of the toilet layout, and yet another justification for the astronomically-high price tag of this trip.

I used to carry a flashlight on these midnight excursions. I figured I could swing the beam to and fro to spot any unwanted guests before they saw me and scare them away. Or else make them freeze as a deer freezes in car headlights and therefore buy myself a few precious seconds in which to hightail it back to bed. But upon reflection I realized that the flashlight did nothing more than act as a signal beacon to any interested predators. So I ditched it and took my chances.

But still, awakening in the middle of the night with the need to go never got easier. And it was made all the more scary by the fact that Glen, in another theatrical attempt to provide the proper *ambiance* to camp life, had managed to locate—or was it *attract?*—the aforementioned leopard who denned up on Whiteface just yards above us directly over the skinning shed. To make sure *chui* stayed put he provided him with a zebra quarter or a set of buff guts every week or so. This leopard had no name, but every evening at dusk we could hear his *RRRRR-uughhh! RRRRR-uughhh! RRRRR—uughhhh!* Unlike the lion, who signals his presence by a loud roar, Chui speaks in a series of coughing, two-tone grunts, which sound like somebody sawing wood in a metal drum. If the grunts got exceptionally loud, we knew it was time to throw him more food.

If we forgot, there was always the lullaby—

Such was the layout of our beloved camp at Whiteface Mountain.

CHAPTER SIX

DAYBREAK

"Knock-Knock!"

It wasn't an actual knocking on a door; tents don't have doors—they have flaps. It was Christoph's voice saying the words..

I rolled over and stared at a centipede crawling along the canvas floor of the tent, a curious peristaltic humping motion that traveled backwards down its hideous body as it propelled itself forward. Was it one of the deadly ones? Probably. Capstick says everything in Africa stings, bites, claws, crushes, impales, poisons, blinds, maims, or runs like hell. If it didn't, it would have disappeared long, long ago.

"Knock Knock!"

The tent flaps unzipped themselves and a pair of brown arms entered holding a tray, which was deposited between the bunks on the floor.

"Jambo, Christoph. Sante."

"Jambo Bwana." Christoph had a great smile. He was a terrific kid. I leaned over and poured the hot water from the carafe into the cup of instant coffee. I hate instant coffee and it seemed ironic that we were drinking it in Tanzania, a country that produces some of the world's finest beans. But then again, we were six hours by road (if you could call it that) from Arusha, right in the middle of the Masai Mara. Things taken for granted even in a town like Arusha weren't available out here. The bunk opposite mine stirred and Larry faced me, opening his eyes.

"Why didn't I hear Christoph?"

"You were still asleep. I guess it's because you were up most of the night. How you feel?"

83

"Like hell. The thanks I get for treating our men in the combat zones in the Persian Gulf."

"You're still pretty sure it's some chemical agent?"

"All but positive. But the government denies it."

"You want to sleep some more? I'll tell Glen."

"Are you nuts Boyer? After all we've done to get here?"

"C'mon then, it's almost five." I said. Pulling on my pants. "I'll see you in the dining tent. Shall I tell John you want eggs?"

"Yeah. Are you going with us today or Glen and Dick?"

"Glen and Dick."

"Lucky you. You know, I wouldn't try to piss off Glen like you're doing. I think he's got it in for you."

"Some people might say Glen has it in for the world. You'd think Dick might have warned us. How many times did they hunt elk together in Wyoming? He must have known about his temper."

"Must have. But he also knows Glen is the best in the business. The absolute best. And an American, not a Pommy."

"Well, Aaron's a Pommy and a nice guy."

"And the assistant PH. Not *the* PH. Better remember it."

I had put on my undershirt, long-sleeved cotton safari shirt, pullover sweater, and a bush Ricket. I exited the tent., and went over to the toilet, which was enclosed in its own structure. However, although it had walls for privacy, it had no roof. I chucked a big rock over the wall and into the head. No growling or spitting. Hopefully, *chui* wasn't in there. Chui, the Swahili word for leopard, is pronounced "chewy." It fits. I walked around and inside, took a leak, and returned to the tent, washing up at the washstand at the side of the tent. Our six long guns rested on the crude table made from mopane sticks.

At the dining tent I entered and sat down. Glen was at the head of the table eating his eggs. His chair was at the far end of the table, which meant it was at the back of the tent facing out over the campsite. Dick lifted his head and smiled at me in greeting.

"Where the hell's Larry?" asked Glen.

"Getting up."

Glen's fork froze halfway to his mouth. "Getting up? Does he want to hunt or not?"

"Don't worry, he'll be along pronto. He was up half the night in the dunny."

"Again?"

I nodded. Glen frowned and returned to his food. He was about my height but only weighed 164. He told us if he forgot to eat breakfast his weight would plummet. He had dark hair and eyes. Intense eyes. Killer eyes. Little did we know (Larry and I) when we signed on with Glen we were dealing with a guy who was one-third Alan Quartermain, one-third Captain Ahab, and one-third Charles Manson.

John the waiter drifted silently into the tent and appeared as if by magic at my side. He bowed slightly. A tall, thin man, I guessed his age to be at least 60. But who knows in Africa? He could be thirty-something, or maybe a hundred, depending on blind luck. I ordered bacon and eggs and more java. Larry came into the tent. Glen looked down at his plate, finished it off in a hurry, and rose quickly, passing all of us on his way out the tent. He looked pissed off.

"Gentlemen, I'm ready when you are."

We ate quickly and left the tent to see Aaron bringing the first land cruiser up to us. Tall was with him. His real name was Talu, but he was tall so we called him that. Great mechanic; could fix anything anywhere. Larry took his rifle from the table and put it in the rack behind the seats. He had only one rifle, a Winchester 375 H&H. A nice all-around gun but a bit light for buffalo. Instead of a two-rifle battery he had opted for a rifle and shotgun because he loves to shoot birds, and the bird hunting on the African plains is incredible. So he added the twelve gauge to the rack as well. This would not only do for birds but the nasty snakes as well. Then Aaron's gunbearers and trackers hopped on behind. These guys were Julius, a Wa'kamba, and Boogie—I'm pretty sure that wasn't his real name—who was a Wanderobo, or bushman. They roared off into the wild green while I strapped on my ammo belt and took my light rifle to the rack.

"Take the heavy as well Rick," said Glen. "We just may get lucky and run into some buff—"

Soon Dick joined us with his two rifles, dropped them in the rack, and sat down behind me on the back seat. I was sitting beside Glen in front, on the left. In Tanzania they drive Brit-fashion—driver on the right side. Beside Dick, Ernest was already sitting in his customary spot clad in his dark green uniform of the Tanzanian state Game Department. All safaris must be accompanied by such an official, who sees to it no rules are broken. Ernest, a native black, had a lot of power and influence. He carried his own rifle: an aging Parker-Hale 458. Glen turned his head around and glared at the very back of the long-wheelbase vehicle, a space of about the size of a card table behind the rear seat where our gun bearers and trackers should now be standing. He leaned on the horn.

"Goddammit Gabriel—where the *fuck* are you!"

Two men in raggedly clothes came running up the compound in the semidarkness from the staff tents. They were wearing old torn-up parkas tightly buttoned up, with the hoods fully drawn tight. And this less than a hundred miles from the equator. But the truth was it was quite chilly out; even with my long clothes and sweater I was shivering. We were almost 9000 feet up on a plateau that makes up the Great Rift Valley, and the dry air of East Africa does not hold heat overnight. But the main reason for the Eskimo rags was simpler, and more tragic: both men, like the rest of the native staff, had malaria. They were probably lifelong sufferers of this horrendous malady and running fevers well above 100. But a day off? Not on your life.

Gabriel was Masai, and had the height and build of a Moran warrior. I don't recall Vincent's tribe, or if I ever was told of it. Vincent was difficult at first, but I realize in hindsight it must have been because he found me difficult. I had much less hunting experience than my two partners and he no doubt felt slighted by being burdened with the rookie. However, as time went on we became close. As for now, they hopped aboard the already moving truck, grabbed onto the bull-bar to avoid being thrown off as Glen gunned the engine, and we careened along the gravel path out of camp and down the slope that curved gently to the left and out into our hunting concession: more than two hundred square miles of prime East African savanna and brush. All reserved solely for us.

As we bounced along, I ducked down beneath the firewall of the Toyota to get out of the slipstream (Glen had the windscreen folded down already). I looked back at the big volcanic mountain that towered over our camp. It was called whiteface because of a pale face of rock on one side. I looked ahead now at the gently rolling horizon. Through the thorn trees I could see the rising tropical sun peering up over its rim.

CHAPTER SEVEN

SIGHTING IN

Early the next morning, right after breakfast, Glen and Aaron took us on a brief scouting trip of our hunting concession, or "block" that was reserved for us. Each year, prior to the opening of the hunting season, all professional hunters and safari outfitters reserve a black of land, leasing it from the government, on which to take their clients. This lease arrangement means that the hunters and their clients have exclusive rights on this parcel of land; no one else may hunt there except natives. Our block was a scant 200 square miles. To picture that more vividly in your head, it is a square of land just over 14 miles on each side. That's a hell of a lot of land, especially since it's the best piece of hunting real estate on the whole continent. Glen and Swannapoel & Scandrol had to pay big bucks for it. That was one reason why these hunts did not come on the cheap. Sure, you can look in Safari Times or other rags that advertise African hunting, and they'll list prices for weeklong hunts that will make you drool. But the concessions are small and game-scarce. The PH's unseasoned and ignorant, and lacking connections with the right people. The camps are dirty, the staff lax, and the food lousy.

And you won't get your trophies. Or at least any you'd really want.

We began by touring the nearest waterhole. This was a big one for East Africa, being a hundred feet or so across. But to us it seemed a mere puddle. However, in a place was magi was scarce or nonexistent, it was a major attraction for game. We climbed out of the Land Cruisers and walked around the water's edge. We were joined by Chris Johnson, an extremely Nordic looking lad of twenty or so who was the acting apprentice PH. Aaron was the Assistant PH, and had finished his apprenticeship some years previous. Presumably if all went well he could go out on his own in a few years and be a full-fledged PH like Glen—assuming, of course, the authorities didn't catch up with him first. Johnson's Dad, an oral surgeon from Minnesota, was a big-time hunter worldwide and a major client of Glen's in Africa. Accordingly, he had arranged for Chris to learn under two of the best hunters now in business. He was a great kid, always cheerful and willing to work like hell. It was mostly from his efforts that the toilets were built. This was during the recent summer months, and could not have been a pleasant experience.

So walking around this muddy hole in the plain were Glen and Aaron, the three Stooges (us), Chris, Aaron's boys Julius and Boogie, Glen's boys Gabriel and Vincent, and finally, Ernest.

Ernest, a black native, was by far the highest-ranking native in camp. He was not even a member of Glen's staff, but a representative of the Tanzanian government. By law every safari had to have one of these government game wardens present. This was to insure that all state regulations would be met—that there would be no abandoning downed game in hopes of finding better trophies, for example. This was tempting, especially in so vast and remote a land. Who was to know, for example, if a freshly-killed Kudu who didn't measure up (literally—by the trophy tape applied to the horns) was to be left to the scavengers and dung beetles? In two days it would virtually disappear, and the hunters could continue merrily onward in search of a better bull. If this were allowed to happen it could mean that for every animal paid for in trophy fees, there could be three or even four animals killed, and the so-called "sportsman" could simply select the biggest head and leave the rest. Ernest was present to insure this kind of thing did not happen. He was the only one of the black staff who was armed and was purportedly a damn good shot. He was also an extremely nice fellow.

But dammit—ALL OF THEM WERE!

That was the single most powerful thing I was to learn on this trip.

Glen squatted down over the soft mud of the waterhole's rim and motioned me over with his hand. Next to his fingers in the mud were tracks that looked like a large dog's.

"Leopard," he said. "Big tom. I'd say about a hundred forty pounds. That's about as big as they get. We'll keep an eye on his spoor. See where and when he comes and goes. My next client's got a leopard tag."

I looked at his cartridge belt. Stuck down in the elastic loops were long brass rounds as big as panatelas. 470 Nitro Express rounds, a rimmed cartridge designed for double rifles. And in the rack, wrapped in canvas, was his Westley Richards double sidelock. A rifle made exactly a hundred years earlier in Birmingham, England, and now worth over $30,000. The double-barreled rifle is the preferred "stopping" firearm of the Professional Hunter. It is a short range, last-resort weapon used to *stop* a charging dangerous animal before it kills the client. Period. And because it shoots two gigantic rounds with double triggers, it can fire these two cannonballs within a second's time. No other firearm can do this. Hence the value of these guns, and their enormous price tag. Also in his belt was a stag-handled, handmade skinning knife. This comprised his tools of the trade. All except his lighter and pack of *Sportsman* cigarettes.

We climbed back into the vehicles and headed off toward a grove of big trees. I was riding with Aaron this time, who told me we were going to sight-in the rifles.

"I've already sighted mine in. Both of them."

He looked at me. "This really is your first hunt, isn't it."

"What do you mean?"

"Well hell mate, you always sight your gun in after a plane flight. Who knows what bugger dropped your fucking case on the runway? Or tried to pry it open? All sorts of things can happen to scopes in transit. This won't take long, and you'll breathe easier for it. Trust me."

Julius took his *panga* and went over to a Baobab tree. He whacked a piece of bark as big as the palm of my hand off the trunk about out eight feet up, then backed off to the side about 30 feet while we set duffel bags on the hoods of the two vehicles and then rested our rifles on them. Using a "rest" for your rifle when shooting long-range is crucial. If your barrel moves a sixteenth of an inch as you squeeze off a 300-yard shot the bullet will miss by ten feet. Larry shot first with the only rifle he brought: a 375 Holland & Holland. This was his heavy gun, and he would make it do for all sized game, because for his other firearm—being an addicted bird hunter—he elected to bring a twelve-gauge pump shotgun. This was to prove useful—even a lifesaver—later on. He shot at the chipped spot on the tree. Julius went up to inspect the damage, finally shaking his head.

"*Hapana,*" he reported.

"What's he saying?" Larry asked.

"Hapana means no. He's saying you missed the mark," replied Aaron. "The mark, an even perhaps the tree. Try again."

The second shot grazed the bark an inch from the chip. Julius held up finger and thumb an inch apart. While Larry adjusted his scope Dick got on deck and sent two rounds from his 300 Weatherby an inch apart within the white mark.

"*Piga!*" shouted Julius as the first round hit the mark. The second hit at just over an inch from it, and Julius held up his thumb and finger to show the distance.

"Good show Dick. Okay Rick, your turn. Now just try to get close to the mark—"

His condescending remark pissed me off, but I said nothing. After all, I had been practicing a lot. But the way this trip was starting off I might just miss the tree, and then any comebacks I might make now would boomerang on me. "I'll do my best," I said as I laid the Winchester on the duffel bag and sighted at the center of the white target of peeled bark. I squeezed and the rifle came back smartly against my shoulder. Even with Magna-ported barrel, it did kick. But I was pretty used to it.

I felt as if I put it on the money, but Julius, after examining the tree from the ground a while, turned in bewilderment, spoke something, and shook his head at us.

"He's saying he thinks you missed the tree; he can't find a sign of the bullet hole."

"That's strange; I thought I was bang on."

"Well then, try another. If that doesn't do it we'll check the scope out—"

I shot again and Julius examined the slash mark. Then he gave a little jump of surprise, turned smiling and said "*piga-piga!*"

"Ha! He missed it the first time. He's saying you hit it twice!"

Julius held up one finger and waved it. Aaron was excited.

"Well that's some shooting. Hey, I thought you couldn't shoot."

"No. I can't *see*. And I'm also colorblind. But if I can see the target I usually connect."

"Well connect you did. The single finger means the hits were almost on top of one another. Good going."

For the first time in days I was somewhat heartened. The only remaining shooting was to sight in the big bores. For my buff gun I brought the 458 Winchester, a cartridge legendary for its power and stout recoil. On both ends, it was a punishing firearm. Dick had chosen the 416 Remington for his heavy gun. It was a step down from the earth-shattering 458, but bigger than the 375 Holland & Holland. He shot first and put two into a space the size of a quarter. But the group was at the extreme lower right edge of the white patch, so he had to fiddle with the scope a bit to get the group in its proper place. I shot and my group of two shots was one "keyhole, which meant that the two bullets had made one elongated hole.

We waited until Larry got his group together and piled into the trucks again. An excellent bird hunter, most of Larry's experience with hunting was limited to shotguns, with which he was superb. I knew also he hadn't shot the big 375 much over the summer because he hated the recoil. I spent most of the summer, and the entire year preceding it, shooting both rifles to acclimate myself to getting slammed in the shoulder each time I squeezed off.

Aaron looked at me. "Never tell me again you can't shoot."

"I guess I won't."

We returned to Whiteface for the best time of the day: Attitude Adjustment Hour. Pronounced *AAHhhhhhhh!* We started with a Tusker apiece to slake our thirst (a preventative measure—the bloody heat can kill you out there don't you know—), then followed it up with gin and Scotch while Christoph and Theodore built up the fire. So there sat in our khaki hunting jackets and desert boots, drinks in hand, cigars going, looking into the flames and coals and up at the blood-red clouds of the sunset, musing over the day's events. We realized we had a hell of a lot of land to cover, and the necessity of early to bed, early to rise made total sense.

After an hour or so Aaron summoned us to the table, where John was waiting by the tent fly, clad in his usual black trousers and white coat. He bowed to us slightly as we entered. "*Jambo. Jambo Bwana.*"

"*Sijambo*," we answered and seated ourselves. The meal was grilled impala chops with béarnaise sauce. There were cooked cauliflower and mashed potatoes and fried plantains (which we had with almost every meal—a staple of Africa) accompanied by a South African Burgundy red. How the staff could come up with this I'll never know. But they did. Lord only knew what *they* had to eat, though, probably Alpo meatloaf.

No, in all honesty, they got more than their fill of fresh meat and animal fat, which are not only sought after in Africa, but worshipped. When they couldn't get fresh meat (between hunts), they always had biltong. Biltong is meat that's usually too tough to cook (like an old daga boy Mbogo bull, for example) that's been soaked in vinegar and salt for a day or so and then cut into strips and suspended on Acacia thorns to dry in the sun. It's a form of beef jerky, and highly nutritious. But natives will go to any lengths to get fresh meat and fat. All the early elephant hunters talk of seeing natives appearing out of nowhere as soon as a big bull was downed. Before the tusks could be chopped out they would assemble at the site. When the ivory team was through removing the big teeth they would slice open the belly with their pangas and *walk inside* the carcass, stripping the loose-hanging fat from the organs with the sides of their hands and stuffing it into their mouths. They could clean an eight-ton elephant carcass almost meatless in a few hours, leaving with bundles of meat wrapped in bloody rags balanced in their heads.

Make no mistake, as dangerous as the staff jobs on safari were, they were paradise compared to life in either a Masai village or the animal existence on the fringes of a city like Arusha. That was the major reason why, though abused, they bore it stoically, and never resigned.

We wrapped up the meal with cigars and snifter of Black and White around the campfire. Aaron came up to join us. We offered him some Scotch. It is tradition that the clients bring the booze and allow the guides to drink their fill. The old story goes that it was a way of PH's sharing with each other the true nature of their relationships with their clients. If things were hunky-dory, the hunter, when asked how his new clients were, would answer "topping!" or "decent chaps—quite!" or something of the sort. If things were a bit sour but the basic relationship was still holding, albeit by a thread, he would answer, "well, let's just say I'm still drinking their whiskey..." and leave it at that. Then, if things had gone totally down the chute, the answer would be a hesitant grunt, a headshake, and a hasty "afraid we're not even sharing cocktails. Rum show. Can't wait til it's over."

Aaron sipped, leaned back in the director's chair, lit a Sportsman, and told us all Glen was impressed when he'd told him of my marksmanship. "He expects all one-shot kills from you I'm afraid Rick. I know you won't let him down, now will you?"

Oh shit, I thought, remaining silent and staring into the flames. That's all I need now. That's sure to jinx the whole hunt.

"Well, we'll get a chance to see you in action bright and early tomorrow," said Dick, slapping me on the back. "Let's see if your skill level stands the test of—-*what the hell's that noise?*"

We fell silent and heard a low, coughing, two-tone grunt. It sounded like somebody sawing wood with a big lumberjack crosscut saw: *RRRRR-uughhh! RRRRRR-uughhh! RRRRR—uughhhh!* Over and over and over again.

"Aw it's nothing. Just Glen's pet leopard."

"Pet leopard. You're shitting me," said Larry. "You've got to be shitting me."

"Afraid not. But no worries; he's quite harmless as long as we remember to feed him. Right now he's just letting us know he's here. Perhaps he wants to join the party. What say guys? Want to ask him down for a toddy?"

CHAPTER EIGHT

SAFARI

Which takes us back to that first morning when Larry and I were awakened by Christoph's pleasant voice saying Knock-Knock at 4:30 A.M.

Since there are no wooden doors on tents, the knocking must be done *a capella*, as in a knock-knock joke. So there we were just after five in the morning, still shaking the sleepiness form our eyes, watching the pale sun rise above the long brown plain dotted with acacia trees and savannah grass. Several peaks rose in the distance. From their curved, Fujiesque slopes I could tell they were volcanic in origin, and lent the place an even more mysterious and exotic aura.

Glen (A.K.A. "Hard On") was driving, with Dick seated next to him. I was riding right behind them in the elevated second seat with Ernest. Standing behind him, holding onto the backs of our seats and sweeping their keen raptor eyes in every direction were H.O.'s trackers. Gabriel, his number one man, was Masai, about six foot three, dark complexioned, and silent. He wore Western clothing, but sometimes visited the local Masai villages, mostly, as it turned out, for homebrew (*pombe*) and pussy (*gume*). For this he was often in trouble. The Masai are a closed society; outsiders are forbidden to have sex with the women or even fraternize with the men. Gabriel was not an outsider, but his clothing, his job, and his attitude seemed to piss off the elders of these villages. Not to mention a few cuckolded husbands as well.

The other man was Vincent. A man whose tribe I never knew, he was to become my favorite of the staff. A man of iron courage and great tenderness, he was working to put his two sons through college.

95

Very black and lean, he was all business. He suffered from Malaria, and when I gave him some medication to help ease the pain and fever he was almost moved to tears. Remember: these men never got a day off, no matter what. *Never.*

Two hours passed without sighting anything we could shoot. We saw lots of giraffe, which were all over the place, but we had no interest in them as trophies and they were expensive anyway. The seemed so vulnerable, standing there munching on branches 20 feet high and staring stupidly at us. But they could run like the wind once they got moving, and could lash out with their hoofs to a distance of twelve feet or so with enough power to crush a lion's skull. So nothing fucked with them. We saw the glorious Greater Kudu with its gorgeously marked head, tawny gray-tan coat and beautiful lyre-shaped horns. The most beautiful antelope in the world except for the giant Sable. All three of us wanted one of these badly, but their tags were very expensive and we didn't have them on our permits. We were each signed up for a zebra, and these we also saw, but at too great a distance. Due to his lack of horns and ample meat, any and all carnivores hunt the zebra, so it's wary indeed.

Just when I felt the day might turn out a total bust a warthog burst from cover and ran right across our path.

"Get him! Now!" shouted H.O. Dick, who had his 300 Weatherby laying across the hood of the Toyota ready for action, did his best to swing it like a shotgun and connect, but he was nowhere close. And I sympathized with him, a rifle with a high-power scope and that recoils like a machinist's hammer can't be swung like a 20-gauge shotgun. The big pig ran into heavy cover, with us going after it. But it was no use.

"They're hard to hit. Closer to the ground and traveling fast, they've got burrows all over the place," Glen explained. "When they go to ground they turn around at the tunnel's entrance and back in ass-first. That way, if a hyena, or leopard tries to follow it inside, they'll slash its face to pieces with those monster tusks. They may be funny-looking but there's nothing funny about trying to hunt them."

If Dick had connected with the pig and brought it down, I would then have changed places with him to get the next opportunity. As it was I sat tight and waited. An hour later, just before ten in the

morning Vincent leaned forward and tapped Ernest on the shoulder.
"*poli, poli...*"

"What's that mean?" I asked.

"It means, slow down." But H.O. had already gotten the message, and also probably also already seen the lone zebra standing beyond the low wall of kasaka.

"Get on him—" he told Dick.

The Weatherby was steadied on the duffel bag and Dick settled down for the shot. But somehow I could tell it didn't feel right to him, and he asked Glen if he could get out and park the piece atop a fallen tree that was just a few feet in front of us. Glen nodded and Dick crept out there, kneeling now behind the tree. The zebra was standing perfectly sideways to us, his head turned in our direction, watching us. Though over a hundred yards distant, he could not have presented a better target if he'd just read a book on animal suicide.

It still amazes me how most ungulates will strike this sideways pose and look at a vehicle for as long a time as necessary (or even *more*) for the hunter to assume a shooting position, acquire the target, estimate the range, breathe deeply, and squeeze off the shot that will end their life. I finally found out why.

The animal *is* suspicious. That much seems certain. But he's just a little too dense to figure out *why*. So he stands there, fascinated by the distant sound of the vehicle's engine, waiting for signs or developments, yet ready to run at an instant's notice. Now, if he faces mostly *away* from the intruder he can make a faster getaway. But he can't see the intruder as well. If he faces *dead on* he presents a very small target, which is to his advantage. He can also see the strange whatchamacallit better. But standing with his feet thus planted, he cannot start a getaway run nearly fast enough. So he does the best combination of possible stances: he places his body and feet crosswise to the intruder so that he can run away or sideways instantly, and yet he is not facing away from the intruder because to do this means jerking his head around at an awkward angle to watch the strange thing that confronts him. So there you are. Or rather, there he is.

And that Burchell's zebra stood just like that long enough for Dick to plant a 180-grain Nosler Partition bullet right into his boiler room.

The animal bucked at the impact and took several small, jerky steps forward. At least one of his shoulders was broken. Perhaps two.

Anyway, his lungs had been pierced. By the time we drew the Toyota up he was on his side, turning to his back and trying to roll over, working his feet in the air and coughing blood and phlegm. I had never before seen such a large animal killed in this fashion. The zebra continued to thrash and work his feet, staying on his back perhaps because it somehow eased the pain. It gave several short gasps, then a long groan, its big head shaking as if in a seizure. Its entire body stiffened, quivered, then collapsed in a relaxed heap after the death rattle worked itself out.

The two boys were on him fast with their knives and pangas, cutting the 700-pound body into quarters and flaying it, saving the head and capeskin intact for Mimu the skinner. They stowed the body parts—including the foul-smelling innards, which Glen wanted for lion bait—in the back of the truck, climbed back aboard, and on we went.

With Yours Truly riding in the On Deck Circle.

I didn't have long to wait. As we entered a heavily overgrown section of trees and scrub an hour later Gabriel raised his hand and pointed dead ahead. "Kongoni," he said. Glen stopped the vehicle and glassed the area with his binoculars. I did the same, and saw a group of antelopes that resembled misshapen Impala. They had the same coloration, but were larger. Most noticeable were their heads. They were, well, ugly. Long and straight in the snout, with no brow ridge, or stop between their forehead and noseline, they appeared to have all just run into a wall headfirst. Their horns, while the color of an Impala's and ringed the same, were not long and gracefully curved. Instead they came out of the heads sideways, then twisted up and back like milk cows. They looked weird and stupid, created, as has often been said of the camel, by a committee.

"Get on him," said Glen, lighting a cigarette and settling back in his seat. Something in his demeanor made me suspect he was not going to be much help in this endeavor. That maybe he was even waiting to see me fuck up.

So I got on him. I sighted through the scope and tried to settle crosshairs for a classic lung/shoulder shot. Problem was the brush hid the lower part of the animal; all that was visible was his neck and head. And neck shots are always tricky. If you connect, your quarry drops like a sack of wet laundry. But if you miss that spinal cord he hops right away because the neck is mostly muscle.

"I can't see his chest from here," I said.

Glen reached back and took Dick's Weatherby from the rack. "Shoot where you think it is; I'll back you up."

"Won't the brush deflect the slug?"

"Yeah, but not that much at this range."

I fired. The animal jumped twice and bounded off. But it was the behavior of his comrades that was most interesting. They mock-charged us, stamping their feet and lowering their horns in our direction.

"He wants to fight!" shouted Vincent with a grin. Glen gunned the truck and we shot forward through the brush, making a hissing, crackling noise loud enough to wake the dead. This was my first experience crashing through brush; until now we had been following roads and trails. The truck bounced hard, and everybody held on. Once through the growth we came into a clear spot. Gabriel and Vincent jumped down and began tracking the blood spoor through the grass. They didn't have far to go: less than sixty yards away the dead animal lay on its side. Like most shot animals, it had fallen on the entrance side of the wound, leaving the blown-out exit hole visible. This is where all the blood had come from. I got down and knelt over the Kongoni. It was larger than I thought. Glen said it would weigh 400 pounds at least—three hundred dressed. Vincent and Gabriel were talking excitedly as they slit the belly open, gutted it, and began skinning. Frankly, I didn't think it was all that great a trophy, but I didn't say anything. Wouldn't do to piss off H.O. so early in the safari.

"Why are the guys so excited about this? I asked. "It's not as big as the zebra."

"Not as big, but much better eating," he answered. "The Hartebeest's flesh is the best there is, except the Eland's. It's everybody's favorite eating. Which reminds me—" he glanced at his watch—"it's almost lunchtime. Gabriel! *Arakasana! Kwenda!*"

"Are you pissed off at him?"

"No. Arakasana means 'fast game,' or hurry up. Kwenda means 'we go.' I was telling him to get his ass in gear."

They chucked my skinned and disassembled Coke's Hartebeest into the rear of the Land Cruiser on top of Dick's zebra and we bounced off over the savannah again. After thirty minutes I realized the terrain looked slightly foreign. I asked H.O. if we were returning to Whiteface.

"No, it's the other direction. I want to keep going this way to see if we can spook up some impala, or maybe another zebra for you. Okay Bwana?"

"Fine by me. How about you Dick?"

"Don't mind me; I'm just along for the ride. But I thought you said something about lunch, Glen. Did you pack us box lunches?"

"No such luck. I think we'll stop at Dimitri's"

Dimitri? Who's Dimitri?"

"A Greek of course. Or couldn't you figure that out?"

"What's a Greek doing out in the boonies of East Africa?" Dick asked.

"Running a gem mine," Glen answered.

"*King Solomon's Mines*! That's what got Dick and me both hooked on Africa to begin with."

"Oh yeah? Well these aren't diamond mines, they're Tanzanite mines, and he's just up the way a bit."

"What's his place like?" I asked.

"Uh…interesting. It'll stick in your mind. So will Dimitri."

CHAPTER NINE

DIMITRI

We didn't catch sight of Dimitri's camp until we swung around a wide curve to the right and saw what appeared to be a ring of brush arranged in a circle. As I was to discover visiting many Masai villages in the bush, this was the *boma*, or *manyatta,* the protective circular fence of gathered thornbrush that (supposedly) protected the village against marauding nighttime lions, leopards, and hyenas. We entered this ringed enclosure through a rough cattle gate and swung to a stop not far from a dining area covered with a roof of twigs and sticks. There was a table set up beneath this arrangement (which to me resembled the shade porches found in our desert Southwest and in Mexico) at which four or so people were having lunch. We had apparently timed our arrival to the minute. We left the vehicle and walked toward the portico. A heavyset man who was sitting at the table's head rose and came out to greet us, a wide smile on his dark face.

"Ah, Glen! Yes, and how are the Great White Hunters this morning, eh?"

There was something about his tone of voice that threw me. It was pleasant, almost humorously so. Was he complementing us, or teasing? It seemed there was a streak of irony in his booming voice—that we, of all people, could not possibly be Great White Hunters. At least from my perspective, I was thus convinced. We shook hands all around. I noticed Dimitri had bright blue eyes under his black eyebrows. A blue-eyed Greek? What the—

101

Rick Boyer

I remembered a quote from one of Joseph Conrad's works—I forget the source—but of course he was expert on out-of-the-way places. I mean, you can't write stories with titles like "Heart of Darkness," or "The Outpost of Progress" and be referring to St. James Street, or Piccadilly Circus, can you now? Anyway, he claims that in any remote spot on the globe such as, say, the south Java coast, or the Island of Mauritius, "you' always find a minute European-style trading colony with the following always represented: an Englishman, an Indian, a Jew, a Chinese, and a Greek. And why not? These were the nationalities that ran the local trading stations and shops. The English were always known as the Shopkeepers to the World. Same with the Chinese, who generally ran the local laundry as well. Jews were and still are known for their role in the trading of precious materials like gems, gold and silver, silks, furs, and so on. The Greeks did a little of all of it.

So here was Dimitri, smack dab in the Masai Mara in his own boma.

"Won't you have a seat gentlemen?" He clapped his hands. *"Tssebe! Chai! Arakasana!"* Shades of Sidney Greenstreet in Casablanca; all he needed was the cigar and fez. In a heartbeat Tssebe came running up with a pot of steaming and four cups. We were seated by then, and I realized I was hungry.

"Eland and rice, gentlemen. I think you'll approve!" I soon cleaned my plate of the last of the big helpings. Eland was indeed delicious, a combination of the tastes of beef and veal, and like all African game, 40 percent less fatty than its American counterparts. I tasted a hint of curry in the meat and gravy. After eating I noticed Gabriel and Vincent talking with some of Dimitri's staff boys around a fire. The fire was almost invisible because it was only coals; no smoke or fames issued forth. This was the typical African bush fire: the wood is so dry here that it lights instantly and burns down to the last cinder, giving off mounds of heat. I had only worn my khaki shooting jacket (The one item I failed to pack was my *light jacket,* and I missed it every morning and evening. But who would have suspected it would be needed in August just south of the equator?

I excused myself from the table and went over the fire, standing above it and smelling the tangy fumes of the mopane smoke that wafted about at our feet.

"Feels good, eh Vincent?" I asked.

102

"*Ndio!*" Yes, he answered. They were still wearing their parkas. First I realized I was hungry, then chilly. Now I realized I was tired. The first-kill experience had worn me out. Don't ask why. I half staggered back to the dining porch and told Glen I would like to take a wee lie-down whilst they chatted. Dimitri immediately volunteered his tent, so, lead there by one of his boys who opened the flap for me, I lay down on an air mattress and soon was fast asleep, the smell of burning mopane wood and the soft talk of the natives drifting in and out of my dreams. I slept for almost an hour, and felt much refreshed when I woke up and made my way over to the dining area. But it was deserted. Going in the direction of voices, I soon found Dimitri seated behind a wooden table, on which were piled...gems!

They were rough, field-grade stones of course, not yet cut to brilliance and symmetry. But I had a hunch that someday they would be worth a fortune. Where had he gotten them? The answer came a few hundred feet away, where I found myself staring down into deep vertical pits hewn from the red earth. Men were down in there, clawing and shoveling at the sides and bottom of each pit. Men above then hauled in ropes that brought buckets of earth to the surface. There big screens sifted and separated the wheat from the chaff, and the good stuff made its way over to the wooden sorting table where our blue-eyed acquaintance examined the stones through a loop, weighed them on a brass balance, and put them in various boxes and compartments.

Yep. Straight out of Conrad.

"Bwana!" cried one of the boys running up to Dimitri. He handed him a plastic baggie that was rolled up. Dimitri took it and handed it to me. "There you are, Rick. I believe you requested this of Aaron before your arrival, yes?"

"What the hell is it?" I took the bag, excited. It did seem that Dimitri was a gracious host, but a gift of a bag of Tanzanite's was certainly above and beyond the call—.

I opened the bag and looked in. I saw a bunch of greenery. One sniff told me what it was. Dope. It smelled rather potent even though it was almost half stems and seeds. I pinched some with my fingers. A tad sticky, but not much. It would work though.

"*Ganja*. Thanks, Dimitri. How'd you get it so fast?"

"Word gets round. Aaron stopped in four or five days ago and had a chat with James over there—" I turned and saw a blond kid raise his hand up at me. "James is my assistant. Anyway, nothing is too good for our friends the Great White Hunters. I hope you have a wonderful time here."

We thanked him and his staff and left, but not before Glen had the boys free up a hindquarter of Dick's zebra and the same from my Kongoni. "It's always good policy to give fresh meat to a camp," he explained. I always try and keep Dimitri happy, and Monty and Colin too. You need good neighbors out here; things can get rough fast, and you need people on your side."

We pulled out of Dimitri's mining operation and swung back onto the road.

"That Dimitri was quite a guy," Dick mused, lighting a cigar.

"Yeah, he's a character," said H.O. "But you've got to watch him, too. Didn't it strike you he was maybe a little too charming?"

"Absolutely," I said. "Like he was trying to impress us. However, he is generous."

"Well, maybe. All I know is he took Aaron's 375 and never returned it. Said he wanted to buy it but wanted to test it out first."

"Will he buy it?"

"We don't know; Aaron hasn't seen it since. We know Dimitri killed a buff with it week before last." There was pause. "I guess sooner or later we'll see how it all turns out."

Finally, I thought as we meandered into the heat of the long, tropical afternoon, Glen was beginning to loosen up. He seemed much less authoritarian. Could it be he was finally revealing his inward, gentlemanly self?

But alas, it was not to be. Soon after Dick spooked a Kongoni of his own and nailed it, I was in the on-deck seat when we spotted an Impala in the brush ahead. When I say *we* spotted it, I mean they. That is, everybody in the truck but me. Why? Because being red/green color blind, I cannot tell a brown animal from the green vegetation. So there we were, me with my 458 in my hands (which I had been holding simply because Vincent had yelled: *"Buffalo! Shoot him!"* twenty minutes prior and I still held onto the thing, just in case) peering into the brush and seeing...nothing.

"Can you see him now?" asked Glen. I shook my head. I had a dire feeling the H.O. PH was going to emerge again. "Look, see that thick candelabra tree? Well, he's right to the left of it and back a couple feet. See him? *See him?"*

I admitted I could not see shit. This did not have a mollifying effect on him.

He jerked my 300 from the rack, popped off the safety, and leveled it in the direction of the tree. "Well sport, one of us is going to shoot him. You or me. Which is it?"

"Let me just..." I was concentrating now, trying so see something—anything—that looked like a deer-sized mammal. Then I saw them...four or five of them. But I noticed they did not have horns. Needed the horns. Horns were what it was all about. Where was the buck? Don't pass the buck, goddammit! The buck stops here! No counterfeit bucks!

I was anxious now, and sweating. The sweat was collecting in my eyes and blurring my vision. I could sense H.O.'s blood pressure rising by the second. I had to make a shot to save myself.

I will shoot as soon as I see the buck I told myself. The scope swept past the small herd. Suddenly there he was! I held my breath and squeezed, bracing myself for the hellish recoil of the 458—the last fucking rifle you'd want for an Impala.

The gun went off with a cannon's roar, and Glen went sailing out the driver's seat, covering his ears and screaming in pain. Oh shit—And then I realized what had happened. Prior to the trip, while sighting in my rifles, I took them to a gunsmith in Greenville, SC to have them accurized, stock-bedded, and Magna-Ported. Magna-Porting is a process by which two small rectangular holes are made through the barrel's muzzle on each side. These sideways holes allow a lot of the hot propellant gases to escape out the sides of the rifle instead of the front. Result? Less recoil, since the blast does not drive the gun back into your shoulder with full force.

Result No. 2? An undesirable one: anybody sitting, standing, or remotely hanging out to the **side** of the firearm gets a super-duper earful blast from the cartridge. It's a fact all guides and PH's HATE the magana port system. It may help the hunter, but boy does it hurt *the guides!* So here was Glen, who failed to notice that my elephant gun was ported on the side, getting a full dose of 458 at about two feet.

"GOODDAMMIT! YOU FUCKING IDIOT! WHAT THE FUCK DO YOU THINK YOUR DOING? DON'T YOU REALIZE MY HEARING'S ALREADY 40 PERCENT GONE? HUH?"

"I'm terribly sorry."

"SORRY? SORRY? YOU HEAR THAT DICK? HE'S SORRY!"

"I'm really terribly sorry. I thought you would cover your ears like you usually do."

"COVER MY EARS?" He turned to face the boys now. **"YOU GUYS KNOW WHY I DIDN'T COVER MY EARS?"** Back to me. **YOU KNOW WHY I COULDN'T COVER THEM? GUESS! BECAUSE I WAS TRYING TO HELP YOU SHOOT THE IMPALA, THAT'S WHY!"**

He stomped around the truck for five minutes or so. All I could do was murmur my apologies and wonder if the guy was for real. Where were all those nice father figure Brit PH's when you needed them? I'd like to know...

Then we went up and inspected the Impala. Shot perfectly through both shoulders. A hole in the carcass you could drive a Sherman tank through, but lets not quibble. Then, as the boys began loading the fourth trophy of the day into the truck, a strange thing happened. I felt a slap on my back and turned, amazed, to see a smiling Glen Schacht. "Hey Bwana, forget it! It's all out of me now. Anybody who knows me will tell you I get pissed off all the time, but it never lasts. Now c'mon, let's get back to camp and clean up!"

On the ride back I glanced around towards Dick occasionally. He was usual, low-keyed, silent self, but now and then he gave me a wide grin and the thumbs up.

We got back to Whiteface with the sun again at the horizon, but this time going down in a sea of read and purple clouds. I grabbed a tall Black & White and soda, found a seat at the fire, and joined Dick, Larry, and Aaron. Larry had taken a zebra and a Kongoni. So we all had two under our belt on the first day. Since we only had six on our licenses, we were a third of the way there in day one. Would we finish in three days?

"Not on your life, chaps," assured Aaron. "Don't you see? The more you shoot the fewer choices you have left. As you go, the narrower becomes the list of permitted species remaining. Follow? And you've taken easy ones so far. Wait for the Grant's gazelle. Talk about a long shot! Same with the Tommy, only it's even smaller."

"Then...there's our old friend Mbogo..." mused Dick.

Mzungu Mjinga

Aaron took a hefty swig of Beefeaters, rattled the ice in his glass. "Don't let's talk about ugly old *Mbogo* chaps. It may spoil our supper."

CHAPTER TEN

KASAKA

Looking back on it, I know now I should have been suspicious on the fourth day of the safari when I got roused out of bed extra-early that something…interesting, (not to say shady) was up. There was an electric charge in the air. You could feel it in the raised hairs on the nape of your neck. You could see it in the faces of the trackers, generally as inscrutable as a Zen statues or Haiku sayings. There was a front moving in for one thing. I always feel a tension when this is happening. People tell me it's from too many positive ions in the atmosphere. Maybe so. All I know is, once the storm begins to break I feel an immense relief in my nervous system. But I did not feel that yet—not by a long shot. Glen was strangely silent at breakfast. He didn't even chew anybody out. Uh-oh—that was a sign right there. And he lighted his after-breakfast cigarette at the table instead of waiting until he got into the Land Cruiser. After breakfast I took a cup of java to go in a plastic travel mug and lighted one of my petite coronas to get me going full-bore.

"Take your big rifles too," said Aaron casually, almost as an afterthought. I cornered him between the dining tent and the gun table. "So what gives, Chum? Why the heavy artillery? You know we haven't seen diddly-shit in the past two days."

He brightened and clapped me on the shoulder. "Ahh! Our luck's about to change. Good chance, anyway. Yesterday some boys in the next village told us a group of W'Kamba spotted a good-sized herd of buff not far from here. Maybe twenty to forty head. Some good bulls in there. If we hurry we can catch up to them before they pass through to parts unknown. Savvy?"

I nodded at him and picked up the big Remington, then thought of something. "Hey Aaron, did you sell a Whitworth rifle to Dimitri?"

"Well," he paused, "I suppose yes and no. He told me he wanted to buy my 375, a Whitworth. We agreed on a price too. But he has yet to pay for it. And already he's shot an Eland with it. The one we ate day before last. So In a way we've consummated half the deal; he has the gun but I don't have my money."

"Well, do you fully trust him?"

"Not by a shot, sir. I tell you, Bwana, he's not on the square, that one. He's one to keep an eye on—" he walked away, then looked back over his wide shoulders. "Chao!" he called, and ambled over to his truck where Larry, Julius, and Boogie were waiting. I waved to them all.

"Better move your ass, Boyer! You'll be left behind; today could be lucky day!" Hard-On was calling me. Lucky day, eh? As Huck Finn would have paraphrased it: "So I clumb into the truck, but I warn't too brash about it."

We were off in a jerk and a rush, with me riding in the rear seat with Ernest and freezing my ass. Mornings were not just chilly here, they were damn cold. We drove for the better part of an hour at good speed; I judged we were at the furthest limits of our block, or even further afield. We had entered a region of sandy plains and brush and low-growing Acacia trees. It was cloudy and cool when we got out of the trucks. I was surprised to see Aaron, Larry, and company there as well. This must be the spot the W'Kamba had reported to our Masai neighbors. We got out and stretched our stiff legs in the cool air. I drank from my coffee mug and watched Glen disappear around a mound of Kasaka brush. I had been seeing this stuff everywhere, and now realized it was what Muad was talking about during the photo safari. The dry brush that snapped and popped when you went into it, and sounded like fireworks. That snagged and tangled you up. That was the snakes preferred abode.

Oh yeah...*THAT stuff*—-

Aaron and H.O. and their boys were kneeling down now, examining what looked like cow shit. It looked like it because it *was* it. Big brown cowpies, Glen stuck his finger down into one of them. What was he going to do? Pull his finger out and taste it?

"Warm—" he said to Aaron. "I'd say less than an hour old. Let's follow these tracks. C'mon Boogie—"

110

The tiny, black Wanderobo walked down the tracks in the packed sand. He did not do it bent over as we see in movies. He simply walked them up, eyes focused on the ground but posture straight, as calmly as if walking to lunch. We followed, and didn't stop until Aaron halted and held up a cautionary hand. Boogie was bent down now, and Aaron followed his lead.

"All kinds of stuff out for a stroll this morning," said Aaron. Dick and I crept up behind him and Glen. I couldn't believe what I saw next. My heart doubled its speed because I knew there was only one animal on earth that could leave spoor this size. Aaron was sticking two fingers of his left hand into a turd the size of a bowling ball.

"*Tembo*," whispered Vincent in my ear. I nodded and leaned forward.

Aaron stood up and looked around. "Not as warm as the other, and with that mass it should retain heat. I'd say the herd passed through here last night sometime." He turned and faced back to the Kasaka brush. "But we know for certain that the buff are still in there."

Glen stood up. "Gabriel—bunduki sante." Gabriel sprinted off to our truck. I asked Vincent what he said and Vincent held up his hand and arm as if aiming a rifle. I nodded back. Gabriel returned with a cartridge belt slung over his shoulder and Glen's 470 Westley-Richards Nitro Express, a 98-year old gun worth more every year. Glen broke the double gun and popped in two bazooka-sized cartridges, snapping the breech shut and flicking on the safety. Meanwhile Julius had brought Aaron's Winchester bolt-action 458.

"Well, go get your guns gentlemen," growled H.O. "We're not going to do this for you. We want to make sure you get all the excitement you're paying for...right Dick?"

"Oh absolutely," replied Dick, turning on his heel. I followed, and soon the five of us were armed to the teeth, apparently in preparation for an excursion into the thornbrush after *You Know Who*...

"Well Rick," grinned Larry, "you ready for this?"

"No." Why lie? I remembered Muad's words of warning. How the buff would be in there during the day, and perhaps the night too, and the only way to get him was to crawl in after him. At maybe 1/2 M.P.H. compared to his 10-12 m.p.h. And what he would do to you when he got to you. "Fuck that," I had remarked. "Yes, Sah. Fuck *all* of that!" was his reply.

"Well, just follow me then," he said, and followed Glen who was already entering the dried jungle growth. Immediately I heard the staccato snapping and crackling of dried branches which could wake the dead. Well, at least I had them to hide behind...

Just as I was working up the nerve to enter what was to possibly be my tomb, I felt a firm hand on my shoulder that turned me around. I was staring into the concerned (or was it angry?) face of Vincent.

"*Kwenda*," he said, and turned and walked away. Kwenda means 'we go,' but this was not a request; it was a command. Good; he was leading me away from this bad dream. I followed eagerly, but was soon dismayed when he walked up to the edge of the kasaka fifty yards or so from the other entering party and walked in, motioning me to follow. Uh oh...and he didn't even have a gun. But then I looked directly behind me and there was the friendly face of Ernest, bearing his trusty Parker Hale 458.

Okay, but my question then was, since I was the least experienced hunter, why was I paired off with these guys instead of Glen or Aaron? It just wasn't fair—not one bit. I had a vision then of my yet unborn son, due to arrive sometime in October. What would happen to him and Ginny if I got trampled to jelly in here and they sent me home in a coffee tin? Or maybe it would be so bad I would get trampled thin as filo dough—then rolled up gently like a Greek pastry and dropped into a mailing tube and sent home like an unframed poster print.

No doubt Aaron would stick a telegram in with it, of course:

DEAR GINNY:
RUM LUCK STOP. RICK HAD RUN-IN WITH BUFF STOP. HERE HE IS—AFRAID A LITTLE WORSE FOR WEAR STOP. HARD CHEESE & REGRETS—STIFF UPPER AND ALL THAT STOP. TALLY HO—AARON BROOME, P.H.

I wondered how she'd take the news. Then I wondered how my son (he was to be named Rick, after me—lucky tyke) would feel about all of this later on. I pictured him in class being called on by the teacher.

Teacher: Now Ricky, what does your Daddy do?

Ricky: Nothin'. He's dead. Went off to Africa and got himself kilt by a buffalo.
Teacher: Well I'm so sorry to hear that. He must have been a very brave man, your father.
Ricky: Naw. He was just a jerk. Spent all our money to go to Africa and crawled into a bush and got trampled thin as paper. A real loser. Can't wait til my Mom remarries.

I didn't like this vision, and strove to shove it from my head. But before I could do so I noticed Vincent was now deep into the dreaded Kasaka, still motioning me to follow him. I turned around and saw Ernest motioning with the barrel of his rifle for me to do the same. He was not pointing it at me. That is, not exactly, but it was a close enough imitation to make me wince. A 512-grain slug sailing through my kidneys from two feet would certainly do some serious damage.

"Kwenda!" repeated Ernest. His face was pleasant, but his voice firm.

"Actually, I'd rather not thank you."

"*KWENDA!*"

I turned and walked in. Or tried to. Instantly I was aware of being gripped on all sides by tangles and "wait a minute" thorns. Below the footing was treacherous; deep mats of clumpy vines several feet thick made every step a challenge—the risk of tripping great. I could see far enough down into these tangles to know that they could house hundreds, thousands of snakes. No doubt including our Four Friendly Fanged Fiends from the snake farm…

And so on we crept. If any animals at all were in here I would be amazed if they didn't hear us approaching. All I remember doing most of that painful, duckwalking trek was that I constantly repeating in my head the following refrain:

"Oh Heavenly Father, I am heartily sorry for having offended thee…"

Because this was, in all honesty the one time in my life when I was positive there was at least a 50/50 chance I was not going to live to see the sunrise. Soon Vincent stopped and peered ahead, then motioned me up to him. My legs aching mightily (I had been squat-walking for forty minutes or so, but barely moving), I joined him.

"Buffalo—" he said in the faintest of whispers. "look—"

I followed his pointing finger, and saw...nothing. It was the same problem I'd head earlier with the impala; I could not distinguish the animal from the brush. Also, I was expecting the Cape Buffalo to be jet black in color. This is not true; they are actually a dark charcoal gray in color, but appear black in dim light, or many other colors depending which kind of mud they have been rolling in.

I shook my head at Vincent. He frowned.

"See? A cow. She is looking at us right now."

And after a few more seconds, I saw her face materialize out of the brush. The sweep of the horns, the wide, wet nose, the giant, sideways twitching ears. And the coal black eyes that bored right through me.

"He looked at me as if I owed him money..."

As I was looking into those coal-black eyes I was sure only of one thing: I did not want to proceed further, Muad's warning's and description of the Kasaka were too accurate to be ignored. At any second that cow could leap to her feet and come at us like an express train while we staggered and fell in the brush.

Vincent started forward again (totally unarmed—not even a stick in his hand, and barefoot, mind you—*barefoot)* and said over his shoulder *"Kwenda."*

I didn't move. "I'd prefer not to actually. Thanks awfully."

"Kwenda," came a deeper, more authoritative voice from my rear.

"I believe I'll take a raincheck."

But Vincent kept moving, and I felt a slight nudge at my back. What was this role reversal anyway? Was I a prisoner of war or something? I mean, weren't they supposed to be working for *me?* What the hell was going on here? Then I realized that if they backed out and left their client without a shot they'd have to answer to H.O. himself. I knew him only slightly at this point, but it took an IQ of just slightly higher than an oyster to imagine what he might do to them if this happened. Of course for the first offense it wouldn't be that bad. For starters perhaps flogging followed by impalement.

So on we struggled, and cursed the bread and waited for the light. Duck-walking is not fun even on a level carpet. In a dry swamp it's torture. My thighs were burning up. My mouth was dry, my body soaked with nervous, sour sweat. Then Vincent pointed at my hands. "You shake, Bwana. I do not like it when you shake—" *"I don't either!"* I hissed. *"Let's get the fuck out of here!"* But they would have none if it. So on we went, with me repeating my desperate refrain to the Almighty, apologizing to Him, to Ginny, and to everybody to have been cocky and stupid enough to decide to come on this misadventure in the first place.

As I fought through the Kasaka I noticed the barrel of Ernest's 458 swinging right and left as I cradled my own heavy rifle in my arms. His gun barrel was making a back and forth arc right behind Vincent's kidneys. A 458's slug weighs in at 512 grains (as opposed to a 30-06 slug's weight of 165) and has a muzzle energy of over 4000 foot-pounds. At this close range it would just about bow poor Vincent right in half at the small of his back. And my rifle, being a Remington (which I'm not fond of), had a safety mechanism which was a simple throw-lever type. This meant that if this lever somehow got caught in the brush and I didn't notice it, it could disengage. Then, if there were any pressure on the trigger, from any source whatsoever, the round would fire. Goodbye Vincent.

But was my concern over what might happen to poor Vincent? Was I really worried about him?

Why of course not. He was a mere hireling, whose presence was justified only to do my bidding and the heavy lifting. And—oh yes—the *dying*, if that were needed.

What I was really worried about, of course, was *me*. Yours Truly. The One and Only. The *Sine Qua Non*. The Center of the Universe. You get the point…

I was worried, of course, that the guy behind the Center of the Universe (Ernest), might have a mishap with his 458 and blow *me* in half. This was the cause of the concern. This is what could ruin my entire day. The fear was somewhat mitigated by the fact that his rifle was a Parker Hale, and had a Mauser action like my beloved Model 70 Winchester. The safeties on these babies were the three-position type that could not come undone unless the shooter flipped them sideways twice.

Still, it was unpleasant being soaked in one's own sweat on a cool, cloudy morning, with nothing in one's ears but the pounding of

115

one's pulse and the crackling of millions of tiny firecrackers as the brush broke and shattered all around us.

Then Vincent stopped and held up his hand, I actually saw him turn his head to and fro and sniff, letting the faint breeze (and presumably, the odors they brought as well) against his face and cheeks. He squatted, frozen like this, for perhaps half a minute. Then he turned to Ernest and me and pointed back in the direction we had come from. When we hesitated—mixed signals are always confusing—he passed by both of us in a hurry, leading the way back out of the thick stuff, again looking over his shoulder at us.

"Kwenda," he said hurriedly. *"Kwenda-Kwenda—Imekwisha!"*

Ernest followed him and I brought up the rear. It was then I realized the cause of Vincent's concern.

Behind me was a growing crescendo of noise and confusion. It was a distant hiss, growing closer. *This must be what a Tsunami sounds like,* I thought as I went into a high-gear duckwalk. Either that or a waterfall you're approaching in a calm river. The noise was growing by the second. Ernest turned around and motioned me in front of him. I gladly accepted. Now Vincent was duckwalking and backpeddling with everything he was worth, attempting to put distance between us and the approaching noise.

I turned to Ernest. "What does *Kwenda-Imekwisha* mean?"

"He saying to you and us: let us go *now;* it is all over!"

"Why? Why is it all over?"

"Many Mbogo coming! We must go. *Go now!"*

Well, he didn't have to tell me twice. I swam through that Kasaka using every limb and muscle I had, and some I'm sure I didn't even know about. We stumbled on, fell down, retrieved our guns, and kept stumbling, all the while conscious of the ever-growing thunder and commotion at our back.

Finally, we stumbled out, exhausted, onto the edge of the hard-packed earth that bordered the Kasaka jungle. I could scarcely breathe as we backed away from the mass of dark, intertwined sticks and vines. A hundred or so yards into the brush we saw a flock of birds explode out of the thick cover of the Kasaka and take flight.

"They are coming for sure now, Bwana," said Ernest in a low voice. "Come with me."

Then the noise took on a new character—an added dimension. The sound was so intense it was surrealistic, and then I remembered what I had asked Muad just a week previous as we toured the Lake Manyara Park and photographing the buffalo. I remembered asking what it sounded like when they charged through the high brush at top speed. His answer had been: *"Sah: like the world is coming to an end!"*

Now Ernest led me running and stumbling back over to Glen's vehicle and we climbed in. I noticed he did not rack his gun but kept it at port arms, ready. Then he aimed in the direction of the wall of brush we just escaped from. I did the same. There was no more than twenty yards distance separating us from the Kasaka. The sound grew unbearably loud now, and I could feel the ground shake the Land Cruiser.

Then the herd exploded from the brush and charged in our direction. Ernest was shouting something into my ear but I could not hear for the racket. Then on both sides of us were huge dark shapes shooting past, kicking up dust into a smokescreen. Twice the vehicle was bumped by a passing animal was rocked so much I thought it might tip over. I had been in the company of scared, running cattle previously and always, during those episodes, heard the moaning and mooing of distress, which generally exchanges between the cows and their calves. But in this instance the animals were in complete silence except for the unearthly racket caused by their mere passing. None of them charged the hunting truck, nor even appeared to notice it. They simply boiled out of the brush and, almost before we knew it, disappeared.

The silence felt in the wake of their passing was an echoing void you could hear. I recall finding myself half ducked down—half sprawled really—on the backseat—the seat that was elevated behind the driver's seat in front. Right behind me was Ernest. In the back Vincent had crouched in the bed behind the big spare tire that was fastened upright on that side. If one of the buffs had decided to jump into the truck we all could have been killed. Fortunately that hadn't happened. I looked at my hands. The shaking was worse. "What happened?" I asked.

"Something frightened them, Bwana Rick. That was a stampede. If we had stayed in the Kasaka we would all be dead now— " he turned his head and spoke over his shoulder "Sante, Vincent!"

After we waited in silence for awhile we got out and walked around. As might be expected I was dying to take a leak, so that was the first thing I did. I walked around a spell, thanking the Good Lord for having delivered me, and cursing Hard On extra thoroughly for being gung-ho and bullheaded enough to have put us into this situation in the first place, when a thought suddenly struck me. I walked up to my two comrades in arms.

"Hey you guys—where are Dick and Glen?"

They shook their heads, looking at the ground,

"Where's Gabriel, Vincent? Wasn't he with them?"

He simply shrugged. I wandered around the car a few more times to stretch my legs. I was having a lot of difficulty with my right knee especially. I have reoccurring bursitis in it and it was especially inflamed during this safari. Thinking back, I'm pretty sure the cause of this flare-up was the seventeen-hour plane trip from Chicago to Arusha. During all that time we were never to fully stretch out our limbs. This bad knee was to be the cause of a very interesting adventure later on. Just as I was leaning back to stretch my back, and wishing we were on our way back to Whiteface for a much-needed soothing Tusker or two and a lie-down, I heard a vehicle approaching at speed.

Seconds later Aaron's truck, now loaded also with Dick and Glen and Gabriel as well as its original occupants (Aaron, Larry, Julius, and Boogie) swerved around the edge of the brush and slammed to a stop in a cloud of dust. Everybody got out and there was a lot of milling around and, from the direction of H.O., a lot of cussing and chewing out. In the midst of this verbal barrage I notice Dick slip quietly away to the opposite side of a big bush. Then I listened as Glen ranted at the natives, Aaron, and even himself at the botched hunt.

"….FUCK! Well…this could be it gentlemen. Because let me inform you that we've been seeing very few buff around here lately. That's not our fault; that's just the way it is sometimes. Now that these have slipped away there's no telling when—if ever on this fucking trip—we'll see any more and I—*Vincent* **are** *you* **listening** *to me?*

"Yes Bwana."

This was the first of many incidents which led me to believe that Vincent was Glen's favorite whipping boy—something that drew me even more to this silent, wiry, and extraordinarily brave man. But H.O. wasn't finished.

"So we get out here, and we find buff sign, a lot of it. The W'Kamba are right. So we enter the kasaka and what happens? The fucking buff stampede because *somebody*—(and here he stopped to glare in Aaron's direction)—forgot the plan and took his party into the brush from the *wrong side* and trapped the fucking Mbogo and their cows and calves in the brush, and then we all closed in on the motherfuckers and it's a fucking miracle **we're all not dead!**"

Then there was a pause for emphasis.

"Aside from this minor fuck-up, the plan worked perfectly," he concluded, then whipped his baseball cap down on his head, drew it down tight in front by yanking at the bill, then stomped off back to our car.

Meantime I had noticed that Dick was still absent. I decided I better check on him. In the state H.O. was in there was no telling. In his present state he could just drive off and leave my comrade to the darkling plain. And then before daylight he would be transformed into *fisi*'s-feces.

Speaking of feces, as I rounded the bush I saw my companion *en la stance ridiculeuse...Le stance de fait un merde.*

Dick Manning, foremost ophthalmologist in Pocatello Idaho, veteran of numerous hunts with the notorious H.O. Glen Schacht (and who therefore, should have known better) was squatting there behind a mopane bush with his pants down.

I sauntered up to him. Downwind. (I was picking up a lot of wilderness tricks from Vincent and the guys.) "I say old chap, who gave you leave to leave your spoor on the moor?"

He looked up at me. He was not smiling. Beads of persp. were formed on his grim visage. His hands were shaking; his bent knees wobbly. He looked all done in. And mostly scared and shaken as hell. So there! *I was NOT the only one.*

"*Rick...it wasn't like this in the video. In the video it showed...*"

"*—you don't have to tell me, pal. I know.* In the video it showed the hunter—a kindly, father-figure guy who was actually pleasant to be with—instead of this *Bull Simons Wanna-be* we're saddled with—

and the client—a guy not nearly as skilled, dedicated, or deserving as us, scoping out a herd of grazing buff in an open field at about seventy yards. They are actually sitting down comfortably chatting about which one of the easy thirty or so shots to take. Then the client pops a prize bull right where it should go and bingo! He's got a Rowland & Ward trophy. No, he's not slogging through Serpent City on all fours with the second tracker's gun barrel up his ass."

He looked over his shoulder nervously. "What if they come back? I'm kinda stuck here for now—"

"Fear not," I said, drawing back my bolt just far enough to see the bright yellow gleam of the brass cartridge up the spout. I closed the action, flipped off the safety, and stood twenty yards or so to his back just in case that very thing happened. And it could. They could have left a calf or two behind. All African animals are loyal parents. If they're not—even for an instant—junior becomes the featured item on the menu.

Finally Dick was ready to return to the truck. We ambled back to H.O.'s harangue about us being late and not listening to him and blah, blah. I just climbed aboard next to Ernest and racked my rifle. He slipped me a wink and smiled as we sped off toward Whiteface, and I bumped fists with him.

Maybe it wasn't the Swahili handshake, but it was close enough. I was prepared now to sit back and let the warming breeze wash over me, cleansing me of all the bad memories of the dreaded Kasaka brush and Glen's cockamamie idea to go in there to flush out the buff.

But I was premature in my optimism because just then there came a commotion behind us. Glen turned and followed Gabriel's pointing finger. Vincent was yelling something in Swahili, but the word Mbogo stood out clearly. Why now? Frankly, I'd had enough of the brutes for one day. Glen leaned on the horn. Thirty yards in front of us Aaron and company turned their heads in time to see our truck swerve around in a giant arc of red dust and haul-ass in the direction we'd just come from. Glen yelled at us to unrack our rifles. "Closest man gets the first shot!" he screamed over the din. "Aim low in the chest and forward. Don't go for the head, and watch for the big bosses: those are the horns you'll want."

We gained on the retreating herd; there was no doubt in my mind now it was the same one we'd jumped in the brush not ten minutes earlier. As we crept up alongside the galloping animals, which had a

120

loping, hobbyhorse style gait, he motioned for Dick to take the first shot. *"That one!"* he yelled, pointing down and to the side. But neither Dick nor I had the faintest clue which one he meant out of the thirty head or so running and jumping beasts, which were to the last one at least partly obscured by dust clouds.

Dick raised his rifle and tried to aim, but in doing so he was forced to let both hands free from the "bull-bar" that topped the rifle rack. It was this bar that we held onto when things got bumpy. And bumpy they certainly were right now; the truck was going almost forty, which was awfully fast for a place with no roads. And a vehicle with no seatbelts. I watched Dick get bounced off his seat twice, but only slightly. It was the third time that made me grab the back of his collar and pull him back down to the seat. The look he gave me over his shoulder confirmed what I suspected: that if I hadn't on instinct done this, he would probably have been thrown off the truck and into the running herd. And they would have ridden right over him. *Ridden roughshod* is, I believe, the expression used in such cases. He tried twice more but never got a shot off. Each time he lined up his scope (and a scope of *any* power is a silly thing at close range—you're better off shooting *blindfolded)* his ass left the seat.

As for Yours Truly, I was, true to form, being a total chickenshit—simply hanging onto the bull-bar for dear life and confirming my earlier decision never to try bull riding.

Glen, seeing a looming patch of Kasaka ahead, gunned the engine one last time in an attempt to catch the escaping herd. But it was no-go, when the buff saw safety, they went into high gear and pulled away from us, veering to the right and smashing, crashing, exploding into the thicket with such force that a sea of birds filled the air above them.

An hour later, as we disembarked from our Land Cruisers and approached the dining tent with *Tuskers* in hand, John sensed the mission had not been a successful one. He knew Bwana Glen would not be in a good mood, so he was careful to stay ramrod straight and silent as he served us, talking in a whisper.

"Well you guys," said Glen after we finished. "Did you redline your fun meter?"

"I never want to do that again," I said solemnly.

"Me neither," intoned Dick.

121

"I could be persuaded to pass on it," echoed Larry.

"Well then, let's hope our luck shifts and Mbogo decides to come back to the Masai-Mara. If he doesn't, and you still want to get your buffs, that means we'll have to charter another plane and fly down to the Selous and get them there."

The others thought it sounded great. But not me; I was just about out of funds.

CHAPTER ELEVEN

FAMILY TREE

As I recall, it took me forty-eight hours to decompress from my experience in the Kasaka with our friends Mbogo and the Four Fanged Fiends. I know I was not alone either. Proof of this was revealed by the ritualistic squatting behavior of Dick, and the moaning and thrashing of Larry in his fitful sleep. It was not pretty. I also could not help but notice the alcohol consumption had increased alarmingly; the level of the precious amber fluid in the bottles of Black and White and JWR plunged as a canoe going over Victoria Falls.

In a word, we were not happy campers.

I was certain, being the sensitive and perceptive soul that I am, that Glen sensed our discomfort. But did he do anything to alleviate it? Why certainly not. To H.O., Africa was Africa, by God, and if you couldn't stand up to it, may you perish in the Darwinian struggle. Served you bloody right. His answer seemed to be more of same, only speeded up and intensified: *earlier* to rise, *more* hunting, *fewer* naps and lie-downs, *less* stuffing ourselves at table even though the food was delicious. Presumably the next step was to put us on half-grog and deny us our smokes too. Well, there was a limit. After all, who was footing the bloody bill?

It appeared that somebody was going to have to talk with the bastard and set things straight. Precisely. Give him a good talking to. Rattle his cage. Put him in his ruddy place. And I didn't particularly care how severely it was done, either. Or who did it.

As long as it wasn't me.

"Are you crazy, Boyer?" scowled Larry as he crawled into his cot, pulled up the freshly ironed sheet and woolen blanket, and began writing in his daily log. "The heat got you or what? Going against him's like going against Captain Bleigh. Or Idi Amin. He'll have you dead in two days out here, maybe less. Think of how many ways a man can meet his fate in these vast plains where corpses are reduced to beetle dung in hours? Why, the possibilities are endless. All he has to do is get you isolated from everybody else and *bingo!* No more Rick Boyer. Might be a snakebite. Or perhaps a stray lion or leopard. You could fall into quicksand, or get mired in a mud hole. Then there are really sneaky ways that take some time, like perhaps a scorpion in your bed."

"He'd never get away with it; the boys would tell on him—report it to the authorities. Or else Ernest would tell, and Glen would lose his license and be forever banished."

Larry stared at me. "You really are pathetic, you know that? Okay now listen: *One*—"he grabbed his index finger, "even if the boys did tell Ernest or did report it themselves, you'd still be dead. Got it?"

I nodded. He did have a point.

"Okay. *Two*—" he grabbed his middle finger. "It's unlikely the boys, or Ernest, would report your sorry death to anybody who mattered. Know why? Because you're not important. What's important to these guys is their job, three squares a day, and sleeping somewhere a lion can't eat them at night. They're getting that working for Glen and that's all they want. So forget anybody reporting your loss. Now tomorrow's important; let's get some sleep and you stop worrying all the time. Two more days have passed since the Buff in the Bush—time's running short and that's what's making Fearless Leader so short-tempered.

Next morning we rousted from bed by Christoph's usual spoken *"Knock-Knock,"* and leaned over between the cots to pour the boiling water on the coffee in our cups. We met Dick in the tent, and noticed that he even looked a bit down in the mouth. We needed to shoot some game and resume filling up our tags.

Here was the reason: we had paid top dollar to come to Tanzania, the most game-rich country in all Africa, and the one with the most Buff, and the biggest. Mbogo was Tanzania's trump card. The license for this great trophy was also small: a mere $600. Why, the zebra and impala were only $100 less! The reason for this low trophy fee was so that Tanzania could use Mbogo (the most popular of the Big Five for hunters worldwide) as an incentive to hunt here. The catch was this: everything else here was ridiculously expensive. There was a 100% tariff, for example, on *all imported goods,* with the government taking it all. This meant that if Aaron wanted a box of 458 cartridges for his rifle, which cost a minimum of $80 in the States (for a box of twenty rounds of ammo, which works out to $4.00 per round), the actual cost of the same ammo for him would be as much as $200 per box. Our Scotch—which could be bought in North Carolina for about $30-35 a quart, was $70 in Arusha. You get the picture. SO…if we could not locate and kill Mbogo, we would still be stuck with the extremely high cost of this hunt and come home sans the all-important trophy, the Golden Fleece we sought.

Needless to say, nobody was cheery over this prospect, least of all Glen, who prided himself on his reputation for delivering the goods, and whose responsibility it was to get us to within shooting range of these beasts.

So everyone was keeping clear of His-honor H.O., including Aaron. A quick wave of his hand showed me that Glen intended I go with him and Dick again. I was puzzled at first as to why he kept me on his truck. I knew he was close to Dick, having hunted with him often in Idaho previously, and that Larry and I had gone to school together, so the logical move would have been to pair us in this fashion. But he didn't. Then I figured out why: he did not consider me a good enough shot to go with Aaron & Co. And I suppose I could not blame him. After all, I had taken only two animals so far: a Kongoni at rather close range (and wounded him with my first attempt), and an Impala that I not only could not see, but had, in bringing him down, almost totally deafened H.O. in his remaining good ear.

Yeah, I guess I could realize why he didn't trust me on a very long leash. We ambled on in the Land Cruiser for two hours, not spotting a damn thing except some small mongoose (mongeese?) that darted across the paths in front of our vehicle much the way possums do in the South. I could tell from Glen's stony silence that his blood pressure was rising. Finally Gabriel saw an Impala. We circled around downwind and finally gave Dick a good shot. He brought it down on the first one, and by the time we arrived it was dead. *Kufa.* As the boys were dressing him out H.O. complemented Dick on his marksmanship, saying how good it was to have a client who could bring down game in one shot...*for a change.* This jibe was not so subtly directed at me. But I shrugged it off. After all, he did have a legit gripe against anyone who blasted his eardrums as I had. On the other hand, one would think a P.H. with his sterling reputation (mostly invented and advanced, I assumed, by those who had not personally hunted with him) could not have failed to notice that both my rifles had been magna-ported.

Be that as it may, I sat back in the warm-up seat with Gabriel and shared some *goro* with him while Glen shifted into high gear and changed direction.

"We're getting the hell out of here. Rick, you've got your Impala. You need zebra next, sand we haven't seen any around here lately. I know where there are some, and some Grant's gazelle too. Grant's are a slam-dunk, if you can place your shot from a distance. The distances are often great but the country's flat and barren. It's alkali desert where we're going, in the heart of the Masai Mara." He looked at his watch. "We ought to be there in about an hour and a half."

Goro is a homemade dry snuff made by the natives. It's pure crushed tobacco, with no flavoring. Gabriel kept his stash in a plastic Kodak film canister. I was soon pleasantly buzzed, and we felt the warm, dry air rush over us we sped along. We made one very interesting stop on the way, however.

Just before we plunged down off the escarpment of our hunting concession we drove through a grove pf acacia trees and thick scrub. What was different about it was the addition of the giant baobab trees. These grotesque giants have enormously swollen trunks and stunted limbs. Like most African trees, the leaves are so small as to make the tree appear dormant, or dead. Also, the branches grow in confused, gnarly masses, which heighten their malformed, diseased appearance. And yet, despite their sick, surrealistic appearance, the baobab is a life giver...and a lifesaver.

Inside the swollen trunks, separated from the air by a skin-like bark that is easily pierced, is a pulpy, wet interior. This pulpy heartwood is damp enough to relieved thirst if chewed by man or beast. In addition, the tree's high water content makes it very attractive to honeybees, which select this tree almost exclusively to nest in. As might be suspected, the bee-eater bird also nests here. The observer who draws closer to the tree will also see clumps of vegetation hanging and swaying from the limbs. These suspended nests are the home of the weaverbird. Finally, since elephant in need of water pierce the thin bark of the wide trunks of these trees (which may be fifteen feet across) with their tusks, these trees oftentimes leave openings and hollows in them which provide shelter and safety.

So this ridiculous-looking tree is a combination barrel cactus, tipi, beehive, birdhouse, and aviary. The Wanderobo tribe, those small, dark bushmen who roam the savannah in search of grubs and bird's eggs, often make the Baobab their home.

It was to one such tree that Glen took us. The first thing Dick and I noticed was the triangular opening in the base of the tree, whose trunk was twelve feet across. Vincent dropped to all fours and peered inside this opening, then crawled in. His head reappeared and he said to Glen: *"Hapana."*

We crept up to it and looked inside. The dirt floor was lined with dried grass. In the center of this living tipi was a fire-pit with charred sticks and cooking stones in its center.

"A Wanderobo family lives in here," Glen told us. "In the evenings they crawl inside and set those big rocks—see them over there in a heap? —in front of the doorway to keep out the leopards and hyenas. Come on in—"

So I followed him in, and Dick followed with some effort. He's a little wider in the beam than either Glen or I. All four of us could all fit in there comfortably, and we're not little people. The Wanderobo are small. Not as small as the Hottentots of Botswana, but pretty damn small.

"Isn't Boogie a Wanderobo?" asked Dick.

Glen nodded. "It's an interesting story how he came to join our staff. Aaron was out leading a party of clients three years ago when they spotted vultures wheeling a mile or so distant over a thorn thicket. He thought it would be a novel idea to take the clients to the

127

scene to see whatever it was the birds were after, since this gathering of scavengers is a key part of the African experience."

He paused to light a cigarette and recline on the straw-matted floor, leaning on one elbow. "So off they go, and soon happened on the carcass of an Eland. It had been dead several days and was well bloated and plenty ripe. Just the way those griffon vultures like them. The hyenas had been at it, and also some lions. In fact there was hardly anything left. But what drew their attention was the little guy, stark naked and obviously starving, hunched over the carcass eating the raw, swollen entrails as he tried to fight off the wild dogs at the same time. Well, they brought him back to camp—more dead than alive—riding way in the back because he stunk so bad, bathed him, gave him new clothes the rest of the boys chipped in, and fed him the first decent meal he'd had in weeks. As he recovered he was so grateful he outworked everybody else in camp. Later Julius discovered he was an excellent spotter and tracker and…he's been with us ever since."

After resting briefly in this unusual dwelling, we exited the tree-trunk to see Gabriel plucking strange-looking white fruits the size of gumdrops from the lower limbs. He gave one to me and I found it didn't have much taste but did have the same consistency as those miniature marshmallows you buy in a bag. Glen pointed to the rear side of the trunk. Protruding from it at one-foot intervals were stakes half a foot long. Glen told us it was crude ladder made my driving Mopane sticks through the thin bark of the Baobab and into the pulpy heartwood, thus allowing the Wanderobo to easily scale the thirty feet or so to get to the honey hives.

"Their only weapons are crude slings and pebbles and sharpened spear-sticks. But with these they can usually manage to bring down several birds that nest in these branches. And look, you can see the smoke hole in the trunk that makes their chimney."

We hung around the tree for another quarter hour before taking off for the desert country in the heart of Masailand. Glen looked at me. "Now, Boyer, we're going to see if you really can shoot."

CHAPTER TWELVE

LONGSHOT

South of our campsite by considerable distance begins the Masai Steppe. It differs considerably from the Masai Mara in that is flat and bleak, with very few trees and the ground almost exclusively covered by white sand and dust. Consequently, the glare of the sun, even on hazy days, is intense. For the first time on safari I exchanged my standard sunglasses for the mountain-climber-specials I bought just for the occasion. The lenses on these glasses were so dark they appeared opaque. When you put them on inside you are functionally blind. It was only the super-bright light of the Masai Steppe that allowed your vision to become normal. In addition to the black glass, these glasses were also unique for the two leather flaps at the sides that attached to the stems. These effectively shielded your eyes from any glare (and blowing sand and dust) coming from the sides. With these on, and my surplus Cold War East German binoculars, I could get a great picture of all things near and distant. I noticed Dick, ahead of me in the shooter's seat next to Glen, was likewise scanning the vast plains that lay stretched away from us in all directions. It was not a total desert; now and then in the distance patches of brush and low scrub trees were visible. But the general the landscape was bleak, hot, dusty, and forbidding.

We saw Masai along the road (or what was supposed to be a road—actually we could have driven about anywhere we wanted). They were driving cattle, hauling magi or firewood (they held the water in old plastic engine coolant jugs, 3-litre soft drink bottles—anything that was unbreakable and would hold magi), or simply walking in groups.

The primary thing about them that caught my eye was that the women did all the work. On countless occasions I saw a woman bent low, almost double, under a load of sticks and brush that had been piled on her back while her husband walked ahead of her bearing only his walking stick or his *kuki*—the Masai spear.

It entered my head that, in the name of world progress, I should get out of the Toyota and approach the Moran, grab him by his flowing robe and enlighten him on the women's movement. I could say "see here, my good fellow, don't you realize what an ass you're being? Why this poor woman behind you is doing *your* work. For shame! For *shame* sir! Now I demand that you turn yourself about immediately and carry that load for her. Do it now, or I'll report you to Gloria Steinem, Melissa Etheridge, Diane Feinstein, and the high priestess of them all…Hillary Rodham Clinton. So there!"

And then in my mind's eye I could envision what would happen next. Why, he would drop his spear and murmur apologies to me (as well he should!) then make his way humbly back to his overburdened wife, take the load of firewood from her back, and lead her, hand in hand (much as Jimmy Carter led Rosalyn along Pennsylvania Avenue after his inauguration—a gesture so sensitive, so humble, so *au courant* I was overcome with joy and hope, and I wept…), along the path to their domicile, where they would live happily ever after. Because, in the words of a famous stateswoman (albeit known perhaps more for her ambition than her brains), we must never forget that it takes *a child to raise a village.*

So I leaned forward and asked Glen if he'd mind stopping the truck a minute so I could get out and have a few words with the Moran. See if I could enlighten him. Bring him into the twentieth century.

But, as I might have expected from H.O., he refused, claiming that all I'd get for my trouble would be a spear through my middle. And that I was a dumb shit, and a pussy to boot. It just shows you that some people will refuse enlightenment.

Sometimes the Masai rode bicycles, and the time they made on the level, hard ground was amazing. They whizzed along, their great tartan robes billowing out behind them like Merlin's cape, their great smiles—gleaming white teeth against the reddish, nut-brown skin, and their jaunty, arrogant hairdos and bead ornaments. Yes, they're cocky. Certainly, they're vain. But we'd all be too if we were that tall and straight, and strong, and could kill lions with a spear and shield, with *no help*. Of course they're in fantastic physical shape anyway, walking or running an average of 18 miles a day.

The Masai were the subject of a heart study performed by leading university a couple decades ago. Since their diet is virtually vegetable-free (with the exception of occasional fruit and some ground millet) and consists almost exclusively of cow's milk, cow's blood (drunk warm, fresh from the vein, in gourd bowls), and meat, contemporary wisdom on cardiovascular disease would suggest that these people would be particularly susceptible to the world's number one killer.

So the research jocks from this university's med school came over to Kenya and Tanzania, weighed the natives, took blood samples and body fat measurements, and the like. The most interesting thing they did, though, was to perform autopsies on recently deceased Masai, both male and female, from children to old men.

Here they got their big surprise. To begin with, most of these deaths were from causes other than heart disease. Malaria, yaws, sleeping sickness, typhoid, diphtheria, cholera…many maladies that either are uncommon in the West or that are now preventable in developed countries. There were also many deaths by accident, snakebite, alcoholism, miscellaneous infections, parasites, and wounds suffered from wild animals and even wilder native enemies. But, despite the length of this study and the large number of autopsies performed, it was a rare native indeed who showed any of the classic signs of heart disease: the clogged coronary arteries and hardening of the blood vessels that are hallmarks of the disease that fells more people in the developed countries than any other.

Why of course, they agreed, the answer is that these people don't have nearly the life expectancy we do—their causes of death are more similar to those of our ancestors a hundred years ago. Face it: both cancer and heart disease are diseases of degeneration; therefore these statistics aren't valid.

But, there was a kicker: all their blood cholesterol levels were sky-high.

So what gives, they asked themselves. Then it occurred to some bright boy to examine the arteries themselves, by age, and see if indeed they became narrower and more brittle and clogged-up with age. After all, that was the pattern in the West. How could people be so different from one another? The study revealed something that set the research team back on its heels: the older the subject being autopsied, *the larger were the coronary arteries!*

Uh oh! It was time to write home to mama. Time to throw out the rulebook.

After the study was completed the only plausible explanation to the so-called immunity of the Masai to heart disease was the fact— only revealed by field observation of the daily life of the natives—that they walked constantly, could run immense distances if necessary, and stayed rail thin.

And so began the walking, running, biking phenomenon in America and elsewhere that began in the eighties and continues to this day. So I mused on this and other things we could no doubt learn and benefit from these "underdeveloped" cultures.

"Kidogo!" shouted Vincent. *"Kidogo Dumi!"* The truck stopped with a lurch and Glen had his Leica glasses up and focused in a heartbeat. Sweeping the scene before us, even though my ice-climber specs and Zeiss-Jena optics, I could see nothing. Not a damned thing. Whatever it was, it was either very small or very distant, perhaps both.

"What does *Kidogo Dumi* mean?" I asked Ernest, who was riding next to me.

He bent down and whispered in my ear so as not to disturb Glen's concentration. *"Dumi* mean boy-thing." He held his finger out from his fly like a penis.

"You mean a male?"

"Ndio!"

That meant yes. So it was a male something or other. "What about *Kidogo?"*

"Little thing. Little male thing is out there."

"A Grant's?"

He shrugged. "I think a Grants. But very far away, Bwana. Hard *Piga."*

I turned to watch Dick line up his Weatherby across the bonnet of the Land Cruiser while he squinted behind the scope. Watching how the barrel was pointed I again raised my glasses and this time saw a teeny white speck on the horizon. Good God! How many yards away was that? Over 300. Maybe 350. And the animal was small. I could see the horns clearly against the white sky. Then I noticed it was doing its "curious ungulate" stance, facing directly sideways to the vehicle, head turned in our direction, looking dead at us, listening with its oversized, twitching ears at the strange grinding, thumping noise it could not fathom. Both Glen and Aaron swore that the running engine of a vehicle was the best hypnotic for hooved game yet invented. Apparently the critters were never able to figure out whether it was a mating call, a challenge from a rival bull, a lost calf, or an approaching carnivore. Or perhaps all of the above. In any case, the distant engine noise was enough to keep them transfixed for several seconds at least, usually quite a bit longer. With the rifle readied Glen cut the engine and sat back, not saying a word. As Dick's right hand tightened around the stock, we all placed our palms over our ears, elbows out, waiting, just like the white-smocked Nazi gun crew in the '60's movie: *Guns of Navarone.*

As these magnum and big-bore hunting rifles go off, the concussion is so overwhelming at close range that you are less conscious of the actual firing than of the deafening emptiness of it's aftermath. It is an echoing, hollow, emptiness, a surrealist silent-movie dreamscape of faintly ringing ears and dropping adrenaline levels, as if some great and nameless Power Spirit has left you.

There was a full second or two pause as the bullet, screaming through the hot, quivering African air at 3000 feet per second, spoke. Then Vincent, eyes glued to the far horizon, spoke.

"Hapana—"

A miss. Glen cursed, gunned the engine, and we roared off in pursuit of the fleeing antelope that was visible to me only as a faint patch of bounding white.

"Get on him!" shouted Glen. This meant the shooter was to make sure a fresh round was chambered and the rifle was already pointing in the general direction of the distant animal. I now saw Dick's contorted face, sweat pouring down it, his poor jaw being pummeled continually as it rested on the butt stock that in turn rested on the bouncing bonnet of the Land Cruiser. Now and then he raised his head up to search the distance with his glasses, but mostly we all followed the shouted calls Vincent and Gabriel behind us, whose eyes seemed to me to be better than those $1000 Zeiss binoculars.

Finally the bouncing, darting white speck far ahead settled down again. The car drew to a halt and Dick snuggled down, tried to control his breathing, and got his target in the crosshairs. Only this time it seemed he was a bit more nervous than before. A follow up shot after a clear miss lowers the self-confidence of the marksman, and he's also fighting frustration and anger. These tend to eat away at that crucial, Zen-level concentration that long range shooting demands. And also, I was not forgetting that this animal, he Grants gazelle, is only about 30 inches high at the shoulder, with a scant 5 inches or so body target from brisket to withers.

Once again the squeeze. Once again the Kraut gun-crew covers its ears as they prepare a salvo to the destroyer convoy far at sea...

BLAM!

One again the ringing in the ears, dammit. Once again the pause of flight—

"Piga—" reported Gabriel. And once we again we took flight in pursuit, but this time after a wounded animal. But not as wounded as it could be, it turned out, because we were awhile finding it again. It was wounded for certain, but by no means anchored. Finally Glen spotted it jump-running in low brush, trying to escape.

"He's shot through the shoulder," Glen said. "We'll just ease up on him slowly so your next shot can be from close up. Don't need to rush now as long as the hyenas don't find him first."

When we were within a hundred yards of him he was buckling over every third or fourth step. This is the scene no hunter wants to witness, or prolong. It took no time for Dick to place a slug right through his vitals and bring him down. We walked up to him and took a look. Nice buck, with good horns that had bulk and a fine curve. It was clear Dick's first round had gone too high and at an angle. He'd clipped the top of one shoulder blade, resulting in a wound that neither bled extensively nor entered the heart-lung cavity, the so-called "boiler-room" of game animals. This was the reason the antelope had run for so long. We took pictures and put the Grants in the back of the truck.

"Okay Rick, your turn in the hot seat," growled Glen. Goody goody. I climbed in next to Captain Ahab, my 300 Winchester loaded with five rounds of Federal Premium Safari-Grade ammo. Each round was tipped with a 180-grain Trophy-Bonded bullet. The bullet that Glen, who, we must remember, spends his lifetime hunting both North America and Africa, recommends as the best all-around big-game bullet made. Fired from the big cartridge case, they would zing along at over 3000 f.p.s.

"I'll tell you why I think African game is so fucking tough, Rick," he said as we whirred along, the wind in our hair, our asses bouncing half a foot off the seats with each rut or bump. "You know half the killing effect of a bullet is not the wound itself, but the shock effect."

"Shock effect?"

"Yeah—the shock wave the impact of the bullet sets in motion when it strikes the animal. Mammals are about 80 percent water, right? Well, picture something striking your body—even something as lightweight as 180 grains, which is a quarter of an ounce—at over three thousand feet per second. What happens? A shock wave is set in motion that travels through all the fluid in your body, from your toes to your head. This is what knocks you down and out, and often kills you. It ruptures cells and tissues throughout your body. Now why animals over here are so hard to put down, even small antelope, is the fact that they are only sixty percent water."

"Because it's dry here?"

"Right. And a drier animal means less shock wave, therefore less shock effect. Therefore the wounded animals just don't go down."

Hearing a discourse on how tough it would be to get a trophy even if I connected wasn't exactly what I wanted to hear. And of course, after watching Dick's difficulty in hitting the first antelope I was beginning to think I would be better off right now spending my time back in camp dozing in my cot, cuddled up with a couple cold Tuskers or maybe a liter of JWR. Boy it would sure beat this. The sun was coming down full force now and all of us were dripping sweat. Fortunately in the low humidity it didn't hang around and make your clothes stick to you, but it was unpleasantly hot.

"Grants!" Vincent shouted, waking us out of our stupor. He pointed off our starboard bow, and we were off in a cloud of dust and a flurry of bumps and swerves. This animal leaped in giant bounds, changing direction without warning, skirting brush heaps, soaring over ten-foot termite mounds and sailing through trees. Glen had the Toyota floored, and we went jouncing after our quarry, scarcely able to hold on to whatever we could find to avoid being thrown out of the truck. I'll never understand why hunting vehicles don't come equipped with seatbelts. I'm positive I came close to being thrown out of them numerous times during my ten-day hunt. Finally I heard Vincent say *"poli...poli..."* which means *slowly*. We looked ahead and saw the reason why; the animal had stopped and assumed the broadside "shoot me" stance, staring at us with curiosity, his body perfectly positioned for a classic heart-lung shot.

The problem was he was too far away. Way too far. Glen looked through his rangefinder and said the distance was between 420 and 450 yards. A long shot for any species, but especially far-flung for an animal as small as a Grants. So we crept ahead, going *poli-poli* and gradually shortening the distance. But after about 50 yards the bugger took off, bouncing away again like a distant white yo-yo...or perhaps a cotton ball on a pogo stick because all we could really see of him from so far away was his white rump patch. After several such attempts, Glen shut the car off and turned to me.

"Good luck Bwana. I guess you're going to have to do it from here."

"From here? Are you crazy? I've never made a shot half this long."

"It's all we got, unless you just want to turn back now and forget your Grants. Hell, try it; you could get lucky. I'll spot for you—" He crouched down behind his binoculars and waited for me to set up. "Don't take too long, Rick. He's been patient with us so far...but I got a hunch next time he's going to go all the way to Mombassa."

Soon I had the crosshairs centered on the buck's body. Then I moved them forward so that they were in line with the back of his foreleg. Then down so that my bullet would hit on the lower third potion of the body. I began to squeeze. The animal began to jump and dance. He wiggled and wriggled like a rubber puppet. And yet he wasn't moving; he still stood. His form came and went, split in half and slid sideways with each half going in different directions. Then the pieces came together again, like the image in a camera's viewfinder.

I was going insane.

No, wait. I knew what it was. Heat. The air between us was dancing in the rising thermals of hot air. The heavy 10X lens of my scope was a telephoto lens; it magnified the effect of the heat shimmer, and now it seemed impossible to shoot.

"Come on, Bwana!" hissed H.O. "Time's a wasting—' he's about to be outa here!"

"I can't fucking focus on him because of the heat waves."

"Do the best you can, goddammit! This is your only chance."

"I feel a breeze from the right. How far should I hold at this distance?"

"Seven to ten."

"And the drop?"

"Since you're dead-on at 200, hold four high."

"So I raised the rifle to compensate for bullet drop, putting the hairs just at the top of the animal's back, then moved them back so they rested closer to his ass than his shoulders. Seemed weird to me, but hey, this was the longshot of longshots. This was beating the Derby favorite at 300 to one. This was the Powerball Lottery...the Irish Sweepstakes. This was insane, was what it was.

I squeezed, feeling the fatigue and tension win, I was shaking, I was fucking shaking, and my sweaty hands were slipping now. The animal had ceased to be an animal—now it was a blob of bright finger-paint that was smearing itself around on some kid's easel.

This would never work. *Could* never work. I was a jerk for even trying it. I was a jerk for even coming on this fucking safari. I was a triple jerk for having the fucking *IDEA* to come on the safari.

The gun went off. And silence followed. A lot of it. There would be a full half-second before the slug would even reach its destination. How could—

"Piga!" shouted Gabriel. And none of us, especially me, could believe it even for an instant. H.O., obviously in shock, turned to me. A faint grin began to appear on his face. "I don't fucking believe it," he said, and turned the key in the Toyota. As we were driving toward the downed animal, in no hurry now, I felt Dick slapping me on the back. Both boys were chattering. Ernest clapped me on the shoulder and said "Piga Rick. Piga Rick. Piga Rick."

Not only had I hit the little critter, I had knocked it dead as well. We piled out of the vehicle and took pictures, The sun was going down over the Masai Steppe now, and the wind, still warm but beginning to cool down, was blowing all around me and through my hair as I knelt holding my Grants white Glen and then Dick took photos. It was a beautiful buck. Bigger than Dick's—but not by much—and with gorgeously shaped horns.   We had a two-hour drive back to camp, so off we went again. I sat in the back seat. As Dick climbed aboard he remarked "Well, if I hadn't seen it with my own eyes I never would've believed it, Rick. Great shot. Great."

"Yeah but it was also luck."

"No. No it wasn't. You've got to be good to get that kind of luck. Don't ever forget it. Now let's get back to Whiteface and gloat and tease Larry to death, shall we?"

"Great idea." And then I realized that the safari had suddenly become a great idea. I was having simply a bully time, and would not have missed it for the whole bloody world. So there!

CHAPTER THIRTEEN

LIONS IN MY LAP

OR

"The SOUND of the FURRY"

Okay. So I showed them I could shoot. My name around Whiteface was now *Piga Rick,* and I was already developing my swagger, and polishing my British accent. When asked about the accomplishment by Larry, Aaron, and the boys, I had a ready supply of comebacks and remarks.

#"Yes, a bit dicey don't you know, but the little bugger was cooperative, I'll give him that. Stood as still as a lad at his first communion, he did. One in the brisket and he was all in."

#"Yes, well I'm afraid I must decline to give you the particulars on technique, me dear fellow, as I plan to go into competitive shooting when I return to the States. I'm sure you'll understand..."

Yes, I was cock 'o the walk, for a while at least, and basking in the glory of it. Oh yeah, they'd thought I was a tinhorn, that I couldn't see or hit diddly-squat. Well, I showed them. And especially—*most especially*— I showed H.O. himself.

But two things intruded on my newfound glory. The first was, and I could not help but notice (as I peered down at them from my pedestal) that my associates began avoiding me. Not only that, they were becoming downright rude. In fact I believe I heard the distasteful phrase *flaming asshole* on more than one occasion. Since I knew this was merely a reflection of their envy and immaturity, I ignored it. I even offered to teach my tentmate Larry how to improve his long-range shooting. But this apparently irritated him all the more, perhaps because he had shot fifty-something deer on his three farms (boy, those surgeons must make a lot of money—), and he suggested that I stick the barrel of my Winchester up my ass and touch it off.

The second incident that rather threw a damper on things was a close call that made the Mbogo Madness in the Kasaka seem like a game of Ring Around the Rosy. It certainly was the nearest that the three of us (Glen, Dick, and Yours Truly) came to handing in the old dinner pail.

And it involved our old pal, Simba. Of Africa's Big Five (Elephant, Rhino, Buffalo, Lion, and Leopard), three are grass eaters and go after people only under threat (perceived or actual) or when they're cornered or wounded. And, as with any animal worth a damn, you're in serious trouble if you mess with a mama of any of these three species when she's got junior nearby.

But the last two, the cats, kill for a living. And one of these, Chui, does it for kicks as well. You might call it the Dark Continent's version of Art for Art's sake. Now, as I recall I mentioned in an earlier chapter that Chui was especially dangerous because of his ability to slink, climb and hide. This is true. Chui CAN hide in your sleeping bag, and wait for you to climb in so he can sing you a lullaby with his fangs…

BUT: Chui always hunts alone.

Lions don't. They're the only feline that lives in packs, called prides. These family units number between 4 and 12 animals, and always include young. Believe me, they are nothing to fool with. We seldom saw lion when hunting in our concession, and we never saw leopard. Of course we heard our own pet Chui every night in camp as he began his evensong, the guttural, cough-grunting roar that echoed down the stony slope of Whiteface Mountain to our cozy campfire spot. But we never saw him. With lions it's another thing; it's not that uncommon to see one or even two when hunting in the daytime when most other animals should be afraid of you. If you see more than a couple, look out.

It was toward the end of the final week of the safari—with none of Glen's and Aaron's clients having filled a buffalo tag—that Glen decided to take more drastic action. Now, I didn't like the sound of this strategy one bit. After the Kasaka/Mbogo stampede episode I was ready just to let the whole thing slide. I mean, sure, it had cost us a bundle to come to the one country that had monster buff, but what the hell. I mean, I'd had the African experience, right? Did I really need the ultimate hunting experience? The joy of being impaled on those monster scimitar horns, or ground to library paste beneath those nasty hooves? I could skip it, thanks.

But then, don't forget, we didn't have the usual mediocre P.H. The standard reasonable, understanding, patient, father figure Brit type. No. We had Glen Schacht, AKA Captain Ahab, Charles Manson, and Hard-On through and through. So before Dick and I knew what was happening he corralled the two of us as we sat after lunch smoking cigars in the shade of the dining tent (as was our wont) waiting to go out for the afternoon's go. Larry wasn't with us; he never was, because Aaron hunted straight through the day. Anyway, we got in the truck and headed out. Shortly, we arrived at the waterhole, which we visited often because it was our bulletin board, our kiosk in the wilderness. A cursory walk around its perimeter revealed the tracks of all the different animals that had come to drink the previous night. The expert trackers could tell the species, sex, and generally the approximate age and weight of each animal as well. I walked around, commencing to daydream a bit in the heat of the afternoon sun, but then I noticed Gabriel busy chopping brush and hauling it to a pile in front of the huge solitary Baobab tree that sat on a low rise some eighty feet distant from the waterhole. He motioned me over and I went over to help him. I supposed at first we were to build a fire for some purpose or other, but he told me otherwise.

"Bwana Glen wants to build a hide here so you can return after dinner tonight and wait in the dark," He said.

"Why?" I asked, feeling my jaw drop. "Are you kidding me Gabriel?"

"No Sah. There is no buff so far. Bwana Glen thinks they will come in the night. You will be here in the hide to shoot when they come to water."

He said this last word WAW-tah, "and after hearing him speak, I pitched right in to lend a hand. It was the British accent. There's something about the British accent that makes me think whoever's got it is an authority, or has authority, and therefore to be trusted. I blame my mother for this. When I was a kid she used to take all of us boys to the local theatre to see those old classic British comedies—the J. Arthur Rank Productions whose hallmark was the half-naked, sweaty guy banging a giant gong just before the credits rolled. Anyway, these light comedies, starring the likes of Alec Guinness, Terry Thomas, Alistair Simms, Robert Morley, and Ian Carmichael were a stitch.

My mom loved the British and everything they stood for, mostly because in those very dark days of the 1940's the British were the only ones to stand steadfast against the advancing Nazi hordes. Therefore, in her eyes for the remainder of her life, they could do no wrong. Some of this attitude must have rubbed off on me. Give me a chap in starched khakis or a Bobby helmet barking commands—preferably wielding a swagger stick—in that crisp, correct voice and I'll hop right in line right behind Tommy Adkins. *Right Ho!*

Before long we were all working on the "hide," which, I assumed, would be called a "blind" in America. To me hide was a better term because it *hid* you, which was the purpose of the contraption after all. And since you want to see out of it, why would you call it a *blind?* We worked for the better part of an hour, tying stout limbs together with sisal rope and interlacing them with fresh-cut branches. When finished it was a an elongated circle chest high, about nine feet long, and four or five wide—the perfect size, Glen said, for three men to sit comfortably side by side in the camp director's chairs and keep eyes peeled at the waterhole which, I took it, was abuzz with activity at night. One last touch was added just before we left: Gabriel and Vincent constructed two circular viewing holes as wide as coffee cans in the brush wall so that we could see out from our positions sitting in the comfy directors chairs.

Apparently well pleased with the project, Glen directed all of us back to our vehicle. We would spend the few hours left in the afternoon hunting, then return for supper, after which we would be driven out to the waterhole by the boys and left there until they picked us up three hours later.

This sent me wondering, and worrying. I was used to viewing the Toyota trucks as our safe havens in the wilderness, or chariots, if you will. True, they were not enclosed vehicles like Maud's photo truck, but they sure could run fast of needed. I didn't like being marooned out there at the waterhole in a pitch-black night with no truck. What if the boys got into the Scotch in Glen's absence and went on a toot and simply forgot us?

And there were a few other details as well. Once was the fact that while sturdy for a hide, the structure was essentially a concealment wall of leaves and branches, and scarcely five and half feet high. It was a house straight out of the Three Little Pigs. The entranceway was simply a gap in the elongated circle three feet wide. Any pissed-off animal on the veldt could come storming right in and leap onto our laps. The structure was, like the house of the First Little Pig, made of straw.

But my main worry became evident right before we left the place to return to camp. We were in the truck and Glen was backing around to head back in the direction we had come. I was sitting next to him in the front seat, and turned my head to take a distant look at the hide. Sort of check out its effectiveness. Of course it stood out like the Great Pyramid to my eyes, but that's always the way with blinds, er, hides. It would certainly do to break up our outlines and make us fade away. It would not conceal our scent, however, if the wind shifted. Still, this didn't distress me so much as the sight I saw leaving the waterhole. It was the sun, heading past its noontime zenith and beginning its long course down towards the western horizon. It would be a magnificent sunset, that was for sure.

Except that the sun was going to drop down directly behind the Baobab tree, and its golden rays would shine right through it, and silhouette us in its glare.

"I'd go easy on the booze tonight gentlemen," cautioned Glen as he walked past the fire circle. It was Aahhh! time. Attitude Adjustment Hour. I was nursing my third Tusker, and decided it would be my last. And I would skip the red at supper as well. One must make sacrifices in these situations. Throughout dinner I was anxious. Hunting at night was one thing. By itself it was to me unsettling to some degree because I knew that for all the beasties, nighttime was the right time. That was when the Terrible Trio: Simba, Chui, and Fisi, came out to play. The second thing was the absence of the hunting vehicle. Gabriel and Vincent were going to take it and skedaddle once we were ensconced in the hide; we'd be alone out there in the dark with no way home, and I had never seen a cell phone or radio in the truck. The third item was the hide itself. Somehow I didn't feel that confident that a five and a half foot wall of sticks and straw could protect us from a charging one-ton buffalo. It seemed to be a no-brainer—even a novice in physics could see the point.

But as I stepped from the truck with my heavy rifle I glanced over at the Baobab I noticed the setting sun, and it was with a heavy heart that I trudged over to the enclosure which was to be our little hideaway for the next four or five hours. As I watched the boys set up the three chairs and lay the canteens down at their bases, I had a feeling time would pass slowly indeed. We seated ourselves with Glen farthest in, Dick in the middle, and me at the entrance end. Since I was convinced from the start that a straw wall wouldn't keep anything bigger than a Dik Dik out, I knew it didn't matter. I also assumed that this would be a much safer way to hunt buff. We would let them come to us, pot one or two as they stood broadside, then watch the rest of the herd take off. Then we could saunter out from the hide and examine the trophies.

Why had I misjudged Glen in the first place? Wasn't he the one with experience? Who was I to question his expertise? Shame on you, Rick. Shame!

The boys handed our heavy rifles to us over the hide: Glen took his 470 double, Dick his Holland & Holland 375, and I my Remington 458. Looked to me now like the Three Little Pigs had a nice surprise waiting for the Big Bad Wolves when they showed up. I was all confidence...until I turned around.

"Glen," I said as politely as possible. "I still think that sun's going to shine right through these branches and leave the three of us outlined against the sky."

"Don't worry about it," he growled, lighting a cigarette. "I've hunted this way from here for years—why are you an expert all of a sudden? Just do what I say when I say and it'll work out fine." He took a paperback from his pocket and opened it, spread it out on his knee, and began to read. Glen was an avid reader. He got into the habit while sitting in hides like this one. Hides are used mostly in leopard hunting. In this type of hunting situation you bait the cat by wiring a ripe, stinky, maggot-filled haunch of antelope securely to a bough high in a tree near the hide. It's important that the bait be wired on tightly so the cat cannot simply retrieve it and scoot. It must stay up on the bough to feed long enough to allow a good shot from the hide. Anyway, Glen said these nighttime stakeouts were boring without a book, so as long as the light held, he read and smoked. That's another thing: all PH's claim that smoking doesn't spook the game. The reason, they say, is that the animals are accustomed to smoke because of the continual brushfires. It's true that brushfires occur constantly on the savannah lands. The Masai start them deliberately to encourage new growth which their cattle thrive on. But I question this entire line of reasoning. I KNOW my sense of smell is not one one-hundredth as keen as any of the animals on the veldt. Yet even I can tell the difference in aroma between burning grass and tobacco smoke.

Be that as it may, Glen continued to smoke and read, read and smoke, not even glancing up from his novel. I spent the time glancing around, watching the francolins and sand grouse flying home for the night, hearing the calls of hornbills and go-away birds. Way overhead two griffon vultures were sailing home on still, silent wings. I leaned over and peered through Dick's peephole (I noticed, to my chagrin, that I was not given one). The waterhole was deserted in the fading light. So where were the critters? Didn't they realize it was time for a drink? Cocktail hour? What was their problem?

Then I noticed my right knee was acting up again. I'd had this problem for some months prior to the trip—even visited my orthopedic specialist. He said to exercise it and flex it, which I had been doing. But I noticed that after sitting in an upright position for more than 20 minutes or so caused the joint to cramp and hurt. The discomfort was severe enough that I found myself involuntarily straightening it out three or four times to relieve the pain. This I did, and massaged it a bit until it felt better. I remember thinking then that I hoped we wouldn't remain all night because prolonged sitting really caused it to act up. I continued to look around me and every few minutes lean over to the right to stretch out my leg, look through the porthole, and then resume sitting.

It wasn't long, however, before the light level began to drop alarmingly fast. This was due to our proximity to the equator. The closer to the equator, the faster is the earth's perceived spin because it's the farthest point from the axis of spin. That's why objects weigh fractionally less at the equator: centrifugal force pulls them slightly away from the ground. In the case of the sun, this faster earth motion means that the heavens rotate faster, and this is especially noticeable at dawn and sunset, when the sun fairly storms up and drops like an anvil. It was now nearing dark, and faster and faster. I felt my knee calling, so I leaned over, massaged and stretched it, and once again looked though the peephole—

Now, sometimes you see things that you're certain must be a mistake. So you shake your head and look again. I believe in the film industry this is known as the
"double take." Assuming this is the case, I found myself doing a double take, rubbing my eyes, and peering out again. Nope. No mistake here. Down at the waterhole, less than a hundred feet away, six lionesses were on their bellies lapping the dirty brown water. *Six* of them. That's five plus one. Two times three. Three times two. Three plus three. In short, a *lot* of them. **Too many.**

I remembered now what Ohljome told me about his uncle being rubbed out by a lion striking him from behind. How you're dead before you know it. There were three of us, two of which were greenhorns in Africa. Sure, Dick had shot a lot of game, but none dangerous that I knew about. And he shot them from a distance. Believe me, shooting an elk at 200 yards is a lot different than stopping a charging lioness at sixty feet. Sixty feet is thirty yards. The lion does the hundred in just under four seconds, which means he can cover sixty feet in between one and two seconds. I knew I couldn't work the bolt on the big Remington nearly fast enough to get a second shot off in time. In fact, this custom-shop rifle generally jammed on the second round. Glen had a double rifle, and from what Aaron told us, he was aces with it. Great: he'd better be, because Dick and I with our heavily scoped bolt-actions were no match for six charging cats at a short distance. Of course, not to worry, we had the bloody HIDE between the beasties and us. Great: a wall of straw less than a man's height and eight inches thick. Why of course it would stop them, why shouldn't it? Just because a lioness can jump an eight-foot boma with a 200 pound calf in her mouth should have no bearing on what—

"Pssst!" said Dick *sotto voce.* "Glen says to look out the hole. There are six lionesses at—"

I nodded back, making the sign of the cross. *Our Father, who art in heaven...*

Mzungu Mjinga

"He says to sit still. Don't move a muscle. Don't talk—"He held a finger to his lips and sat slowly back in the director's chair, but I noticed him slowly easing his 416 up from its resting place into his lap.

Charlie Manson, who had decided maybe now would be a good time to put this month's Book Club Main Selection aside for the moment (bless his grisly heart), was now sitting up all alert, a look of definite concern on his Captain Ahab face. He too slowly drew his Westley-Richards double up onto his lap. I saw his thumb deftly slide over the tang safety as if caressing it. Then he turned to us slowly, and grinned a wide grin.

Swell.

Now I was more conscious than ever of my vulnerability sitting next to the so-called "entrance." Actually, the whole damn thing was an entrance when you're talking about *Felix Leonis*. And I couldn't see shit either, because I had been denied a peephole. I slowly leaned sideways to ease the tension on my constantly throbbing knee again, and took another peep. The lions were still drinking, crouched down at the muddy water's edge just like giant kitty cats drinking from a saucer. Some lolled on their sides. I noticed there were three adult lionesses and three juveniles. I also noticed the one thing that gave me some reassurance: all of them had big round full bellies; they had obviously just returned from a kill. This was good news; they were stuffed and lethargic after feasting and wanted nothing more than to return to the pride and crash. Then they would, in the manner of all cats, sleep for ten to sixteen hours. Great—all we had to do was stay hidden and wait till they drank their fill. Then they would saunter off with their swinging bellies and fetid breath and we'd sit back and wait for the buff to take their place. Pot a couple and wait for the truck, and then we'd have our tags filled. Maybe Glen wasn't so dumb after all. I felt the knee acting up again and leaned over to move it and rub it a little.

"Don't move!" came a quiet but extremely urgent whisper from the other end of the hide. In my half–bowed position I rolled my eyes up to see Glen looking anxiously out his peephole, holding up the big double gun now, glancing my way with tiny flicks of his eyes. I glanced back at him, continuing to rub my throbbing leg.

"DON'T...FUCKING...MOVE!" came the urgent request again, in a low gravelly whisper much like a Mafia enforcer might use as he's urging you to shove your bare feet into a washtub of wet cement.

I returned to my uptight—excuse me, I mean up*right*—position as unobtrusively as possible and waited, rifle at ready. I felt dampness on my forehead and under my arms. Great. Nervous sweat. If the wind shifted and the *Simba Sextet* got wind of the sour odor of man-fear, it would take them less than a second to hippity-hop up the hill and over the blind and into our laps.

The voice of authority from the far end of the hide continued. *"When I say 'don't move' I mean it. IT COULD MEAN YOUR LIFE!"*

And with those words, the uncertainty and apprehension turned to real, deep-down dread. After a few more seconds Glen said, "We...have a problem..."

And that's when we heard it.

Now, if you've never heard a lion roar in the flesh, so to speak, believe me when I say you are missing one of the wonders of the natural world. I heard it for the first time at Chicago's Lincoln Park Zoo, a zoo famous for its cat collection. I was at the other end of the zoo, perhaps half a mile away, when the lioness let fly, but believe me when I say it got my attention. Now, when the lead lioness roared at us, it was squarely in our direction, from a distance of...from a distance of...

Then I paused to think a second. Certainly it sounded closer than the waterhole. I decided to lean over and glance through Dick's peephole again, no matter what Glen had told us. I could not believe what I saw, and recoiled in horror. She was on her feet, walking straight for us, forty feet away and closing fast.

"Get out of here!" Glen yelled. The old lioness stopped, barred her teeth, and spat. I got a good look at her face this time...up close and way too personal. She had a bad case of Ugly. Her face was all cut up and scarred, witness to the countless fights against rival females for the alpha position in the pride. I believe that's where we get the expression "cat fight" for a woman-on-woman scuffle. Anyhow, she must have been a great fuck because she sure wasn't comely. She looked like Mike Tyson.

But the good part was that the three young ones took off toward the waterhole and kept right on moving. Well that was good news anyway. But the three old timers were still there, single file, holding their ground. Then I remembered another thing Ohljome mentioned that day at the coffee plantation: *Terri*-tree. The main reason lions kill people: to defend their territory. And here we were, interlopers at their waterhole, an extremely strategic spot in their territory.

Glen remained sighted down over the 470, no doubt centering the front bead low in the middle of the lead lioness's chest. He spoke to Dick quietly, urgently, without taking his eyes off her for a second because he knew what could happen if she saw him shift his gaze (a sign of submission in the wild and, though we are loath to admit it, a similar sign in us), and what could happen in that second:

"I want to save both barrels if they charge. If she keeps coming, shoot at the dirt eight feet in front of her; there's a good chance the blast and the flying dirt in her face will scare her off. It usually works—"

Dick nodded and stuck his Winchester out the peephole, flipping off his safety.

I flipped mine off as well. There was a good reason: I thought there was a chance that one of the Terrible Trio might skulk around to the back entrance and order takeout.

Shit. First Buffalo in the Bush and now Piggies in a Blanket. Who was the Mensa candidate behind these schemes? Bright Boy Schacht, that's who. Well I would show him. I was going to report him to the Professional Guide's Association as soon as I got back to Arusha. IF I got back. It was looking increasingly doubtful.

Another snarl from Ma Barker on the other side of the greenery—this time accompanied by the requiem choir behind her. My hands were so sweaty now I couldn't hold the rifle stock.

"Goddamit you bitch! I said get the FUCK out of here!"

And I'll be damned, this time it worked. The old bitch snarled, spit again, then turned on her heels and trotted off, her gal-pals in tow. It was awhile before anyone spoke. After a few minutes, when it was apparent they weren't coming back, I exited stage left via the entranceway and walked over and took a much-needed leak. Soon Dick joined me, and then we went back into our pathetic little cocoon and waited again. Very soon it was full dark, and Glen drew out his night-vision binoculars and passed them around. These were interesting toys, but I couldn't see how they'd do us much good when it came time to shoot anything because we still had use conventional scopes on our rifles. We did see a pack of hyenas slink down to the water to drink, their eyes glowing eerily in the dark. The glasses made everything green, which added to the surrealistic quality of the performance.

Soon we heard a distant rumble and whine that grew louder and louder, until finally the piercing beams of headlights cut through the brush and trees and the truck rumbled to a halt. Two jiggling flashlights made their way over to us. Vincent and Gabriel gathered up our chairs and canteens and rifles, and soon we were once again ensconced in the relative safety and mobility of the Toyota Land Cruiser. As we returned to camp, the hot wind rushing over us, I was glad to be alive. It was the kind of intense gratitude that only happens after a close shave. And then I realized why I was enervated throughout this experience. It was the continual stress of the dangerous and unexpected. We literally did not know what was behind the next bush or tree, what lurked just over the horizon waiting to trample or pounce. What ghastly creature was making its way up your pant leg or down your shirt collar. In short, when you were going to be unexpectedly *on the menu*.

As Fats Waller was so fond of saying:
"One never knows...do one?"

CHAPTER FOURTEEN

LUCY'S HOUSE

The next part of my misadventures was marked by a major change: I shifted from Glen's truck to Aaron Broome's, and so was teamed with my old college chum, Larry Dietrich. This would be enjoyable of course, but I would also miss Dick Manning. I wouldn't especially miss Hard On Manson, however, and I think, looking back on it, that it was the words we exchanged the morning after our close call at becoming *Simba Supper* that had at least a little to do with this logistical shift.

It started at breakfast with Glen remarking that it had been my fault that the lions had charged the blind because (1) I was wearing a light colored hat at the time which stood out in the dark foliage, and (2) I kept moving, and the motion caught the eye of the lead lioness. I answered that while these may have been the immediate causes, Glen had, in my judgment, been remiss in not heeding my earlier observation about the falling sun's rays coming directly on our backs and shining through the hide, thus outlining us in their glare. Glen stopped chewing then and glared up at me.

"One week in the African bush and he's a fucking expert!" he said, pointing accusingly at my chest. "Listen Boyer, when you have as much experience as I have, then you—"

"Glen, now you know I mentioned the sun, and what it could mean. That's all. If you can give out criticism, then you should be able as a good sport to take it as well."

Needless to say, he did not receive this comment with equanimity. As a matter of fact it seemed to increase his H.O.F. (Hard-

151

On Factor) by more than a few notches. He then terminated the discussion by announcing I was going with Aaron and Larry and for Dick to get ready pronto. We still hadn't a single buff yet and there were only three days left.

Aaron told me I had better take my heavy rifle as well as the 300 in case we did run across some buff, so I hopped out of the truck, retrieved it, and got back in, only to hear Glen bellow at Aaron: "remember, no buffalo hunting."

"Now why the hell did he say that?"

"Well sir, I suppose he's still pissed at you. He's not at'll used to clients back talking him like you do. You better watch it, laddie."

"Look: am I working for him or is he working for us? I mean, who's paying him anyhow?"

"Oh, haven't you heard? You're paying him. And you're also working for him. How's that strike you?"

"Not well. And I'm leaving Tanzania without a buff or a chance at one."

"According to the Boss, you guys had your chance at about twenty of the buggers and you blew it."

"In the thick stuff? No. No way I'll ever do that again."

"Well, they just don't amble along the prairie in broad daylight nibbling grass like they did in the Old West, now do they? What was that? 'Where the deer and the antelope play?'"

"What do you think Larry?"

"I think Glen has sized you up for what you are: a chickenshit asshole. But then you were thirty years ago, so why should anybody be surprised? I'm only surprised Dick and I agreed to go with you."

He and Aaron laughed. Let 'em. I was considering I was down a zebra. Larry still had to score a kongoni. Then the three of us would all have our tags filled except the Big One. "It doesn't look like we're all going to get buff anyway."

"Oh, I'm not so sure. Glen gets really pumped up when there's not much time remaining. He'll even take clients out with sleeping bags and spend the night in the bush thirty miles from camp so as to get an early start next morning."

This did not sound particularly attractive to me, especially considering our luck at the waterhole. "Let's go get me a zebra Aaron. What say?"

"One zebra, coming up sir." He pronounced the animal's name *Zeb*-rah, not zeeb-rah. We continued to jounce along the savannah, now and then ducking low in the truck to let brush and low-hanging trees brush over our heads, then checking for parasites that may have hitched rides on our scalps. Dangling amidst the branches of one candelabra tree a weathered snakeskin eight-feet long writhed and fluttered with the sound of tissue paper in the hot wind.

"Mamba skin, intoned Aaron in a bored voice. "It's been there all season long. My nickname for it is *The Grateful Dead.*"

I mused on this epithet without deciphering it, and told him so.

"Be bloody grateful the bugger's dead."

"Oh. Now where's my zebra?"

"There are several straight on. See them?"

Larry saw them too. Naturally, since I could not see the front seat, I raised my Ruskie field glasses and could make out four or five of the pajama-wearing critters frolicking in chest high growth. They appeared to be 300 yards distant. After attempting to close on them twice, Aaron finally pointed the vehicle at them and killed the engine, motioning me to take the shooter's seat next to him. The windshield was lowered; I flopped down my shoulder bag for a rest, set the 300 atop it, and scanned the small group. Aaron, looking through glasses, told me the second one from the right was the "shooter." That meant he was the trophy. "Get on him, sir, before they run off."

The shot was between 250 and 300 yards, not as far as the Grants shot, and the target was three times bigger, but it was still no piece of cake. I screwed the scope up to full power, set the crosshairs on the point of the zebra's shoulder right where the stripes made a swirl pattern, and squeezed. I had learnt from the antelope just how flat shooting the 300 magnum was—the Grants bullet had struck 6 inches high because I held 10 inches high. That wasn't much drop. I had decided to hold dead-on to the vital spot with this attempt and hope for the best. Zebra are tough animals, like Wildebeest. It takes a good shot in the vitals to put them down.

"Not to hurry you sir but you've not much time—"

I continued to squeeze until the rifle bucked against me. I was thrown back in the seat enough to temporarily lose sight of the quarry.

"Piga!" shouted Julius, and Aaron threw the truck into gear and we raced to the animal before he could regain his feet and run off.

"Sounded awfully hollow to me," observed Larry. "I think maybe you gut shot him, Rick."

"Well I hope not."

"If he's gut shot he'll be getting up shortly," said Aaron. "Look!" He was pointing a hundred yards further away in the brush, where a frenzied zebra was running to and fro and staring at us, making yipping, barking noises. "That's his mate. She's pissed off."

I realized I would be too, and began to regret having shot him.

Before we knew it there was the dying zebra stretched out on the dusty ground, arterial blood pumping rhythmically from the shoulder wound that was exactly where I'd aimed. Aaron said it was a damned good shot. Larry admitted it was too. I still felt lousy about the whole thing. Shit—I didn't know the guy was *married* for Chrissakes.

We didn't have to wait long at all for the stiffening tremble to begin. The thrashing of legs; the spastic, horizontal gallop of futile desperation; then more intense trembling, followed by a guttural gasp and groan…and finally the quiet, slow easing into death. The animal lay still now, a giant pool of dark red blood filling out the hot dust beneath it.

I felt terrible, and it certainly didn't get any better when I looked up to see his mate still there, running in hysterical circles around us, barking for her husband.

Julius and Boogie hopped down from the back of the Toyota, skinning knives in hand, and began disassembling the animal. They cut the skin around all the four lower legs, and then made a skin-deep belly slit, and finally, deepened the belly cut through the muscle and mesentery into the gut cavity.

"You know Glen won't eat zebra," Aaron said, "but the guts make great lion bait, and most of us love the meat."

It was then we made a fearful discovery. Larry, using his thirty-plus years of surgery experience, was first to spot it. "*Oh my….God!*"

"What?" I asked.

"That—" he said, pointing into the billowing, convoluted, multi-hued mass of intestines and organs, "is a *uterus!*"

"You're fucking joking!" said Aaron.

"Nope. Watch this: a post mortem caesarian—"

Larry took out his folding knife and deftly made incisions in the globular reddish organ that was as big as two bushel baskets. Before

154

we knew what was happening, he was dragging a bright pink (pink the color of Pepto Bismal) fetus from the opened belly cavity. There it was, a tiny fetus-calf, hooves, closed eyes, and all, its umbilical cord, now useless, dangling from its tiny belly coiled tightly as a phone cord.

I practically fell through the ground I stood on. As it was I walked over to a fallen log and sat down, resting my chin on my hands. I am not a sentimentalist, but this was really too much. So we'd had it all backwards, the frenzied mate scurrying to and fro at the far edge of the cover was not the female, it was father. The expectant father. Defending the mother-to-be. I felt like total shit. Aaron came over and sat beside me.

"Don't feel too bad. You got your zebra. Wrong gender is all."

"C'mon Aaron! She was pregnant. That compounds it. And we can't take it with us anyway. Girls are illegal to kill—we both know that."

I felt his hand on my shoulder. The younger man looked at me through hardened eyes. "Listen Rick. I'll tell you something. This happens all the time with zeb-rahs. Know why? Because in the field, at any distance, you cannot tell males from females. They're the same size and neither sex carries horns. But most importantly, the male doesn't carry his pecker or his balls outside himself. Even through great glasses, he looks like a female. I tell you this happens quite often—we just don't talk about it."

"Why the concealed sporting equipment? I don't get."

"Zeb-rahs are under constant attack from lions; they're the cats' favorite prey. It's a rare zeb-rah whose hide isn't raked with old claw scars from near misses. Almost all the attacks come from the rear. If the males didn't draw up their genitalia they'd be clawed off. So there's your answer."

"So what do we do?"

"What we're doing. It's all we can do. You want to pot that male ahead of us and make it legal? Take two and keep one?"

The answer was obvious; I shook my head."

"We'll take just the skin and most of the meat back and not tell Glen. Or anybody else. I'll have a set-down with Julius and Boogie and tell them if any of this leaks out around camp they'll get a beating to write home about. Now c'mon—"

We returned to the carcass where the boys were just finishing with the hide. Their knife work had been excellent-all there was to do now was shave the bulk of the hide off using skinning knives to scrape away the connective mesentery and then to pull it off. We had left the entire head, flesh, skull and all attached to the rest of hide since this was to be a rug, into Whiteface for Chume, the skinner, to cape out. This was a delicate task and none of us wanted the blame for screwing it up.

Peeling off a zebra hide is sweaty, time-consuming work. Before we were a quarter way into our task the first vulture appeared on the scene, sailing in on silent wings, then doing lazy circles above us. But when we finished, he was still the only scavenger visible. This amazed me. In the states, especially in the South, one turkey vulture brings scores of comrades at a kill this big.

So we left the carcass in the brush, Baby and all, and left to return to camp. I now had everything on my tag except for the Big One: Mbogo. Larry needed not only a Buff but also a Kongoni. Therefore Aaron told me he planned to take Larry out for a twilight hunt, and asked me if I wanted to go along or be dropped off at Whiteface for an early cocktail hour or nap. I opted for this, since Dick and I could share a cigar and a Tusker or two and then I would get some shut-eye during the late-afternoon's heat. The temperature was in the mid-nineties, which to me would be unbearable in North Carolina. But here the aridity made it tolerable, especially if there were a breeze blowing up the valley.

"But let me show you something first, Rick, that should get your mind off the Mummy and Junior zebrah."

I flinched inwardly again at these words.

"Do you like old houses?"

"Sure. Why?"

"How old?"

"Well, pretty old. I've seen some lovely old houses in Europe. Chateaux in France, Schlosses in Germany, Castles and manor houses on the Isles. Villas in Italy...you know. Then there are some great antebellum plantation mansions in the Deep South, particularly on the river road between New Orleans and Natchez—"

"How would you like to see a house that's a hundred-thousand years old?"

"C'mon Aaron, cut the bullshit—I haven't got the energy to..."

"I'm not kidding. We all think this place, which is less than twenty minutes from here, is possibly the oldest continually-inhabited dwelling on earth. Would you like to see it?"

"Definitely."

So on we drove and soon were approaching a mild escarpment that rose to a short vertical cliff with a longish dark shadow at its base. Aaron fought the truck up the incline using all four wheels and we bumped our way slowly up, the boys in back hanging on with strained knuckles. We stopped and got out, climbing the rest of the way bent over and huffing in the hot air. As we drew closer I saw that the shadow was what I suspected it was: a cave at the cliff's base. The setup reminded me of a miniature version of Cliff Palace, the new-world rock and cave structure at Mesa Verde in Southwestern Colorado. Only this dwelling was much, much smaller. Finally we were standing on a flat ledge at the cave's entrance, the "front-porch" of the ancient home. Aaron and Boogie ducked over and went inside. Larry and I followed with Julius bringing up the rear. We were standing in a low room, the ceiling seven feet at its highest point, five feet or so most places. We had to stoop-walk to get around in there. In the shafts of light that percolated into the cavern dust motes and gnats milled about, giving the dark place a fuzzy, surrealistic appearance, as if the entire thing were recorded on ancient celluloid movie film. In a corner we found two curious skimmers made from short forked sticks with grass mesh woven in the forks. Their purpose escaped me—and Aaron's too—but I remembered seeing them earlier, and then recalled where. It was in the base of the Baobab tree where the Wanderobo family lived. Whether these skimmers served an actual utilitarian function—such as to strain flies from honey, or whether they had some ceremonial purpose I could not say. But clearly somebody was using the dwelling— that much was clear by the fireplace and the smoke blackened wall behind it.

"It's no wonder people like to live here, Aaron," said Larry. "It's waterproof, stronger than any hut or boma, and fireproof.

"Right...and the best part of all: check out the view you guys."

We returned to the entrance and gazed over the terrain we had just traversed.

"Oh my God—" I exclaimed. It took my breath away. I've always been one for views, especially sunsets. What we were looking at now was the golden globe of the sun falling behind the distant slopes of a volcanic mountain. Giant clouds rolled across the red sky, their edges bright yellow-white from the sun's glare behind them. Shafts of golden light pierced the clouds and illuminated the far plain below. The plain was deep purple in the far distance, blue gray closer, then gradually turning to brownish beige, all scattered with acacia trees, whose flat planes of foliage gave the twenty-mile stretch a serene aspect. The view was the best I have ever seen, and that's including the coastline of Big Sur, the California Hills from Nepenthe, The live oaks and the grounds of Oak Alley plantation from the upper gallery and all the ones in Europe. It was no wonder that successive families and clans had chosen this Paradise Penthouse over the millennia. Who could resist it?

Then I thought of something else. This dwelling wasn't 100,000 years old as Aaron claimed. It was a *million* years old, and I knew why. We were in the Great Rift Valley, the place that Peter Matthiessen called *"The Tree Where Man Was Born."*

This was the cradle of the human race. It was in the Olduvai Gorge that the Leakys' first found Lucy, the world's oldest humanoid fossil. This then was Lucy's House. The oldest house on earth. And here I was, standing on its front porch admiring the view and also realizing that the beauty of the view was not the only reason it was important. From this vantage the cave dwellers could see anything heading in their direction from miles and miles away, be it wild game to eat, lions they must fight, enemy tribes, marauding elephants, or approaching strangers.

So here I was, a man from Chicago, one of the New World's most modern big cities, standing on the front porch of the oldest human dwelling in the world. A house that predated the caves of the Neanderthal and Cro-Magnon societies by at least three quarters of a million years—and made the tombs of the pharaohs or the dolmen stones of Britain seem like 1970's split-level ranch houses.

Aaron joined me on the ledge and asked if I'd seen Julius. "Bugger's always going off or dawdling. I want to leave in a few minutes. Damn his hide!"

I stooped and reentered the cave, where Boogie was explaining to Larry in pigeon English the fine points of the place. As a Wanderobo, or bushman, he was from a branch of the Masai tribes that had split off from the warrior/herdsmen race of tall, elegant morrans and had become, over millennia, a series of small clans that eked out a living gathering honey, bird's eggs, nuts and berries, and, if they got lucky, a dead animal that wasn't too ripe to eat. This hunter-gatherer mode of life was undoubtedly the same as the one led by Lucy and her descendants.

And finally there was one thing left to see at Lucy's Pleistocene dwelling: Aaron motioned me over to the very edge of the cliff ledge and told me to look straight down. I drew near the precipice with some caution; to slip and get a compound leg fracture out here—a minimum of 6 hours away from hospital—was nothing to be taken lightly. I got to the edge of the cliff and looked down.

At first I was confused by what lay beneath me. It was a heap of reddish brown…something. Something that resembled a rough carpet without hair. A piled up, wrinkly, bag of old thick leather forced deep inside a pit formed by huge boulders that formed a cone, a giant narrowing funnel of rock. I continued to stare at it, confused.

Until I saw the ribs. There, at one point in the ripped thick leathery shroud, giant pale arches projected from the ancient ribcage. Then, looking at the other end of the carcass, I saw a bright object as big as a 1/pound butter package. This was the elephant's molar, the same giant-sized tooth as the one I picked up the day we hunted Mbogo in the kasaka. I looked in vain for a tusk, but knew it was foolish. Had there been any—even small ones—they would long ago gave been chopped out and spirited away to Zanzibar—that Arab island trading center off the coast of Tanzania.

"What happened to this poor guy?"

"Glen and I have speculated about that. Best we can come up with is that the poor bugger simply tripped and fell. For all their strength, size, and courage, elephants have several great handicaps. They seem to be outgrowths of the very size and strength that makes them feared." He paused, look around and yelled "Julius! We're leaving!"

I guessed that maneuverability would be sacrificed in a body so big, and he replied I'd hit the nail square on the head. "This animal—and the carcass has been here for at least six years we know of—was climbing up this slope and no doubt probed this depression with his trunk. Then he apparently lost his footing—perhaps some rock pile gave way—and fell in headfirst. There's really nothing he could have done at this point. It must have been a slow and horrible death.

"Africa is basically nasty isn't it?"

"Yep. And so is life in general. Fortunately we don't have to deal with it that long. Well, we'd best be moving along Rick. Glad you enjoyed this little side trip."

"Do you realize that's probably the oldest human dwelling on the planet?" I said as we climbed aboard the truck.

"Humph! Never thought about it, but I suppose you're right. I hear that humans originated here. Bloody shithole they chose for it, right? Oh well, go figure. **Julius**! Come on you bloody swine. Julius! Come here!"

The man hesitated, then headed for his place the back of the truck. Aaron was out of the driver's seat now. "I said come *here!* "

Julius approached his master, wincing. Aaron drew his hand back and clipped him across the face with his fist. Julius took the blow without complaint and took his place on the back of the truck. All the way back to Whiteface I was disturbed by Aaron's action. Of course if I offered my opinion I would be dismissed by the PH's in short order. "What the hell do you bloody know Boyer? Best you just keep out of it."

The scene stayed in my mind, however. Not the part of the white man striking the black man, but the way Julius came voluntarily forward to receive the punch, knowing full-well how much it would hurt. In his position, the only option he had was to wince and wait for it.

Then I remembered where I had witnessed the identical scene. It was in Charles Darwin's Voyage of the Beagle. In that book young Darwin is witness to an identical act by an English sailor upon a South Pacific Islander.

As if this—coupled with the zebra episode—wasn't enough to dampen my spirits, we arrived back at camp to bad news.

CHAPTER FIFTEEN

THE PACT

"Hapana Mbogo."

That was the bad news. We'd rather been expecting it though—it's not as if it came as a thunderbolt out of the blue. I guess the most telling and reliable sign was Glen's disintegrating temper. Never the most jovial of fellows, he tended to brood around camp much like Ahab pacing the quarterdeck, staring at the doubloon nailed to the mainmast, and hailing every passing ship: *"Ahoy...good brethren...tell me...have ye seen the white whale?"*

Well, nobody on the arid savannah lands of the Masai Mara had seen a white whale, you could bet your doubloon on that. But they also had not seen—literally—*hide nor hair* of Mbogo. So far we had only that one glimpse—far too up-close and personal—of the blackish bassboat-beasts, and I wasn't going into the kasaka again to drag him out. Ever.

Everywhere we went Aaron stopped the truck and asked the Masai herdsmen if they had seen Mbogo. No. *Hapana Mbogo.* How about fresh droppings? *Hapana.* Does anybody you know, or another tribe close by like the W'kamba or the Nandi, know of any Mbogo?

They shook their heads and walked on, their skinny, bone-pointed cattle walk-trotting alongside, their bells making that weird *tink-tonk* sound as they faded into the brush...swallowed up by the great wilderness.

Two and a half days to go until the plane came to meet us at Monty and James' farm. Two and a half days to get three Buff. That

161

would be enough of a challenge even if the place were fairly crawling with them. But on top of this we now had *hapana Mbogo*. No buff. No buff sighted anywhere in the area, and none heard of from farther away. Glen got on his two-way radio—the one reserved for emergencies, like a leopard clawing or elephant mutilation (they never needed one for snakebite; all that was needed for that was to tell Dmitri or James or Monty or anyone passing through to relay the message to Arusha that we'd be needing a size X coffin).

Blank on the radio as well. Damn! That meant that even down in the Selous Wilderness—the world's premier spot for African game— there was *hapana Mbogo*.

Glen was going ballistic. I heard him chewing out Vincent for the fourth time in a day after our return from Lucy's house. Afterwards I met the dejected Vincent outside my tent and invited him to sit down on Dick's canvas folding chair. He declined, no doubt realizing that this act was tantamount to a black person sitting at the front of the bus in the Jim Crow South . He pointed to the staff end of the camp, so I got up and walked in the direction of the skinning hut. He brightened a bit at this because it meant I was going to sit around the fire with him and the other boys, and perhaps pass out a few smokes. I think I've said it before, but in Africa tobacco is worth more than ivory, at least to the natives.

"Is it Bwana Glen?"

He nodded. "Yes Bwana. Bwana Glen angry because hapana Mbogo."

"Mmmmm. And he's taking it out on you?"

Vincent nodded, and the others did too. I suspected they knew more English than either Glen or Aaron gave them credit for. Maybe a lot more. I handed Vincent and the other three boys a cigar apiece. They were not top of the line, but they were real Hondurans, and strong as month-old socks. The guys puffed mightily and inhaled lungfuls with enough tar and nicotine to fell a 12,000-pound bull tembo. And didn't even grimace.

I liked sitting with the staff. To me, they were as much a part of the experience as the PH's, the trucks, the game, and the scenery. And they truly were very, very nice. I was surprised the first time I approached their campfire, 40 yards from ours, and saw them seated around it. Not one of them stood to come over and shake hands. Of course I interpreted this as rude or ignorant behavior. That is until I learned from Ernest that Africans never rise from their seats (either on a chair or on the ground) when a friend approaches, because rising is a challenge, a threat display, showing the potential intruder that they are on their feet and ready to fight.

I stayed with the guys an hour before Glen came storming up in his truck again, followed by Dmitri in his. The Greek was all smiles as he waltzed into camp. He spied me and beamed. "Ah, Mr. Rick. James has another gift for you. I hope you enjoy!" So saying he handed me another baggie of weed. I thanked him and gave him three Upmanns.

"And how are the Great White Hunters doing today?" He was unprepared for Glen's returning scowl.

"We're doing shitty, Dmitri. Real shitty."

Dmitri. Having fulfilled his mission, made a few parting jovial remarks and buzzed off from whence he'd come, exuding cheer.

"That guy gives me a pain in the ass." Glen grunted as he prepared to take a brief lie-down prior to dinner. He could use it. I also had a hunch he would join in heartily for Attitude Adjustment Hour later on, Mormon or no.

I caught him just before he disappeared behind his tent flap.

"Hey Glen, I'd like a quick word with you if you don't mind."

So we sat in his tent for a full ten minutes. It wasn't long, but long enough for me to outline the pact.

"The way I see it, we've run up against a streak of bad luck here. It's nobody's fault we don't have any buff yet. Not yours, not ours. And we're all so worked up over it that right now everybody's suffering. You especially. Well, I say this is silly. If there's nothing we can do from our end, let's all concentrate on enjoying what's left of the safari. I mean, that's why we came isn't it? For the fun and excitement of it?"

He thought for a second, then pointed a finger at my chest. "You're right about most of it, Rick. But remember, you came to get a trophy. One in particular. And if you guys don't get your buffs I'll have let you down."

"Sure we want our buffs. That's why we chose Tanzania and you. But you won't have let us down. If this place were crawling with buff right now and we came up empty it would be a different story. But the way I see it it's the *place* that's letting us down, not you. This place is empty of buff right now, so the only answer is to go with the flow and let whatever happens happen. Now here's what I say we do: you concentrate on the other guys first. Forget about me for the time being; narrowing it from three to two should take a little pressure off you."

He slapped me on the shoulder. "Great Bwana! You're being a great sport. We'll all work like hell and maybe we can pull it off yet."

I saw him approach his truck where Dick was waiting in the "on deck" seat. They roared off in a cloud of dust and I went back to our tent and had a lie down.

Now I'm not a superstitious man, but the damndest thing happened when I woke up. I saw I had slept longer than planned. It was now close to dark. I slipped into my shit-kickers, put my pipe and pouch into my safari jacket, and sauntered out to the campfire, which Christoph had just lighted. There was Dick, puffing on a Macanudo, a big shit-eating grin on his face. He leaned over in a conspiratorial manner and whispered:

"I've got a buffalo story for you—and I think you're going to like it."

CHAPTER SIXTEEN

HIGH NOON

Dick's buffalo was a good one all right. It was a daga boy, a lone bull kicked out of the herd who was spending his last days alone. I don't know why the alpha cows, who run both the elephant and the buffalo herds, are always deciding to kick the old bulls out when they reach a certain age. I used to think it was because they got achy and ill tempered with age the way most of us men do, and consequently become a royal pain in the ass. I mean, nobody wants a grumpy, nasty old uncle butting his way around in the herd trying too hump the young sweet girls. Disgusting. Reminds me of us, right?

Okay. But then enlightenment struck and I realized that it wasn't mean tempers that exiled the old boys, it was their horniness. I came to this conclusion because all the exiled males (especially of the elephant and bovine persuasion) are still in prime physical shape and pack awesome horns and tusks. They are not to fuck with.

Unless you are a comely young cow in heat. Then it was time (as my idol Teddy Roosevelt used to say*), to MOUNT UP!* Well, I figure it wouldn't take long for the younger bulls to want those old lechers out of the herd and for the high-ranking cows— those grannies, aunts, and moms-in-law—to join them in ousting the old farts and make them wander alone or in small groups.

It was such a daga boy that Dick and Glen had come upon, and Dick had pasted it smartly with his 416 right in the boiler room. We were now looking down at the severed head just outside the skinning tent. Glen had been telling us all along not to go for length in horns, tusks, or the like. "Go for mass," he said. "Always go for mass—the big bulls have it always."

Dick's buff certainly had mass. The neck was very thick. The muzzle very wide and heavy. The face was so blocky, the head so enormous, it reminded me of a giant Newfoundland dog. And yes, the boss was awesome. Extremely heavy atop the brow ridge, accentuating the massive quality of the animal.

But frankly, the horns themselves, though massive as well, were not that impressive. They had nice drop and spread, but the curl stopped far short. I reasoned that given his age and build the animal had spent much of his life fighting, and therefore the horns would have worn down a lot with age. Still, it was a magnificent head, far better than anything you could get in South Africa or Zimbabwe.

So we toasted and I congratulated him, and we sat down again and waited for Larry to return—hopefully with his Kongoni. We expected Aaron and Larry back at any minute. But after an hour, they still hadn't arrived. We finished drinks at the campfire, and still hadn't heard the telltale grinding of Aaron's diesel engine winding its way up the long road to Whiteface. Where could they be? John called us to dinner, and we ate a superlative meal of roast guinea fowl (*Vulturine* Guinea fowl with bare purple heads and necks—hence the name), Francolin (the African plains grouse), and sand grouse (actually a small dove, not a grouse). These game birds were, with the exception of the Kongoni steaks and the buffalo tongue, the most delicious meat we had on the entire trip...and all of it was killer.

Still, after we returned to the dying embers after supper with our snifters of Scotch, it was in hushed tones that we discussed the possible reasons for the delay of our companion and the assistant P.H. Did they run into trouble? Truck break down? Attacked by baboons? Impaled by Masai kukis?

It was with a sigh of relief that we finally heard the distant diesel whine, then saw the pencil beam flashes of the headlights as the truck snaked homeward. Aaron drove the truck right up to the campfire circle, so we knew they had something to show us. And right in the back of the beg bed, there it was. Even quartered, the buff was impressive. The spread of the horns was enormous, almost twice the width of Dick's animal. But again—and I swear this was *not* sour grapes, it did not take me long to see that this animal was the opposite of Dick's. It's horns were longer, true, but they were thin, almost spindly. Also, the bosses were thin and did meet in the center. The head had no mass. True, given another five or six years on the veldt and it would be a magnificent trophy. But as it was, it was readily apparently to me that Larry had taken this bull too early in life. The most glaring weakness in the head was the lack of "drop" to the horns. As I mentioned earlier, as a male buff matures, his bosses thicken until they join in the center and become a mighty battering ram. Also, his horns thicken all along their length. As they grow and thicken, they also begin to grow downward as well as out, so that the sweeping curve at the bottom of the curl falls (ideally) below their jaw line. Then the horns curve up again, and in again, giving them the look of Napoleon's hat. The top inward curl should be at the same height as the buff's head, ideally even the jawline, but never higher. If it is, the animal resembles a cow rather than a bull. Larry's bull had horns without much drop or thickness, and they curved up above the head, making them look like horns on Elsie the milk-cow.

Again, this was not sour grapes, and I had no wish to belittle the head. But, there it was. I suppose if I were in his position (and I was…I was the *only* one who still was) at this late stage in the safari I would have done exactly the same thing and potted the beast. After all, the horns were long, the head was big. It was just that the shapes and curves and mass were wrong. Better an imperfect trophy than none.

But he was happy, and we toasted him, and then I went to bed. I wanted to get a good night's sleep. With the strain and tension of tomorrow, I would need every minute I could get.

The next day passed so slowly it was as if time were standing still. No wait: as if time were moving backwards. I knew when ten A.M. rolled around that twenty fours hence we would be breaking camp, packing all our gear, and heading back to James and Monty's farm to meet Nigel and the plane. That was it; the hunt would be over. If I didn't get my buff today I wasn't going to get one. So why did I do the noble thing by making the pact with Glen? Why indeed? Was I a chickenshit or a sucker? Easy answer: *both*.

Glen explained to me that word had come over the sands that there was a sizeable herd of Mbogo down on the Masai Steppe, beyond where I'd killed the Grants, high up in the slopes. They had been feeding and resting there for several days. If we got there soon enough in all likelihood they would still be there. Some very good breeding bulls had been seen in the herd.

"It's a long drive from here, Bwana Rick," he said, lighting a cigarette. He blew the smoke out of his mouth and it wafted away down the hill toward the acacias. "Between one and a half and two hours. We should leave here about three thirty this afternoon. You nervous?"

"Yes." There was no point in lying.

"Great. That's how I want you. Nothing worse than an overconfident hunter. I want you sharp and ready, but not shaking."

"As long as I'm not in the Kasaka I won't shake."

"Good. Now, two things about how we'll hunt him. One, it will be just before nightfall. Therefore the window of opportunity is small—a matter of a few minutes really, between quick dusk and night. Secondly, we'll be in thick cover, which will allow the boys to get a track on the herd and allow us to move in close. We can walk in this cover but it'll be thick. So with the cover and the falling light, we've got to hit him and hit him good. Break him down so he can't get up. If we wound him and he runs off, everybody's in big trouble."

"I understand. And if I fuck up the first shot I may not get a second."

"Maybe you will, maybe you won't. But Aaron and I won't wait to find out; we'll go for his shoulders and hips and knock his legs out from under him. A big buff bull can go forever even if heart-shot, but when he's shot through the shoulder and hip bones and they're shattered, he falls down and doesn't get up. Follow me?"

"Yep. So what you want from me is to hit him low in the front of the chest with my first bullet. Right?"

"Exactly. All we need is *one good shot*."

Well, this made me feel better, but now I obsessed with the "one good shot." I went over and over in my mind all the books and articles on shot placement. I remember Aaron's telling me to visualize in my mind's eye the fictional tennis ball that hung right between Mbogo's forelegs about 8 inches back from the front of his brisket. If you visualized this correctly, then shooting from almost any angle was made fairly simple: the farther back you shot from relative to the animal, the farther back must be your entrance point, aiming forward between the forelegs. If the animal were quartering away, you shot at the rear end of the ribcage, thus angling the bullet up through the tennis ball from behind. If he were coming dead on, you aimed low under his chin and squeezed. This was the easiest shot—if you pulled it off fast enough. But a charging buff generally had you *hors de combat* by this time, impaled on those giant curved javelins, tripping over your entrails as they squirted from your ruined belly.

The best shot was the sideways body shot that always varied little from animal to animal, from the tiny Thompson's gazelle to the buff. Place your sights at the rear vertical line of the foreleg, then follow that line upward until you were a third of the way up the height of the animal's body. Then squeeze off and let the bullet do the rest. Why was this a great shot? Because it hit the biggest vital spot of all: the heart-lung cavity. If you were a bit too far forward, not to worry: you still hit the shoulder joint, anchoring the animal, while sending bone splinters from the shoulder joint into the heart-lung area. If you placed it too far back, you hit only the lungs. Not as fast a kill, but still lethal.

The diciest shot of all was, of course, the *stopping shot*. It is for this lifesaving shot, and this shot alone, that the flawlessly-constructed, immensely-powerful, and ridiculously-expensive double rifle was developed in the last century. This is what they developed double rifles for, and that's why PH's still pay a king's ransom for a good one. The stopping shot is needed to save your life or the life of your client. When the buff is charging you at full steam (30 miles per), head up, hate in his beady eyes, nothing can stop him but a brain shot. But how do you hit the brain of an animal that has bosses over the top of his head two inches thick that can deflect even the largest slugs? And horns that hang down strategically placed so they cover the sides of the brain cavity?

The only answer is to shoot Mbogo right up his nose. The slug will go up the nasal cavity and into his lower brain. And he will drop in his tracks.

Of course one has to stand his ground unflinchingly and squeeze this shot off milliseconds before he feels himself levitated and penetrated simultaneously. Stiff upper lip, dontcha know?

Well fuck it. I was going to kill my Mbogo any way I bloody well could, cheating if I had to. In fact, preferably cheating. So there.

Hmmmm, follow-up shots. They were important in hunting dangerous game. I dragged the Winchester into the tent, inserted a full magazine of cartridges, and worked the action. I worked the bolt fast: unlock, back—forward, lock. Over and over and over again, each time reloading the magazine. The Model 70 action, a Mauser derivative, functioned flawlessly. The rounds stripped from the magazine, fed into the chamber, extracted flawlessly, and snapped out of the rifle in a flash. Perfect.

Except for one thing: this was NOT the rifle I would be using tonight. I needed the 458 Remington, which had been jamming repeatedly on the second round.

I dragged this gun into the tent, loaded it up, and worked the bolt. First round extracted fine and ejected with a pop. Fine. But when I tried to move the bolt forward again it would not feed; the cartridge hung up on the magazine lip and would not chamber. Great. Swell. The *follow-up round* of a dangerous game rifle (costing $1000, and from the Remington custom shop, no less) *would not chamber*. Well La-dee-dah. I wanted to melt the sumbitch down right then and there.

I mentioned this to Glen and he dismissed it, saying that it was probably just the follower spring in the magazine. "Sometimes they put the spring in backwards and it makes the rounds point too high and hang up. Don't worry about it."

Don't worry about it? *Don't WORRY about it?*

I returned to the tent for some shuteye. Dick and Larry were out bird hunting with Aaron and the boys. Now was my chance to get the sleep I had missed last night due to unforeseen tremors. But I couldn't sleep thinking about that damn spring. "For want of a nail the shoe was lost..."

I opened a bottle of prescription downers and popped one. It was now before lunchtime. This would allow me to sleep, then maybe half a one as we took off would keep me in a mellow enough mood to face onrushing death with some semblance of dignity. Well, it was clear after forty minutes one downer wasn't going to do the job. I popped another, and sometime later I guess I drifted off...

"Well Rick, you ready?" It was Glen, emerging from his tent. I replied I was—as I would ever be.

"Relax Bwana. Everything you've done on this safari has been better than anyone ever expected—especially you. Now grab your heavy and let's go."

"What about the magazine spring?" I asked, seating myself beside him.

"Fuck the magazine spring. Just remember what I said: all we need is one good shot. Now look behind you: here comes our company. If it'll make you feel any better, you'll have three rifles backing you up: Aaron, Ernest, and me. And we've got Gabriel and Vincent plus Talu. Don't feel so alone now, do you?"

I sure didn't. It's amazing what a hunting party the size of a small town will do for your self-confidence.

We drove for a solid hour past the Masai villages I had become familiar with, the landmarks, the great trees, the familiar escarpments and mountain peaks. The land became yet drier, more sand-colored and bright in the lowering sun. We passed Masai men riding bicycles and wearing digital watches. They waved and smiled at us, yelling "Jambo! Si Jambo!"

Later on we stopped to pick up a man who needed a ride back home to his village. He was dressed in a red robe, but he had shorn off the long, braided locks of the Morrans—he was too old now to be a warrior. He was retired now, and his duties were to spend time with his wives, with other men's wives (if they didn't mind, and usually they didn't), to teach the young men the old ways, and make sure his wives kept the fires going and had food and homebrew ready for him always. I think his primary occupation was drinking *pombe*—Masai homebrew. It seemed the life of a retired Masai was the life for me.

He spoke excellent English with a British accent. This valuable skill was no doubt another holdover of self-shame and culture mutilation the British inflicted upon him during their filthy Imperialist Adventure.

"Have you read much Ernest Hemingway?" he asked me when Glen told him in Swahili that I wrote books. I replied that I had indeed.

"Have you read *The Green Hills of Africa?*"

I said it was what brought me here.

"I met Mr. Hemingway when he was here. He wrote that book about his stay in a camp not more than three miles away, right over there." He pointed to the horizon.

"But he wrote that book in 1933," I said. "You just don't look that old."

"No. I met him in his later safari in 1953, twenty years afterwards. I was only four or five at the time."

"Was he a nice man?"

"Very. Some people said he was not so nice a lot of the time. But he was always nice in Africa because he loved it so. He drank a lot of whiskey."

"So I've heard. Hey Glen, can you strop a sec? I gotta take a leak."

Aaron, Vincent, Talu and I walked over to the side of the road and realized our hitchhiking friend had joined us. So there we were, hoisting aside robes and unzipping flies, pissing on the roadside in the Masai Steppe. We climbed aboard again and headed off. Twenty minutes later we were at his village, and he and I got out and shook hands. Aaron got a picture of us standing together in front of his mud and straw hut. I still have the picture; it is one of my favorites. I never got his name, nor he mine.

It was late afternoon when we slowed the truck and wound our way down a rocky streambed toward large trees in the distance. It was more an arroyo than a streambed, since it was mostly dry. We left the truck, double-checking to make sure we had all our gear. I left my camera behind, thinking it was a sign of arrogance and would therefore anger Diana. All I had were my binoculars, my heavy rifle, my ammo belt with its two pouches (one for soft points, one for solids), and a specially made hunting shirt Ginny had made by sewing a heavy-duty PAST recoil pad into the right shoulder area. On my feet I had my new Nike running shoes. Yep, you got the right word: RUNNING.

Mzungu Mjinga

We left the truck parked at the edge of the arroyo. I was worried about leaving my camera bag and rucksack in the vehicle but Glen assured me it would be all right. Then we slowly, silently, made our way down to the small stream, and waded across. I was struck by the professionalism of the crew. Nobody talked. Nobody made a sound, even going through the water. The animals must therefore be quite close, I reasoned. I reasoned incorrectly. We were only beginning what would be a long, exhausting climb. On and on we climbed silently upward, sometimes going directly up a rather gradual slope, other times making switchback turns, zigzagging up the steep ones. All the while the hot dry air of the savannah-steppes gave way to air that was increasingly damp and cool. The higher we climbed, making even our footfalls as silent as possible, the thicker was the vegetation. Finally, as we began to enter a mountainside forest, Aaron came up beside me, grabbed my arm, and drew his head next to my ear. In a voice barely audible, in an utterance below a whisper, he told me: *"From now on, stay **very** close to Glen—"*

CHAPTER SEVENTEEN

THE BLACK DEATH

Now I knew it was for real. Now was the moment. All that had come before: the childhood wishing intermingled with bad dreams, the adventure books, the videos, the beginning of hunting when I moved down South, the target practice at the range, the saving of money, the preparations and equipment—all this had been leading up to what was going to take place—or fail to take place—within the next hour or so, perhaps the next fifteen minutes. I could clearly, unmistakably hear my pulse in my ears.

Our silent party wound its way up the slope of the mountain. I saw Gabriel faithfully carrying Glen's 470 Westley Richards over his left shoulder. Talu, the handsome young mechanic dressed in his khaki jumpsuit, was nearby ready to lend a hand. Ernest, the government representative in his olive drab uniform and cap, a fixed look of determination on his round, pleasant face. My favorite of all, Vincent, whose lithe body and keen face I found walking to my left, was welcome indeed. Wiry, agile, courageous as a pit-bulldog, there could be no better confidence builder than this man. Glen had sensed our bond and had no doubt asked him to walk there. Or perhaps it was Vincent's own idea—to protect the new man who had given him much-needed medication for his violent attacks of malaria. Just to my right were Glen, eyes darting keenly in all directions, and Gabriel at his side, as Vincent was at mine. Off further to the right was Aaron. Well, if two excellent guides and a total of four rifles couldn't get a buff, who in hell could?

Then I realized that by making the pact with Glen and freeing him up, I had not lessened my chances, but actually improved them. Dick and Larry got their buff by accident—running across them in the wild. On the other hand, we were—if the local buzz was to be given any credence—about to enter a large herd of prime buff where we—I—would get my choice if all went as planned. Was there some sort of biblical parable in all this? I hoped like hell not. Bibles reminded me of the last rites—

It had been a glorious evening, but now the light was fast fading, as it had been out in the blind that night. Minute by minute—second by second, we could see the light level fall. Glen picked up the pace, and finally, we were topping the mountain.

We hadn't walked more than a hundred yards along the ridge when there came a grumbling bellow from the brush somewhere off to the side. I froze and looked at Glen. He waved his hand to and fro, as if shaking it off, then leaned over.

"Buff feeding—" he whispered right in my ear. "Keep with me—"

We continued to walk slowly along, and I noticed the boys had disappeared. Where were Vincent, Talu, and Ernest? Had they panicked and taken off? Would not blame them. No siree—

Then Vincent appeared as if by magic by my side and made sign language at Glen and Aaron. Glen turned and followed him and I followed as well. Glen had his Leica glasses out now, scanning the thick growth in the gathering gloom. Aaron leaned over. "He tells us there are two great bulls just over that hedge-like growth there, feeding. At least one has a great boss. C'mon, we'll set up the shot."

"What's your favorite position?" asked Glen as we approached the hedge.

"Reverse cowgirl," I replied, convinced he was trying to lighten the tension.

He glared at me. "Goddammit wiseass, I mean *shooting* position!" He said it in a whisper but it was strong enough to get the point across. I answered sitting. So they found an elevated spot another sixteen or so feet back from the hedge that had enough elevation so I could sight the rifle over it. I sat down, elbows on knees, and looked through the scope. All looked good.

"Safety off?"

I remembered I had the bolt uncocked, so I drew the bolt handle up and then lowered it. "Ready," I whispered, and Glen nodded back, then leaned over me, glancing now and then through the binoculars. I noticed he had the double rifle in his left hand ready to go.

"The two bulls are right there, just over those bushes. I'll tell you which one has the best head, just wait until—*there's one*, see him?"

And there he was, just like the videos: big and black and huge. But he didn't look mean. Not yet anyhow. Not unless I shot him badly and put him in an ocean of agony. Then we'd all be chopped liver. I raised my glasses. Oh God, I thought, *the perfect head!*

"Now just wait until the other one raises his head and then we can compare..."

But time ran out; at that instant the one with his head up suddenly snapped it around. And stared right down our throats.

"He looked at me as if I owed him money—"

"*Shit—he's winded us! Pop him in the face Rick! Whack him right now!*"

And I should have. But I waited a millisecond longer. Perhaps too long for the perfect head shot. Because I realized in that lightning flash the invulnerability of Mbogo's head. Since his head was turned quartering to us rather than head-on, I could not shoot him up the nose. If I shot for his nose I would blow off the end of it, ruin the head, and still not hit the brain. I moved the crosshairs to the left and settled them just below his ear. Perfect for the brain cavity. But guess what? The fucking horn was in the way. Son of a BITCH! I'd come all this way just to be foiled by an impossible head shot. And he was the trophy of trophies—

"Whack him **now,** Bwana!" hissed Glen.

And I knew if I didn't kill this buff, Glen Schacht—mild-mannered P.H.— was going to kill me. I moved the crosshairs over still more and settled them just above the angle of his jaw, at the base of the neck, and squeezed.

Things happened very fast after that, and in the darkening void things are still hazy in mind no matter how many times I play the tape over in my head.

The last I saw through the scope was the buffalo jerking his head around and backward with the impact of the massive bullet. His body seemed to follow the turn of his head but I wasn't sure because his buddy likewise took off, perhaps from the report of the 458. And then I was being pushed back by the recoil. I rolled back, going with the force, and fell on my back, trying to work the Remington's bolt to chamber a second round as I went. The fucker jammed. What a piece of *shit*. I made a vow right then—not even knowing if the animal was this very instant goring four of our party—to trade the son of a bitch in the first thing stateside.

"Great shot bwana! We got him!" was all Glen said as he dashed toward the hedge.

As I struggled to my feet I heard two bomb-sized blasts a second apart. Standing up, I realized I could not see anyone, and that it was now just about full dark. I staggered through the brush in the direction of the shots. No Glen. I yelled Aaron's name. No answer. Then, just before a deepening dread set in, Vincent and Ernest appeared next to me beaming and pumping my hand. "Bwana Rick! *Kubwa Mbogo! Kwisha! Kubwa Mbogo, Rick. Kubwa, w'Kubwa!*"

They were saying it was all over, that I killed a very big buffalo, and it was dead. I was naturally rather eager to see it, so I followed the two of them another thirty or so yards up the game trail until we caught sight of the rest of the party in a small clearing. Flashlights blazed and flashed. Several caught us in their glare as we entered the little circle, and there was much clapping and chatter.

Well, there he was, just about exactly as big as a bass boat. And at least three times as heavy. It was not black, but rather charcoal gray with black hair. Vincent, ever the dauntless one, went up to it and stuck a stick in its eye.

"Get away Vincent! Damn you anyway. How many times do I have to tell you to make sure the eyes are open before you approach them? Stupid coon, I ought to—"

Well, it was obvious Glen wasn't long in resuming his accustomed persona. Aaron came up and congratulated me. Then we set three big lanterns on the ground, set the bull up for pictures, and the boys got their pangas and skinning knives ready.

But first, I wanted to touch him. I approached him and felt the hide, ran my hands over the massive horns. I tried to wiggle them but they would scarcely budge—the animal was just too big. I straddled the beast and then sat down on it not for curiosity's sake but to soak up some of its warmth while it was still there. I was freezing, but hadn't realized it until now. When I put my weight on its back he groaned at me! I jumped up and backed off, my Nikes already finding a sprinter's foothold in the turf.

"He's still alive!"

"No Bwana. That's just air you pushed out of his lungs with your weight. He's kufa."

It didn't take long for the night to grow chilly. I wished I had brought my jacket. We snuggled against the carcass, which was still warm and would keep its heat for almost an hour. In celebration I took a drag off Glen's cigarette—the first drag I'd taken in 15 years. Bright lights appeared before my eyes. I reeled and blinked. I coughed. Jesus, no wonder they kill you. Tall (Talu's nickname) was dispatched to go fetch the truck while we were to skin out and cut up the animal ready for transport back to camp. He was gone a long time, and I grew colder and colder, and sleepier and sleepier. The adrenaline had worn off now, and the downers were kicking in full force.

The skinning took over an hour. They began by cutting my buff crosswise through the middle with their pangas. This they accomplished with their pangas (machetes). They whacked at the carcass for twenty minutes to sever it. Then they opened the gut cavity and emptied it. Next they cut the rear half in two, saving both hindquarters for meat. I saw Vincent drag something huge out of the animal's chest. It was reddish white and as big as a honeydew melon. I asked him if it were the heart. He did not understand, so I pointed at the left side of my chest and he nodded. What a heart! Twenty times the size of a human heart, and yet a big bull weighs but ten times what a big man does. It was no wonder they could take several nitro express rounds in the chest and keep on coming. Mind-boggling.

Finally we heard the welcome sound of the distant engine whine. Ten minutes later Talu and Toyota showed up. We unceremoniously tossed Mbogo into the back end—the boys had to squeeze together mightily to make enough standing room—and we headed down the mountain, across the river, over the dry sands of the Masai Steppe and then (by ten thirty) into Whiteface camp, where two very drunk fellow hunters were waiting by the fire for us. As I staggered out of the Land Cruiser Larry and Dick were already admiring the head in the back of the truck. Whistles and ahhhs all round. Boogie and Julius, Christoph, the cook boys, even John came over for a look. I modestly walked away from the group, much as Sir Edmund Hilary must have modestly walked away from the base camp at Everest in 1952—

As I mentioned earlier, the past few days of constant adrenaline high had begun wearing off as soon as we gathered around the fallen buff, and the two downers I had taken earlier in the afternoon to try to get some sleep had began kicking in. Now I was in near collapse. The two tuskers before dinner seemed to put the icing on the cake. I slithered and slathered through dinner, drank a glass or two of red to wash down the buff tongue (from Dick's animal) and veggies and yams, then begged pardon from the PH's and my comrades and announced it was beddie bye for Rickie. I shuffled toward the tent, already dreaming how good the cot would feel after all the tension, the big climb, and the crescendo of the hunt.

CHAPTER EIGHTEEN

LULLABYE

I crawled between the crisp, clean, cool sheets and felt myself falling into those crazy random thoughts that precede sleep. I knew what tomorrow would bring. We would start with a great last breakfast at Whiteface. Not just quick rolls and coffee, but eggs and bacon, guinea-fowl livers, orange juice, fresh-baked bread and toast, and native honey from the Baobab tree.

Then we'll go bird hunting. The most glorious bird hunting you could ever imagine. Better than the best pheasant hunting in South Dakota, the best quail hunting in South Georgia, the best duck hunting in Stuttgart, Arkansas. Oh, Africa's a bird hunter's paradise. And there are no limits, since most people are after the big trophies, birds are forgotten, a minor roadside attraction. We'll have the coolers all loaded up with Tusker and soft drinks. The boys will be our retrievers, running out into the fields to catch downed doves and grouse, francolin, and guinea fowl. The sky will be huge and forever and bright blue with puff clouds, and the tall savannah grass will blow in tan ocean waves— and then the coveys will explode in bright wing beats and we'll swing on them with the shotguns. We'd get them by the droves, then drive into the nearest Masai village waving them above out heads and the natives will come out to meet the truck, all smiles, and take come of the birds and give us beadwork bracelets.

Africa! What can I say? Seven years later what can I say? It's the ultimate outdoor adventure. I hear on the news some people are paying 20 million bucks to go up into space and play astronaut. Now really, I ask you: how can anybody that stupid have made $20 mil?

What's great about space? First off, I hate to fly. Second, who wants to float around in a silly suit trying to fix the Hubble telescope—which still isn't working right—or farting around with that ancient Ruskie "*Mir*" space station that never was worth a damn in the first place. And food? Christ almighty, all they eat is some dietary goop from toothpaste tubes and dump in their pants all day because they can't take their pressurized suits off. To hell with space.

Then we'll leave. But someday, after my new batch of kids gets bigger, I am coming back. Because once it gets in your blood, it haunts you forever.

What was that? A commotion outside the tent. Larrry turning in? Nope, I heard the bunch of them still laughing at the fire circle. A rustling now, closer. Then it came: a low snarl. It was deep, a rumbling basso that echoed in a cavernous throat. *Chui.* I knew he was padding by tent now on silent feet. Then I heard him farther off, giving his telltale coughing grunt. I listened for night sounds. There was wind in the trees, the campfire chatter, and a birdcall here and there. Then I heard something rare: a far-distant trumpeting of an elephant. No doubt she was calling her child.

And then finally Chui again, who I no longer feared. After all, he was just part of the scenery now. His guttural growls sang me to sweet sleep.

CHAPTER NINETEEN

FOREVER SKIES–
FOREVER BIRDS

Next morning I awoke shocked to see it was light outside. Not only light, but surprisingly warm and cheerful. What happened? Where was Captain Bligh? Then I remembered: the hunt was over; we could sleep in. Oh Frabjous Day! Trouble was, I was so used to arising before dawn I couldn't sleep in if my life depended on it. I looked over at Larry's bunk. Empty. I heard a guffaw from the dining tent. They were in there, and the coffee was in there too. I pulled my duds on and exited though the flap. After a quick stop in the head I went in to breakfast. The coffee was there but no breakfast. And guess what? No Glen. No Aaron. Where were they? Neither Larry nor Dick had seen a sign of them, and it was after eight—practically lunchtime by our schedule.

"Maybe you're forgetting how bushed they are," offered Dick. "After all, Glen gets going a little after three each morning and doesn't stop until ten thirty when he shuts down the generator. I bet they sleep 'til noon."

He was right. After breakfast I returned to the tent and fetched my remaining stash of Federal Safari-Grade .458 ammo. The heavy boxes, each containing 20 rounds of the monster cartridges, cost over $70 apiece in the States. Here, because of the 100% import duty, they fetched twice that. The solid rounds were especially valued. I knew Aaron needed them.

183

I approached the hunters' tent warily. I had the feeling that waking Glen would be tantamount to stealing a bone from a chained-up, starving pit-bull.

I announced my presence by saying Knock Knock in a fairly loud voice.

"Bloody hell—?" came a voice. Aaron's.

"Come in Bwana." A much friendlier voice from the other side of the flap. Glen? What had gotten into him? Sleep, that's what. And what a difference it made. The Terror of the Great Rift Valley had become Mr. Sensitive New-Age Guy. I entered the tent and went over to Aaron—tapped him hard on the shoulder. "Wake up you damned Pommy! I bring you a farewell gift." So saying, I dropped the heavy boxes on his mattress. He was obviously pleased. I asked them if they were getting up and was informed that they would get up today when they damn well felt like it.

"From here on out we sleep, Bwana," said Glen. "Sleep maybe ten ours a day or more until the next hunt starts. But not today; by the time you guys finish breakfast I'll be in the car with Gabriel on the way to Arusha. I'll be there in time to meet your plane, which will be just before supper."

"What about Aaron?" I asked.

"He and Johnson are taking you guys bird hunting on the plains—you'll never forget it. A perfect end to a perfect hunt." He paused a second, then added, "Actually, you did quite well, Bwana Rick."

I wanted to thank him but found myself speechless. I tried to manage a Jimmy Stewart "Aw shucks," but it didn't come out. "Good leadership," I said finally, and Glen rolled over and closed those Charles Manson eyes.

"Kip in then. I'm going back to the tent for breakfast—if we're having any today."

"Oh don't worry; John and the boys have it underway. And we'll be in to join you shortly."

Our head waiter John, ever resourceful and ever diligent, took our breakfast requests but was keeping a watchful eye on the tent where the PH's were sleeping. He did not want to begin the meal without them. But soon they emerged and joined us, and in less then twenty minutes we all were sitting before plates piled high with steaming scrambled eggs, sausage and ham, fried potatoes, fresh oranges, plantains, and homemade bread with jam and native honey. It was a great feast, marred only by a steady procession of bees swooping into the dining tent to partake of the honey. At first it was cute. Then it became somewhat troublesome. Finally, when John and Christoph were forced from the tent by a horde of the creatures the situation had become serious. And they were African honeybees. The ones that can (and do) kill people. So we hid the honey and sprayed some insect killer at them (hated to do it) until they left. We finished up, had more coffee, and sat outside in the director's chairs and smoked. We all agreed it was too bad the hunting was over. But Aaron, who had appeared behind us, assured this was not so.

"You're all mistaken; there's plenty of hunting left. Today I'll lead you to the best bird hunting you've ever seen anywhere. Tomorrow, when we're back in Arusha, we'll roust up a guide who can take you to the last trophy on your cards: the Thompson's gazelle. A fine trophy and delicious treat. Too bad you guys won't be on hand to eat any of it."

"Where are these Tommy's?" I asked.

"On the Masai steppe where you got your Grants, bwana. You better wear your snow glasses too—it's godawful bright down there."

After breakfast Glen summoned the three of us back to the dining tent, which was now fully cleared out and cleaned. We were instructed to sit in a row just inside the tent on our chairs. Christoph placed a clean straw mat on the ground in front of the doorway. I sensed some sort of parting ceremony about to transpire, and I was not mistaken. Next Aaron came in bearing two boxes of gifts: packs of cigarettes, disposable lighters, snuff, pocket flashlights, dark glasses, several wristwatches, and assorted other goodies. Then he and Aaron found their own places on each side of us. Glen spoke to John softly, and the tall, thin man departed soon to reappear with Christoph and Michael, the tent boys. They seated themselves cross-legged on the mat and waited while Glen gave his speech:

> Christoph, Michael—in recognition for fine service during this safari our clients would like to show their appreciation to you with these gifts, and hope that you both will enjoy the remainder of the hunting season and that they may hunt with you again sometime. You may come forward now and receive your gifts...

He then handed out the gifts, which were indeed received with smiles and gratitude. We all shook hands, and I realized I was finally familiar with that East-African gentle caress of a handshake that everyone, including the stoutest Masai warriors, bestowed on friends and guests. But then something struck me. I leaned over and whispered in Larry's ear:

"Who bought the presents?" Larry only shrugged. I was told only later they were bought in Arusha and stowed before the hunt began. The next staff were the cooks and laundry crew, who numbered five men. I can't remember their names because they never came to our side of the camp, but they too, took delight in their presents and left the mat smiling after shaking our hands. This procedure, and Glen's little speech, repeated itself over and over until everyone, including Chobe the skinner and Ernest the Government Game Warden, were acknowledged. It was no surprise to anyone that Ernest was bountifully bestowed, as befitted his crucial station as the representative of the Tanzanian government. It must be true worldwide, I mused, that government work is the best if you can get it.

After the ceremonies were completed we loaded up Aaron's Land Cruiser and headed out to the pasturelands to hunt birds. In back were Boogie and Julius and Michael Johnson, the likeable, lighthearted Apprentice Hunter. Ernest didn't bother to come along; there were no game regulations on birds and therefore his presence wasn't necessary.

After the ceremonies Glen jumped in his truck with Gabriel and roared out of camp, heading for Arusha—six hours away—after wishing us good hunting. Ten minutes after his departure Dmitiri roared in on his wagon accompanied by James, who was driving, and two other mine workers. "And how are the great white hunters doing this morning?" he said with a formal bow as he disembarked. Same old Sidney Greenstreet in Casablanca

"Well? Ah, that is good. I have business to discuss with Glen, but since he is away, I shall return later. Adieu!" And so James wheeled the truck about and they departed with much fanfare—not to say ruffles and flourishes. Aaron stared after the departing vehicle. "I tell you sir," he murmured, shaking his blond head, "he's not on the square, that one—"

In less than 40 minutes Aaron had us rolling along through knee-high grass and over gently undulating plains. Except for the acacia, baobab trees and distant mountains we could have been in South Dakota.

The only bird hunting I have done is in the South: quail hunting in Georgia and South Carolina, ducks and geese along the French Broad River near Asheville, and doves in any field that showed promise. I especially like to shoot doves because they're such a challenge and when they come on, they come in droves.

Africa has its own version of these counterparts in America. The smallish sand grouse is the counterpart to our mourning dove. Grouse and pheasant are absent on the Dark Continent but the Francolin, a grouse-like bird in the quail and partridge family, is fabulous table-fare. This bird has mostly white flesh and is excellent eating. A larger bird, and perhaps even more delicious, is the Guinea fowl. This relative of the chicken and pheasant is large, heavy, and full of white meat. A ground dweller, it is a lousy flier and can be brought down rather easily by a tolerable shotgunner. In our concession there were two kinds. The regular speckled Guinea fowl and the Vulturine Guinea fowl, the latter being more numerous and instantly recognizable by its bald head and it's bluish-purple plumage. These roosted in dense growth of acacia and thorn brush, but were easy to spot by their bright plumage. We parked the truck and Larry got out with his twelve gauge. Slipping bird rounds into the magazine, he shucked the action and proceeded to walk the plains with Boogie and Julius out in front of him walking in big arcs. I realized that since we had no hunting dogs, the gunbearers and scouts would act in their place, flushing up the game birds.

Larry is an artist with the shotgun, and it did not take long for him to bag a harvest of birds, both large and small. These were placed in the truck and we moved on to another spot. The plains were endless, the birds everywhere and obviously not skittish at our approach. Soon I got my chance, and got a francolin on a going away shot. Dick shot 4 sand grouse in as many seconds, and then Aaron bagged three guinea fowl. But the real kicker was Larry's "sept un coup" with the vulturine Guinea fowl. Sept un Coup is an old French story—also called La Petite Tailor, in which a poor hungry tailor kills seven flies with one swat from his flyswatter—hence "seven in one blow." Actually, Larry only scored a "four-in-one," but it was impressive nonetheless. And the Guinea fowl are big birds.

Next Dick took a turn with the slide-action and bagged six birds of all varieties in fifteen minutes. Then Larry went on deck again and went though a box of shells lickity-split. The birds were now piling up on the back seats and the cargo area of the Land Cruiser. I noticed the guides eyeing them. I knew why; while the meat in camp had been delicious, fresh-roasted game birds are hard to beat, and a nice change in fare. Michael Johnson borrowed the shotgun next, then it was my turn again. We now had bushels of birds! You seldom hear birds mentioned in any talk of safaris, or see articles about them in hunting journals. More's the pity because if you find yourself skunked on a given day (at several hundred $$ down the drain), a few hours spent with a scattergun on the grass-flats will fill the pot and brighten your day.

The boys collected mopane sticks as thick as pencils, whittled points on both ends, then built a small fire near the truck. As I mentioned earlier about the campfire at Dimitri's gem mine and the one at our camp, fires are marvelously easy to make in Africa; the wood is bone dry and lights instantly. Coals come in fifteen minutes with minimum smoke or fuss. The boys had already plucked, drawn, and singed the birds we selected for our lunch. I was expecting them to place the birds in the cooler for twenty minutes or so because I had always been taught that any meat should be chilled out prior to cooking to remove some of the gamy flavor. But everyone scoffed at me, and soon the birds were impaled on the sticks at one end. The other end was then thrust into the earth at a steep angle that placed the meat right over the coals. The boys watched the cooking meat carefully, turning the sticks diligently to brown the flesh on all sides. Soon we were stuffing ourselves with sand grouse, Guinea fowl, Francolin, and even some smallish birds that resembled Carolina warblers! All the staff shared in the meal of course, and we did mighty damage to the monster supply of birds in short order, slaking our thirst with ice-cold Fanta orange drink. We washed up by rubbing our hands in the fine sand, then rubbing our mouths and faces with the sand. When all was dry, we brushed it off.

The rest of the afternoon was pure bliss. The pressure to fill our tags had been lifted; we were in bird hunter's paradise. The natives were grinning and laughing as we rolled and bounced along into one village after another. We drove into these compounds through the opening in the boma, or wall of thorn brush, which every village erects around its perimeter. This wall is eight to ten feet in height and serves pretty well to protect the inhabitants from the two most-dreaded nighttime callers: fisi and chui. Notice I say "pretty well." Thorn brush is nature's barbed wire, but its effectiveness is limited. A hungry lioness can still bound over the boma, scoop up a bullock, and leap out again with the bellowing 130-pound calf in its jaws.

It can do the same with a child, or aged woman.

Once inside we held the birds aloft—their bright plumage blowing in the breeze— the residents would soon crowd around the vehicle, eager to relieve us of our burden of birds. We had to watch the kids; more than once I saw Julius push a boy back from the truck, and only then noticed the child's arm snake back out from the truck's interior. The kids would grab at anything—camera bags, ammo boxes, knapsacks, binoculars, cigarettes—and who could blame them? To them (and their parents as well) it was as if we had everything, and obvious they had nothing.

Along towards 3 o'clock we met Monty near the road to his farm. I gave him a cigar and some birds. Aaron joined us as we lit up and went off a ways from the trucks to chat. I realized then it was hot outside.

"Well it's all in now, eh?" he said. "I suppose we'll see you all out in the field shortly. Isn't that the plan?"

Aaron replied that it was, and that we'd better hurry back to Whiteface, grab our gear, and haul ass back to the airstrip for the flight back to Arusha.

It was on our return to base camp at Whiteface Mountain that the adventure became surrealistic again. In hindsight I suppose it was brought on by my mixed feelings. On one hand, I was delighted and relieved the hunt was over. It was fun and exciting, but stressful as well. I realized that over the previous twenty hours or so my mind and body had been continuously decompressing from the continual adrenaline rushes, the constant "on-alert" status of my nervous system, and the myriad stimulus/response episodes that I had undergone since we touched down on this continent.

But opposing this was a warm, soft feeling of nostalgia that I knew was bound to grow as the time away from our beloved little camp and the wonderful staff who served and helped us—indeed, laid their lives on the line for us, day in day out.

Inside my tent I grabbed my packed duffle, my camera bag, and my small haversack, which had served so well to carry personal items but mainly as a rifle rest on the hood of the Land Cruisers. I heaved these into Aaron's truck, put on my shooting jacket (who forgot to tell me they were for display only?) and wide "White Hunter's" hat (definitely for display only). Actually, I realized that besides the tripod for my camera, the only other item I NEVER used was the Alan Quartermain hat. Why? Well, because the modern African hunt has rendered them useless. In the old days, the hunters, guides, and native staff all hunted on foot. In the hot sun, the Mzungus needed protection from the heat and sunburn. The wide cowboy-style hats were perfect. Also, the brim in front kept the sun out of their eyes when spotting game or shooting.

What's changed? Well for one, today's hunting is done most of the time using vehicles. While shooting from a moving vehicle is prohibited—as it should be—trucks do cover a lot more ground in a given day than do hunters on foot. Is this bad? No, because the trucks stick to the roadways on the gravel flats, and this wide-ranging method allows hunters to fill their tags faster, then return home. The bottom line seems to be that the less time hunters spend rambling around the wilderness the better for the ecosystems.

But, thing is, you cannot wear a wide hat in a moving vehicle with the top down; the hat will blow off in a heartbeat.

The other disadvantage is that a wide hat will also disengage when the hunter enters thick brush stalking game afoot. In the good old days, when the animals were out on the flats, they were hunted by glassing from several hundred yards, then stalking through tall grass and potting them at between one and two hundred yards. This included game such as Mbogo, who, chewing his cud out there on the grass in the midday sun, presented some very nice targets and allowed the hunter and guide to pick and choose their quarry. Not so today. Hunting pressure is heavier and the animals have wised up. As Maud said, they hole up in the daytime and sleep.

I shot my buff in the thick jungle of the mountaintop just as the herd (and also the sun) was bedding down for the night. And my target?

All I saw—all any of us saw—of the animal was his head and neck; the remainder was invisible. So much for the ideal heart/lung shot.

So the wide hunting hat, long the colorful hallmark of the Professional Hunter, has become obsolete. In a moving truck it blows away. In the thick stuff it gets entangled and scrapes off your head.

So the answer?

Why, the good 'ol American baseball/truckers hat of course! Besides being adjustable, these offer the unbeatable combination of a long bill to fight glare and a tight, rounded body that will not blow off or tangle in the brush. Voila! Efficient, yes. Cool looking, definitely NOT.

With Aaron at the wheel we pulled out of Whiteface for the last time. Aaron would return here after we boarded Nigel's aircraft and load his truck with the skins and skulls of our trophies. He would then drive back to Arusha for a late-night arrival and meet us next morning to embark on the Thompson's Gazelle hunt.. Thirty minutes later found us at Colin and Monty's farm, where we again sat on the veranda beneath the bleached horns of the plains animals fastened to the wall. Now I began to feel truly homesick, and could not keep my thoughts from dwelling on Ginny and our soon-to-be-born son, Rick. And—thank God—it looked as if he wouldn't have to relate the sad tale of his fatherless existence to his schoolteacher after all.

Thirty-five minutes after we arrived we heard the faint droning of Nigel's turboprop aircraft. It circled once to get behind the windsock, then touched down and taxied to within a hundred feet of our waiting vehicle.

We touched down in Arusha and repeated the process of ten days previous in reverse order. Glen was waiting for us in his Land Cruiser. We loaded our guns on the racks, tossed our bags into the back, and in less than an hour were back at the Impala Hotel. I had the surrealistic feeling I was in a movie or videotape that was being run backwards. We had a pleasant meal at the Impala, killed quite a few Tuskers (bottles of beer, not elephants), and crashed.

CHAPTER TWENTY

KWA HERI!

"**N**ow how is this thing going to work?" I asked.

We were finishing breakfast at the Impala the next morning after an extremely restful and long sleep in a roomy bed with no wake-up calls in the early morning hours.

"Aaron's on his way over here now from his house across town," said Dick. The skins, which weren't yet completely dry, have been stretched out on his yard. We're going to stop off there and look at them and then head out to the steppes where the Tommies hang out.

"And where's this guide?" Larry asked. "Or is he merely a fictional character?"

Dick shrugged. "Personally I don't give a rat's ass as long as the Tommies are there. Right Rick?"

"Absolutely. But you guys know there's a fifty buck apiece charge for this little expedition today."

They looked at me in consternation, then asked why.

"Well, if I remember correctly, Aaron said something about this guide fellow in town having to be reimbursed for his trouble. So it's fifty apiece. Plus there's another six hundred for the trophy fee, and another—"

"Stop it! I smell a rip-off!"

"Of course you do Larry. That's because it *IS* a rip-off," explained Dick, always the politician. "Obviously, the hunt's officially over; our PH's have packed it in. Aaron's doing us a big favor by arranging all this. I suspect it's really a bribe of sorts to get this so-called guide—who may or may not be one—to take us out *sub-rosa* so-to-speak, and pot several of these little critters."

"A bribe?" I looked at Dick, unconvinced.

"You're surprised? In Africa? C'mon Rick, welcome to the Third World."

"Well I hope Aaron shows up soon—we only have this last day. Our plane leaves at nightfall."

Right about that time a grinning Aaron Broome came into the dining room and joined us. We finished up breakfast and made our way out to his truck—which had our rifles already stowed on the rack—and drove for fifteen minutes across town to a shabby section of Arusha where each dwelling place had high cement or brick walls around it. I wished I were elsewhere.

"Not to worry Mates—it's me neighborhood," said our young P-H.

"You live here?" asked Dick.

When Aaron nodded, Dick asked the obvious question. "Why?"

"Rent's higher than you might think here in the big cities. Crime's higher too. Now we're coming up on my place on the right. See it? Check out the tops of my walls…"

I did, and noticed they were all topped with upright shards of broken glass that had been set into the wet cement as it had dried. I recall seeing this arrangement only in one other place—the French Quarter in New Orleans.

"It keeps anybody with funny ideas the hell off my property, is what," he told us. Now hang on while I unbolt the gate—"

He hopped out and unlocked the massive wooden doorways that swung outward, and we drove through into a little courtyard with a lawn in its center. It was difficult to see any grass at all; it was covered with skins and skulls set out to dry in the sun. We paused here only momentarily for him to use the telephone, and then sped off to a yet seedier neighborhood where he pulled up in front of what appeared to be an apartment building and honked. Soon a smallish man appeared walking toward us. He was bundled in a heavy parka, and had the hood drawn tightly round his head. A brown face with thick glasses looked out at us. He nodded silently and hopped into the car, never saying a word. As I recall, he never said a word throughout the entire morning. Except one. Just sat there on the back seat saying nothing. Probably had the "tip" on his mind.

Once again we drove out past the ostrich ranch and the elegant European houses of the once-landed gentry, and then on to dry, flat steppe country that resembled West Texas; it was hot, the earth shades of brown, gray, and tan, and the monotony broken only by occasional termite mounds and dust devils that danced and weaved about in the distance. Far-off animals were hazy in the extreme brightness, and viewed through our binoculars waved and shimmered—appearing more as chimeras than living animals.

We drove on for another half hour and the countryside became a savannah covered with low thorn brush and sparse grass. Only occasional Acacia trees dotted the land. We slowed, then stopped and glassed the area.

We could see no Thompson's Gazelle, but the place was by no means empty. Way off on our left I caught the sudden flicker of motion through the glasses. It was a pack of golden-eared jackals closing in on…something. Then I saw the pack converge around a low blackish hump on the ground. As they moved in the hump seemed to spring to life: great moving gray and tan flippers waved and flapped on its sides. It resembled a giant stranded whale more than anything. But then the flapping shapes took flight, and a half-dozen griffon vultures were soon gaining altitude on their outstretched wings, wheeling about the carcass, waiting for their time to return to the feast. Not much later we saw a pack of wild dogs hunting in a small pack.

"Look well on those, sir," Aaron advised me. "They've been terribly decimated recently by canine distemper. It's doubtful they'll recover."

Among the other game we saw that last morning out were ostriches, two lionesses, a rhino mother and her calf, and a pack of hyenas. When we saw a Gerenuk standing on his hind legs to browse a thorn tree, Aaron slowed the vehicle. "We're getting close now, gentlemen—the Gerenuk and the Tommy are almost cousins. When you see one generally you'll soon see the other—"

And we were not mistaken. Shortly afterwards Aaron pointed over the hood of the truck. "There, sir. Get on him if you want him—" He pulled up to a slow halt, swinging it in the direction he had pointed. But Dick murmured he could not see anything out there resembling an antelope.

"You might be forgetting how small they actually are, sir. About the size of a large spaniel. See there? Right to the left of the termite mound yonder?"

Dick locked in on the animal and brought up his Weatherby. I picked up the Tommy through my military surplus binoculars, the ones the Soviets had made for their East German border guards at the Berlin wall. They were the best pair of glasses any of us had seen except for Glen's Leica lightweights. The tiny animal resembled a baby Grants at first, until I looked closely and saw the grayish fur around the muzzle, the scarred face and ears, and the thick bases of the horns. This was a full-grown male, and no youngster either.

True to form, the Tommy picked up the sound of our grinding diesel and turned to face us, his body held for a perfect broadside shot. Why don't they ever learn?

"Do make haste sir," urged Aaron. "He could take off any second."

We covered our ears as Dick held his breath and began the squeeze. Still, my ears rang afterwards. I don't like Weatherby's for several reasons. The vicious kick is one. The other is the report, which seems to me to have a higher pitch than most rifles. Perhaps that's due to the extra high-velocity their proprietary cartridges achieve.

But where was our Tommy? He had vanished from my vision. Had he taken off just before the sear engaged? Had he seen the muzzle flash and managed to get rolling before the slug tore into him? I knew Dick did not miss with that rifle.

"He's off for the races I'm afraid," said Aaron. "*Hapana piga.*"

I searched the dry savanna for motion and soon saw our quarry running at a right good clip through the grass, leaping over brush, and...stopping again to look back. Aaron again stopped the vehicle Dick settled himself for another shot. This time the distance was far greater—at least 300 yards out. The little herbivore was a mere speck even in my glasses. Then, before Dick could get the rifle into position on the rest, the animal took off again. And that's when our "guide," who so far had said less than the proverbial cigar-store Indian, jumped up from his seat pointing in the distance.

"*Jeruhiwa!*" he shouted.

Aaron turned in the driver's seat to follow where he was pointed, then gunned the engine and we were off. We chased the antelope for twenty minutes. As the time ticked away, I watched the fleeing animal through my glasses. The guide had been correct; thick glasses or no, he had seen the subtle, telltale evidence of a hit that revealed itself whenever the animal began a leap. His left hind leg tottered ever so faintly. But sadly, the limp was growing more pronounced with each long jump. But to our surprise he kept well ahead of us, and after another several minutes, Aaron admitted he had disappeared.

We backtracked several times over this tracks, but he had vanished into M.M.B.A. "He'll be okay I reckon," Aaron mused. "Any critter that can run like that will recover."

Now I did not fancy myself an expert by any means, but inwardly I disagreed with his assessment. True, if left alone in the wild with a flesh wound in the thigh, or even a nicked tendon, the animal probably would heal with time. But realistically, how much healing time did this little jumper have? We'd already seen the wild dogs and the jackals. Leopards, lions, and hyenas would be out in force once darkness fell. And even in daylight, vultures would circle overhead, telling everyone else on the Masai Steppe there was a tasty treat right below their wings.

We moved on, with Yours Truly in the shooting seat next to Aaron. I was a little down in my spirits, and was hoping we would have a change of heart and continue or search for Tommy #1. But we did not. I wasn't long in my reveries before I heard Aaron say in a low voice: "There's one sir; get on him."

Now, "*get on him,*" means locate the animal with your eyes (or glasses, if he's quite far off), then place your rifle on the sandbag rest atop the vehicle's hood in preparation for the shot. This I did, and cranked the Leupold scope all the way up to 10 power. The gun writers are correct: most people shoot more accurately with a scope in the low power ranges because the "jiggle effect" of extreme magnification is less apparent. Also, the compression of distance and resultant "shimmy" effect of rising hot air currents are also minimized. But when you're trying to hunt an antelope the size of a Brittany spaniel that's maybe 300 yards away, you want some magnification. Also, the day was still quite cool; rising waves of air would not be a problem.

197

My Tommy was quartering away from us to the left, which was perfect since I was in the left front seat. He ran in wide arcs, making giant bounds, heading left then right, then left again. Our truck followed, going noticeably slower but slicing through the radius of every one of his curves. This is why the advantage of the chase always belongs to the pursuing animal: it can see which way its prey is turning and at that instant turn in the same direction. But since it is also some distance behind the prey, the pursuer need not follow in the footsteps of his quarry but can always head directly for it, thus shaving off the curved portion of the fleeing animals tracks. In short, the hunter is continually "heading off" the panicked, zigzagging quarry, ever-shortening his lead.

My antelope finally stopped and assumed the position. He was not totally broadside, but quartering slightly away from the vehicle and ahead of it. I estimated the range at less than 200 yards, and Aaron agreed. I set the Winchester up on my bag and placed the crosshairs a third of the way up the torso behind the front near leg—but farther back than usual since the animal was quartering away. It seemed an easy enough shot. But for some reason I did not then understand—or stop to think about—the vision through my scope seemed less clear than usual. Anyway, I did not wish to dawdle knowing how fast these small, agile creatures could take flight—and how terribly hard it was to make visual contact with again after that happened. So I squeezed off the shot. The gun butt jabbed me in the shoulder and I immediately grabbed the glasses to see where my trophy had fallen.

"Where is he then?" I asked Aaron.

"Gone. He took off like a scalded cat at the report, bwana. It's surprising to see you miss after the way you've been shooting up till now—"

Well there it was: two misses in a row. Mine a total miss—I didn't even connect enough for a minor wound on my buck, which through my scope seemed as large as a billboard. Aaron exited the truck and asked me to follow. He walked in a dead-straight line from the Land Cruiser toward the spot where the buck had stood. I noticed he was sweeping his eyes over the scrub growth nearby as he walked.

"Before you shot, did you get a clear sight picture of the animal?"

"Of course. Why?"

"Absolutely clear?" Then I remembered the slight interference with the picture—a faint vertical obscuring of the reticules and the animal behind them.

"Mum. I thought as much. Look here." He led me almost fifty yards to a dried stalk that had been cut in twain roughly two feet above ground. He then turned and stared once again at where the Tommy buck had stood. It was in a slight down slope—a minor depression on the steppes. "That's about right, sir. Right where your bullet went. I knew you wouldn't totally blow the shot—not at that range. But this dry reed was enough to throw your slug way off target."

"Well I know this happens when your target is, say, way downrange—but my buck was only a hundred yards or so past this plant—"

"More than adequate. The only way to successfully buck brush with a bullet is when your target is, say, twenty feet or less behind it. Now let's get back in and keep going; my guess is he can't be far off."

We picked up on him in less than five minutes. Again he paused, looking back in wonder at the strange grinding noise coming from our truck. I readied the rifle, and four seconds after Aaron turned off the ignition I squeezed off a shot and the animal dropped in his tracks.

Larry gave up his turn, claiming the little antelope were simply too cute to take as trophies. So Dick resumed the shooter's seat, and within another thirty minutes we had our final trophy and headed back to Arusha.

* * * * *

That afternoon the dreamscape descended upon me once again. We arrived back in town before noon, and had lunch at a native restaurant that consisted mostly of fruit, bread, and cheese. Then we prowled the streets of the market district and looked for gifts for our wives. There were many items of ivory, and raw and cut Tanzanites as well. I almost bought a genuine Masai bead bracelet, no doubt in hopes that its charm would transfer to me and make me tall and courageous—not to say fierce. I actually believed this for several minutes before leaving the shop without making the purchase.

Finally, around four, we wended our way back to the Impala and lugged the big metal gun cases down from the storage lockers, finished packing our luggage, and went into the lobby to wait for Glen, who was outside at a terrace table wrapping up our paperwork. He said he would take us each individually. Dick went out first and didn't return until forty-five minutes had elapsed. He was smiling. Larry went next. He returned after only thirty minutes. He too was smiling. Part of this was no doubt because we had decided to give Glen and Aaron a rather substantial tip. This is ordinary practice, and expected on safari. We three decided first what the sum would be. It was generous—enough to buy a decent used car in the states. But then we got going on how to subdivide the tip between the two men. This confused and rattled us, until finally we just let it be, with the assumption that they would no doubt know how best to split it up.

So Glen was probably going to be in a (sort of) good mood. I had that going for me at least. But I also knew my turn was coming up soon, and I had a very strong hunch as to why I was to see Glen last.

It was no secret to anyone at Camp Whiteface that he and I were not exactly on the best of terms during the hunt. In fact at one point things got so strained that out of curiosity I asked Aaron if—to his knowledge—I was the worst client Glen ever had to deal with.

He ruminated on this question awhile before answering.

"Ummmm—I wouldn't exactly say that, sir."

"Well that's good to know. I—"

"—No sir—there was *one* worse than you. A perfect *shit* he was. I tell you, Glen damn near shot him."

So now you know why I was waiting on...on...—*tenterhooks* is the term I believe—before going out on the terrace to see Captain Ahab one last time.

So, after crossing myself, I stepped out into the terrace and sat down opposite Glen at the table. He looked up, his black eyes boring into me.

"Have a good time?"

"Excellent. Can I go now?"

"Can you *go*?" He leaned forward to emphasize the point. "Hell no you can't go. We've got a lot of work to do bwana. Now let's start with the tags and fees—"

*　*　*　*　*

I hoisted the chilled mug of Heinekens up to my parched mouth and took a long, slow draw. It was good. It tasted good and felt great. So great I took another. My comrades in arms, on each side of me, did likewise. Larry looked at his watch.

"We leave in an hour. Let's drink enough here so we won't lose our buzz before they start serving drinks on the plane—"

"Capital idea," I said, lighting a corona. The bar was cozy, a small dim room lined with trophies on the walls and full of hunters swigging drinks and puffing on cigars and pipes. Veddy British.

"Okay Boyer. Let's hear it," intoned Dick. "You came inside with a grin on your face. So who's lying here—you or him?"

"Neither. In fact I would say we parted friends. He told me something he said earlier, on the last day in camp."

"Let me guess," said Larry. "He told you he never wanted to hear your name mentioned again."

I shook my head. "Actually, he said *bwana, you surprised me.*"

Both men stared at me. "You're shitting me," said Larry.

"Ditto," echoed Dick.

"Nope. The truth. And in actuality, he surprised *me*. Admit it: he *is* the best around—you're right about that, Dick. A hard-on for sure, but hell, remember when he said if all we wanted to do was sit around the campfire smoking and drinking he didn't care, but we wouldn't get any animals. Remember?"

They nodded.

Well, Glen Schacht gets the game. That's what a PH is paid to do, and he does it best. Case closed. He also said something else,"

"And what might that be?"

"He said 'bwana—keep in touch.'"

*   *   *   *   *

Twenty minutes later we were called to the gate. We were the center of a relatively small group of Westerners boarding the giant bird. But all around us were the natives, coming from or going to parts unknown. Many hugged and kissed their loved ones, giving that same delicate—almost feminine—soft handshake that I will never forget. Over and over again I heard **Jambo! Jambo! Jambo!**

Then, we walked across the tarmac, we realized there were more groups of people hugging, only this time they were saying another word—one I had not heard before: **Kwa heri! Kwa heri!**

"What does that mean?" I asked a white man walking nearby. He looked very tan and carried himself as if he belonged in this country.

"Kwa heri? What does it mean, you say?"

"Yes. Any idea?"

"Why of course, it means good-bye."

"Oh, thank you."

"Don't mention it. *Kwa heri.*"

"Kwa heri!" I called after him, and walked to the boarding stairs.

* * * * *

Twenty minutes later the plane was aloft. The ship's wings tilted and she began a slow circle over Arusha. I saw the lights fading below as we headed out over Miles and Miles of Bloody Africa to land in Dar es Salaam in 40 minutes. Then we would land in Amsterdam en route to Chicago. Chicago? My hometown. It sounded now like a foreign country.

I would be forever changed by this adventure. They say Africa does this to you, and it's true. For now, however, all I could think about was Ginny and my son-to-be.

I stuffed a pillow under my head, leaned back, and looked out the window.

"Kwa heri!" I murmured, and fell asleep.